LAUGHING GIRL

LAUGHING GIRL

A MYSTERY NOVEL

BY

GEORGE F. WORTS

WILDSIDE PRESS

[1.]

THERE were stacks of silver dollars on the table before her and each time the wheel was spun, it seemed to Peter Storm, the little white ball dropped into one of her numbers and the dealer pushed another stack of silver toward her.

Afterward, Peter Storm wasn't at all sure he hadn't seen her somewhere before—on a train, perhaps, or a plane, with her face glowing with excitement as it was now, her dark-blue eyes half-mooned with laughter and oblivious to everyone about her. Yet she was not a girl he would have readily forgotten, even after a glimpse or two. The impact of her personality was too electrifying.

She was not more than twenty-two. She wore a sleeveless white linen dress in the prevailing peasant style against which her arms, face and throat were golden brown, and there was a small bunch of fresh cornflowers in her hair, above the left temple, one shade less blue than her eyes.

Each time the dealer pushed a stack of silver dollars toward her, she murmured, "I did it again!" Then she laughed at the dealer who was all white—white shirt, chalk-white face and ivory-white hair—and said, "I'm sorry," and, in the same breath, "Isn't it wonderful?" Her eyes when she laughed were sapphire flames and even the dealer was smiling.

Peter Storm found a space at the table and bought a stack of fifty-cent chips and began to play his favorites. The girl was across from him and unaware of him. With her deep clear blue eyes, her rather large laughing mouth, she was either beautiful or it didn't matter.

She hadn't been in the desert long, her skin was too smooth and too soft. After watching her eyes for a while, Peter Storm decided she wasn't married; therefore, she wasn't in Nevada for a divorce. He guessed she was a tourist, here, probably, with her parents to see Boulder Dam.

She lost heavily on three spins of the wheel, then won. She laughed, "I did it again!" The dealer pushed a pile of silver dollars across the table to her. Then her half-mooned eyes discovered Peter Storm's brown face, with its V-lined forehead, its amused green eyes, and her laughter stopped, her smile gave way to an expression of dismay, and in the instant before she recovered herself she reminded him of a girl who has just glanced at a clock and realized she has missed her train.

She opened her large white knitted bag and methodically stored her winnings in it. A stack toppled over and a dollar rolled off the table. A wrinkled old man who looked like a prospector picked it up and said reprovingly, "You shouldn't quit yet, miss; your luck's still runnin'," and she laughed and said, "Partner, my luck's gone. I could feel it run out."

She took the heavy purse to the cashier's window and exchanged most of the silver for bills. As she passed the roulette table, she hesitated a moment, placed a silver dollar on thirty-four, and walked out of the Boulder Club.

Mystified and uncomfortable, Peter Storm watched her until she vanished. He was tempted to follow her. He wanted to know why one glimpse of him had spoiled roulette for her.

There was a ripple of laughter about the table. The wheel was spinning slowly enough so that he could see the number into which the ball had fallen. Thirty-four.

"Watch my chips," he said to the dealer. "I'll tell her."

He walked out into the street. The impact of the desert heat, after the air-conditioning of the Boulder Club, was like a puff of dry powder in his face, and his first inhalation of the hot dry air, with its faint spicy smell of desert brush, seemed to scorch his nostrils. Heat lightning was flickering above the mountains about Railroad Pass.

He saw the girl as she turned the Comanche Hotel corner, and he yelled, "Hey! Wait a minute!" But she didn't hear him. When he reached the corner, she had passed the hotel entrance, walking rapidly.

Beyond the hotel, across an alley, were the fire house and the police station. But she didn't cross the alley. She stopped beside an iron ladder bolted to the yellow brick wall. It ran about fifteen feet up the face of the building to the lower platform of a fire escape.

She looked quickly up and down the street, which was deserted. Peter Storm was in the shadow of the building. Before he could call to her again, she had started to climb the ladder.

She reached the platform and began to climb the steel stairway to the third floor. A hot draft of the desert wind belled her skirt about her knees and she suddenly became a figure of romance and mystery bent upon some improbable errand entirely in harmony with the desert night. And Peter Storm wondered why she had stared at him across the roulette table with dismay, why she had left so abruptly, and why she was climbing the fire escape.

She passed the third floor platform and continued to climb. For a few seconds she was lost to the diffusion of neon lights along the street and, in shadow, became a phantom moving mysteriously against the white glitter of the Nevada stars. Reaching the fourth floor, she deliberately climbed over the rail. Facing the building and clinging to the rail with one hand, she reached out with the other for a window frame just beyond.

Peter Storm was perspiring, and not entirely because of the risk she was taking. He had just realized that the corner window, which was her obvious objective, was the window of his room.

Still holding to the rail with her left hand, she pushed against the pane with her right, opened the window, and climbed into the room.

Peter Storm waited until the light came on. His amusement was gone; he was no longer enchanted or entertained. He was slightly disgusted, for it was evident now that she was merely a bold young woman working against him in a case that already seemed hopeless.

He went into the lobby, secured his key at the desk, and took the automatic elevator to the fourth floor. He went down the hall to his room and listened. Hearing faint sounds, he quietly unlocked the door and went in. He closed the door softly behind him.

The girl whose bright laughter had intrigued him was standing at the foot of the bed busily engaged in rooting through his suitcases. They had been locked. She had slashed them open, and the contents of one of them were strewn over bed and floor. She was disemboweling the other suitcase when she saw him.

The vandal swiftly reached into her white knitted purse, which was lying on the bed, and took from it a small automatic pistol. This she aimed at Peter Storm's chest. Her blue eyes, after their first alarm, became steady and alert.

She said pleasantly: "Please stay where you are, Mr. Storm," and her voice still had the rich, golden quality that had attracted him in the Boulder Club.

Peter Storm took two steps forward to find out if she really meant business, and he learned from the tightening of the muscles about her eyes that she did. What he saw, in addition to her determination, was momentary fear. And he was aware that more triggers are pulled by fear than by courage.

Peter Storm was a tall, lanky young man with a smooth and easy way of moving. He backed away until, with one hand groping behind him, he found the small table on which the telephone stood. He surreptitiously lifted the telephone out of its holder and pressed his palm over the receiver, so that the inquiring voice of the switchboard girl would not be heard by the girl with the automatic pistol.

He waited a moment and said in his deep, slightly harsh voice, "I suppose that gun is loaded."

She said promptly, "It is, Mr. Storm," with only the slightest catch of her breath.

"And you wouldn't hesitate to shoot me if you had to."

She seemed puzzled. Her eyes became more wary. "I wouldn't hesitate, Mr. Storm, if it were necessary."

It seemed to Peter Storm that she was handling the situation in a firm but civilized manner. She was not a nervous girl with a pistol in her hand. She might be a desperate girl but she wasn't nervous and he concluded that she wasn't afraid. Her air was composed and businesslike. Yet she was not hard-boiled. She was apparently well-bred, she was obviously intelligent, and she was certainly resourceful and relentless.

"I don't suppose," she said lightly, "you'd tell me where it is."

"You might as well shoot," Peter said. "There isn't anything of the slightest value to you in those suitcases."

Her smile was brief but charming. She was being as gracious as if they were having tea together. And this interested Peter much more than if she had been brittle with fear, or hard-boiled, because it meant, if this case should prove not so hopeless as it now looked, she was apt to be quite dangerous.

Holding the pistol in her right hand, with her left she was removing what remained in the second suitcase. Her hands were long and slender, evenly and beautifully tanned, and they gave an impression of great vitality.

She took out shirts, socks and shorts. She felt them carefully, then shook them out before tossing them aside. And she seemed to be paying no attention to Peter Storm. Her brown hair with its reddish tint, had a soft wave, and sometimes fell forward when she bent over, and when it did it concealed one eye. And for moments at a time, he saw nothing but the smooth young curve of one tanned cheek.

There were, he reflected, people who would have kept on walking toward her; people who would have said lightly, "Don't be silly; you know you haven't any intention of shooting me." He was not, alas, one of them.

Peter Storm was not a gambler. He had no faith in luck. He had found that the only way he ever accomplished anything was to apply himself diligently and leave nothing to chance.

Watching this attractive, competent stranger gutting his suitcase, he realized that she was obviously fitted for this kind of work. She was daring and ruthless. She typified the kind of person an industrial undercover agent must always match his wits against. But although Peter Storm had been the confidential agent of the Allied American Metals Corporation for three years, and had dealt with a number of amazingly clever adversaries, she was the first he had encountered who was not only amazingly clever, but amazingly beautiful.

As he watched her with appreciation, the door suddenly opened and a big man in khaki walked in. There had been no knock. His face was saddle brown and his small blue eyes were looking for trouble. He was holding a large black revolver in one hand.

"Put that thing down," he said curtly.

The girl promptly dropped her hand. Her eyes were large with surprise, but she wasn't frightened. She looked belligerent.

Peter Storm said in amazement: "What's the meaning of this?"

The intruder's sharp blue eyes left the gutted suitcases, and jerked from the girl's face to Peter's. "What's going on here?" he said harshly.

"Put that gun away," Peter said in an angry voice. "Who are you?"

The man stared a moment and his face became a darker red. "The house detective," he said. "I'll take that gun."

"You'll do nothing of the kind," Peter said. He moved over to the girl, took the automatic pistol from her hand and dropped it into his coat pocket. He turned to the house detective, and said curtly, "Explain yourself."

The house detective's small blue eyes were growing pink. His large square face became a darker shade of red. He had the look of a man whose suspicions are virtually a certainty. He had lowered the revolver to his hip, but the muzzle was still up.

"A lot of suspicious stuff came over the switchboard from this room," he said heavily. "Your light flashed, but no one answered. The girl heard a very suspicious conversation going on in this room."

Peter glanced down at the telephone, which was lying

on the table beside its black cradle. He glanced at the girl with a faint smile in which there was a hint of malice.

"That's odd," he said.

"Isn't it?" the girl said.

"What's going on here?" the house detective said belligerently. "What were you doing with a gun and what happened to these suitcases?"

"Is it customary in this hotel," Peter said pleasantly, "to question what your guests say and what they do?"

"My job," the house detective answered angrily, "is to know what's going on. If anything suspicious is going on in this hotel, it's my job——"

"Is it your job," the girl interrupted, "to burst in upon guests without knocking—with a revolver in your hand?" She laughed suddenly, as if she found the detective a ridiculous spectacle.

The man's face was now brick-red. Before he could answer, Peter said: "You had no right to walk into this room without knocking, you know. I think you'd better go."

"You might have taken the pains," the girl said with amusement, "to inquire who we are. This gentleman is Peter Storm, of the Allied Metals Corporation."

The house detective looked dubious and confused and definitely peevish. "And who are you?"

"I'm Mr. Storm's fiancée."

"Are you a guest in this hotel?"

"I was," she said softly, "until you came in here."

"What's your room number?"

"Two-seventeen."

"How," the house detective said angrily, "was I to know? It sounded like a stick-up to me. What were you doing with that gun? What happened to these suitcases?"

Peter Storm laughed. "Is it your habit to pry into every personal quarrel that takes place in this hotel?"

The house detective's face was now purple. "After this, you better be more careful," he said in a thick voice. "And see that your telephone isn't off the hook. You've caused a lot of trouble and inconvenience."

"So have you," the girl said.

Peter went to the door and opened it. The house detective glared at the girl, then at him, and walked out heavily. Obviously, he had been enjoying his authority, and he was now a bewildered and angry man.

When Peter turned back to the girl, she was taking a pack of cigarettes and a pad of matches out of her white purse. She had evidently no intention of trying to get away. She lighted a cigarette. Her hands weren't shaking.

She was watching him not so much guardedly as with admiration. If he had expected her to be brazen at this point, he was disappointed. She wasn't smiling, but there was a glow in her eyes.

"That," she said pleasantly, "was awfully clever, Mr. Storm—that telephone stunt." She was composed. She said lightly, "Well, I've certainly got myself into a spot. Thanks for not having me arrested."

Peter was thinking of the ease with which she had handled the house detective. "I haven't decided not to have you arrested," he said. "Who are you?"

"My name is Sandra Page. Cigarette?" She held out the pack.

Peter Storm shook his head. "That doesn't explain anything."

"I'm Hilary Logan's niece."

Peter looked as if he were about to laugh. Crinkles appeared at his eye corners. He said, "That still doesn't explain anything, Miss Page."

Her eyelids came down a little, and the impression her eyes gave was one of deliberate hostility. Even when she smiled it remained.

She said with a chiding air, "Oh, come now, Mr. Storm. Honesty is the best policy. You spent two hours late this afternoon with my uncle in his laboratory at Three Tree Ranch. You went there as the representative of the Allied Metals Corporation. No one is supposed to know that, of course. You've been telling everybody you studied chemistry under him at Harvard, and just dropped in to pay your respects. I didn't learn the truth until I went through these suitcases. Your company sent you here to buy or steal the formula for loganite."

"To buy it," Peter Storm said gently. "We don't steal, Miss Page. And we don't carve open people's suitcases."

She said airily: "Yes, I know. Everything fair and above-board. That's why you lie about who you are. And maybe it explains why, less than an hour after you left the ranch, the laboratory blew up and my uncle and his assistant, Simon Ketzler, were killed. And I'm awfully glad to know that you stop at carving open people's suitcases. A nice clean-cut robbery and a nice job of murder—"

Peter interrupted: "How do you know that laboratory was deliberately blown up?"

"When I heard you'd been there," Sandra Page answered pleasantly, "I assumed it."

Peter gazed at her thoughtfully. He wondered just how much he should say. How much did she know? He chose his words carefully: "I was sent to your uncle by my company to close the deal for loganite.

"He wanted us to manufacture the metal because he and our president are old friends. Negotiations of this kind are always conducted secretly. And I did not get the formula for loganite."

Her deep blue eyes were probing and skeptical and hopeful. She sat down on the end of the bed. "If you had got that formula this afternoon," she said calmly, "it would have been to your interest to kill my uncle and destroy his laboratory."

"Not necessarily," Peter said.

"You can't deny," she murmured, "that big corporations can be ruthless. My uncle's first mistake was in not realizing how valuable loganite is, and his second was in trusting you at all."

Peter was watching her eyes, her mouth. He said, "Your uncle and I had only a preliminary talk this afternoon. We went over the laboratory tests my company has been making with the stuff, we discussed its war possibilities, and we came to an agreement on the royalties he was to receive. That was all, Miss Page. I was going back tomorrow afternoon with the contracts, which won't be here until the morning air mail comes in."

Sandra Page got up quickly from the bed. "But if you're telling the truth," she said breathlessly, "that formula won't be found. It was destroyed with everything else. Have you seen what that explosion did?"

"Yes."

"Did you know that there was hardly enough of my uncle found to identify him, and practically nothing at all of Simon Ketzler?"

"Well?" Peter said. "Something must have gone wrong with an experiment and there was an explosion."

"But," she said eagerly, "if someone blew up the laboratory it would definitely mean that someone had been planning to get the formula and had succeeded. And if it's in existence, it's mine. My uncle left me everything in his will. And I want that formula."

Peter Storm nodded. "That's understandable. It's worth millions, and if it does exist and if you can get it and establish that you're Hilary Logan's sole heir, my company will gladly make the same terms with you that we would have made with him."

Sandra Page was smoking another cigarette. She was taking small avid puffs. She cried: "You don't understand. I haven't any intention of selling it to anybody. I want to destroy it. I don't know much about it, but I do know that it's an atomic process for making a metal stronger than steel and lighter than aluminum, and as far as I'm concerned, it's nothing but another war weapon—something to make warplanes fly faster and shells go farther and bombs penetrate deeper. It would make war just one degree more horrible."

She turned to the desk and crushed out her cigarette in the glass pen tray. She turned back. Her face was flushed. Her eyes looked enormous. "If that formula is still in existence, and if I can get my hands on it, I intend to destroy it. But I'll make a gentleman's agreement with you. I trust you. And I need help. On the slim assumption that it exists, will you work with me—and whichever one of us gets it can keep it—if he can hang onto it."

There was no telling, Peter reflected, how much this girl knew, or what she planned to do. To safeguard his own plans, he must not let her out of his sight. He smiled and said, "All right. It's a deal."

"Will you shake hands on it?"

He thought of himself standing on the sidewalk thirty feet below as she climbed through his window, and he thought of her composure when he came into this room, and her calmness when the house detective came in, and he knew that she was many times as clever as she was permitting him to suspect.

He held out his hand and clasped hers. Hers was warm and dry, and the skin felt smooth. Her fingers were strong. She was looking up into his eyes not only with her challenge but with more than a remnant of the hostility that had puzzled him before.

She said softly: "No holds barred?"

"No holds barred," Peter said, and meant it.

"Let's," she said, withdrawing her hand, "pool what we know."

Yes, he thought, that would naturally be her first move.

"I can't contribute much," she said. "My uncle sent to New York for me, told me to fly out, and I landed at the airport here on the afternoon plane. We were held up by bad weather east of Salt Lake City, and it was dark when we came in. When I reached the ranch, the laboratory was in ruins. I heard you'd been the last man to see my uncle alive. I assumed, whoever you were, that you had the formula and had somehow planted a time bomb to go off after you'd left. I think I was mistaken."

"Thank you," Peter murmured.

She went on: "I came back to town and tried to find you. Actually, I wanted to make sure you weren't in your hotel room. Someone told me you'd gone into the Boulder Club. I dropped in, and you were pointed out to me. I started playing roulette, so that I could watch you and make sure you'd stay there long enough for me to come up here and search your things. Then I started to win and I got so excited I forgot all about you until I saw you again across the table. I saw you'd bought chips, and I thought I'd have enough time to go through your things."

Peter Storm had dropped his hands into his coat pockets. His left hand encountered her automatic pistol. He took out the pistol and pulled back the breech block. The chamber was empty. There was no clip in the butt.

He said gently: "You're a smart gambler. The trouble was your luck stayed behind."

Her eyes became large. "Don't tell me thirty-four came up!" she breathed.

"Yes."

She stared at him wildly a moment, then her eyes became half-moons and she began to laugh. Her laughter was free and fresh and joyous. She cried: "Oh, I love that! I did it again! And you courteously followed me to tell me. And saw me climb into this room!"

"Not so courteously," Peter murmured. "I wanted to know why one glimpse of me had frightened you away from your winning streak, and I wanted to know where I'd seen you before."

Her eyes were still half-mooned, and her mouth was still tremulous with mirth. "Ah! Aren't you used to seeing people frightened when they look at you?"

"Only children under six," he answered. "Certainly not girls who brazenly climb in windows thirty feet above solid concrete sidewalks to commit vandalism."

"I'm so sorry, Mr. Storm. I'll gladly buy you two new suitcases. Had you seen me before?"

He said wryly: "I don't know. Had I?"

Her eyes were wide and serene. "I don't know, Mr. Storm. Of course, I've seen your pictures in the papers, but that hardly counts."

He said with distaste: "Oh, yes—the newspapers."

She laughed softly, with derision. "Well, haven't you asked for it? My Aunt Agatha told me that gentlemen who stick their chins out should always carry liniment. If I were the kind that frightens easily, I'd have had an excuse for running, wouldn't I? Or are all these unsavory stories just window-dressing for your job—or camouflage?"

Peter smiled slowly. "Well," he said, "what do you think?"

She was observing his lean dark face, his amused green eyes, with her head tilted a little. And her eyes were gay with a mocking shimmer.

"I'm interested only in that phase of your private life, Mr. Storm, which concerns loganite," she said. "We were pooling what we know, weren't we, or are you being evasive?"

Peter was divided between interest in her motives and amusement at her skill. She had so far said nothing. "When," he asked, "was the last time you saw your uncle?"

"I was awfully young," she answered. "I don't suppose I was more than four or five. I don't even remember him."

"I suppose that explains why you're bearing up so well."

Her eyes were steady and they gave an impression of thoughtfulness and candor. She crushed out her third cigarette firmly in the glass pen tray. "He treated my father badly," she said. "The truth is, that's why I want that formula and will go to any lengths to get it. In a way, all I'm doing is for my father."

She looked at Peter speculatively, as if she were considering taking him wholly into her confidence, as if she were afraid of trusting him, but as if she longed to tell him everything. Her high coloring, the glow in her eyes, the golden richness of her voice, her quick smiles, even the constant small movements of her hands were those of a girl who was warm and sympathetic and generous.

"Temporarily, Mr. Storm, I'm a screwball. Uncle Hilary never helped my father at times during his life when he really needed him. My father feels strongly about loganite—much more strongly than I do."

Peter Storm's curiosity about Sandra Page and her background was intolerable, but all he said was: "I see. But what I don't understand is how you found out about loganite. It's been such a carefully guarded secret. At this end, only two men knew about it—your uncle and Ketzler. He assured me this afternoon that he hadn't mentioned it to anyone. At my end, only the president of Allied Metals and our laboratory chief and I knew about it. As we consider loganite the most important industrial material," Peter added dryly, "since the discovery of glass, my boss will be curious to know how the secret leaked out."

He wondered if she was prepared to answer that one, and when she promptly smiled, he knew he was wasting his time.

"I hate to spoil your mystery," Miss Page said, "but there isn't any. Uncle Hilary wrote reams to my father about his experiments, and to me, too. He told us not to mention it to anyone, and we didn't. That ought to make your boss feel happier."

"He's a hard man to make happy," Peter said. "Another point he may raise is why, if you weren't on good terms with your uncle, he left you everything he had?"

"My father says uncle was very fond of me when I was a little girl." She looked at Peter Storm with the glowing large eyes of innocence. She waited a moment, then said: "If the cross-examination is over, Mr. Storm, perhaps you'll answer some questions of mine. What were you doing in the Boulder Club?"

Again Peter weighed his words, deciding how much to tell her in order to get the most information from her. "I had a hunch about that explosion," he said slowly. "I thought it might have been dynamite. When you came in I was at the faro-bank table talking with a man named Joe Rennow who runs the Clark County Wholesale Supply Company, which is the only place in Las Vegas that sells dynamite. And I learned that your uncle's assistant came into town yesterday afternoon in his maroon coupe and loaded up the luggage compartment with eight cases of dynamite. He also bought a box of percussion caps and a coil of fuse."

Sandra Page was staring at him, and he was sure that her face had lost some of its warm color. It was the first time he had seen amazement in her face. He had wanted to catch her off-guard, and he had evidently succeeded.

"But he was killed in the explosion!"

"Yes. It doesn't seem to make sense, but it may lead somewhere."

She was looking at Peter's mouth and her eyes were busier than he had ever seen them. She said impatiently: "Well, what are we waiting for?"

"Exactly," Peter said. "As a matter of fact, I was on my way to the ranch when I saw you at the roulette

table. My car's still parked in front of the Boulder
Club."

She picked up her purse and walked past him to the
door. She carried herself with pride. With her soft hair,
her clever, tanned face, her golden voice and her
warmth, it still didn't make the slightest difference
whether she was beautiful or not. A girl with her gifts
had nothing to worry about. Sandra Page not only attracted him, she fascinated him.

She glanced over her shoulder. "You came over because you thought you knew me."

"No," he said. "Because I heard you laugh."

A faint line appeared between her eyes, but her eyes
still had that mocking shimmer in them.

"You liked my laugh."

He frowned. "I think I've heard it before. Yes. I
liked it."

She was nodding. "It's a nice laugh. I like it myself.
It's one of the nicest laughs I ever heard. So golden."

Peter Storm grinned, but his eyes were no longer
amused. Just how she fitted into this picture he had no
way of guessing. Her entire story was a very competent
lie. Under other circumstances he might have been inclined to believe it. But, as it happened, he knew that she
was not Hilary Logan's niece. And he knew that she
would double-cross him at the first opportunity.

IN AN apartment overlooking New York City's East River, Brook Van Pell, corporation counsel, put down his empty highball glass and smiled at the girl in sapphire-blue lounging pajamas who sat limply on a davenport watching him.

Brook Van Pell was a tall, slender man of thirty-six, with gray eyes, which were whimsical, and a sensitive, rather wide mouth. He looked as if he were about to deliver himself of an amusing comment, but the girl on the davenport was frightened. He was drunk, and he was in a savage state of mind, yet anyone who did not know him very well would not have suspected it. His color was only slightly higher than usual, and his eyes were clear.

He had started drinking tonight because he was worn thin with worry. He had expected a report hours ago from Las Vegas, Nevada, from the wily individual who was, at present, masquerading under the name of Professor John Medkin—and no report had come.

He had expected a message from Sandra Page, who was supposed to have disembarked in Las Vegas from a plane hours ago, and no message had come. He had telephoned the Las Vegas airport and learned that Miss Page had arrived safely. He wanted to know several things—that she was still safe, that she was at work on the job he had given her, and he wanted, above all, her reassurance that she adored him.

And he was worried because he had sent her there. Shortly after he had seen her off at the airport, he had begun to doubt the wisdom of it. He had sent her to Las Vegas because she was clever and resourceful. She was capable of doing the job—but she was also capable of finding out for herself how carefully he had lied to her.

As long as she continued to believe that he had told her the truth, he could count on her loyalty. Her prolonged silence made him uneasy. He had sent her to Las Vegas to keep an eye on Scott Higgins, alias John Medkin, to report to him at once if Higgins might have double-crossed him.

Had Scott Higgins been up to tricks? Did that account for her silence? Brook Van Pell had selected Scott Higgins for the job because he knew that Higgins was ruthless and always got what he went after, but he also knew that Higgins, if it suited his plans, would not hesitate to double-cross him.

And Brook Van Pell was worried about the representatives of Russia, Germany, Japan and France with whom he had been discreetly in contact. His intention was to sell the secret of loganite to the highest bidder, and he knew that he was being watched, that one or all of his potential customers had grown suspicious, and might, if things went wrong, cause trouble. His experience as a corporation counsel had taught him how delicate and how dangerous an affair of this kind could become.

He had started to drink shortly after dinner, and he had been drinking heavily all night. An hour ago, unable to sleep, jittery with worry, and in a decidedly belligerent frame of mind, he had walked from his house to Carol Dunbar's apartment and awakened her.

He was so drunk now he could hardly stand upright, and when he was very drunk he became suspicious and belligerent, and his jealousy, always a pronounced trait, was aggravated.

The girl in sapphire-blue pajamas was familiar with all these symptoms, and, because of her familiarity with them, was frightened. She had seen Brook Van Pell in many of his drunken rages, and she had learned to watch their development with apprehension.

Carol Dunbar was a slim, pretty girl of twenty-five, with dark hair, large, deep brown eyes, and a soft, bright red mouth.

Lurching toward her, Brook Van Pell said heavily: "You've been keeping in touch with Peter Storm, haven't you?"

Carol Dunbar's eyes grew larger. "Darling," she said soothingly, "I haven't seen Peter, or heard from him or communicated with him since I left Pittsburgh."

"You're a liar," he said, and struck her across the face with his open hand.

That was the beginning, the usual beginning.

When Peter Storm and Sandra Page had collected her winnings and he had cashed in his chips at the Boulder Club, they drove out to the Three Tree Ranch in his car. It was a long gray convertible with a powerful engine that had a low and sinister song. The top was down.

Sandra Page said as they started out: "Is your connection with Allied Metals supposed to be an absolute secret?"

Peter glanced at her thoughtfully and answered: "Pretty much so. Most people don't know about it, and it's better that they don't."

"You mean, you prefer being mysterious?"

"I find it practical."

As they swung around the long curve on the Tonopah Highway, the girl said: "Allied Metals treats its help pretty handsomely, doesn't it? This car must have cost a lot. What will it do?"

"A hundred and fifteen with a tail wind."

"Allied Metals must want you to get places in a hurry. It must be fun to work for them."

"You can have my job," Peter Storm said.

She said with what, in any other woman, he would have called pretty confusion but with what, in her, was only another example of what he would learn to call her damned perverseness: "Oh, I'm not nearly clever enough for this kind of work, Mr. Storm. You must be awfully good. A car like this. An apartment on Park Avenue. An unlimited expense account. It must be fun."

"You can still have my job," Peter said.

She turned to look at him. A late moon was rising over the mountains far to their right. It was the color of Chinese gold. Sandra Page had tied Peter's handkerchief about her hair. A few curls had escaped and were floating about in the rush of hot wind. He glanced at her. She was gazing at him with large-eyed solemnity.

"Really, don't you like your job, Mr. Storm?"

"Not tonight," he said concisely.

"I suppose," she said, "that means you don't like me."

He deliberated and said: "I might fall in love with you. In fact, maybe I have. But I don't think I could ever like you. Wherever you are, there's going to be trouble."

She gazed at him a moment and said: "I wouldn't care if Donald Duck came galloping up on a pink cloud and told you to go to the devil. You are the rudest man I ever knew. Isn't it a lovely night?"

Peter drove two or three miles before either of them spoke. The girl said: "You must have seen Simon Ketzler this afternoon."

"Yes."

"What was he like?"

"I should say he was about seventy, a very kindly-looking old fellow, with shiny, apple-red cheeks and a bald head. While I talked to your uncle, Ketzler was working at the other end of the laboratory, paying no attention to us. He was finishing up some torsion tests. I gathered that that was his job—testing the physical characteristics of loganite. Your uncle said that Ketzler had had nothing to do with the atomic experiments. He'd worked for your uncle two years, and he looked trustworthy."

Sandra Page was watching his face. "What's your guess?"

"I haven't made one."

"I have," she said promptly. "He was working with someone. They planned to steal the formula, blow up the laboratory and kill my uncle. But whoever Ketzler was working with double-crossed him."

"It's a possibility," Peter said.

"Someone has that formula and we're going to find him."

Peter wished he shared her optimism. He was not at all sure there was anything in the dynamite theory. He had not been prepared for this sort of thing. He had anticipated no trouble, no complications. He had been in Reno when word came from Dan Ryan that he was to proceed at once to the Three Tree Ranch, near Las Vegas, and close the deal with Hilary Logan.

It was no fault of his that the secret was out. And it was no fault of his that he had failed to secure the formula, yet he blamed himself. He should have anticipated the leakage and he should have anticipated the destruction of the laboratory, either by accident or plan, and the death of Hilary Logan. A man who engaged in this kind of work should anticipate everything.

He wondered how he would proceed with the investigation once he had reached the ranch. And he wondered what was to be done about this girl. With her cleverness, she would make a useful ally, and, with her cleverness, she would make an exasperating and dangerous enemy. It was certainly his duty, first of all, to see to it that, if the loganite formula existed, she didn't get it before he did.

They were skimming up a long grade. They passed the turnoff to Charleston Park. A few miles beyond, a hand-made sign proclaimed in neat, square, amateurish lettering that Three Tree Ranch was six miles.

Peter turned the long gray car off the highway onto a desert road yellow with dried and pulverized clay. Dust rose in a pale and mighty billow behind them. Heat lightning flickered again in the vicinity of the Arizona line, and ahead and off to the left, beyond the gently swooping valley bottom, was a cluster of glittering lights.

Three Tree Ranch lay on the alluvial fan which ran in a long neat slope for miles from the base of the black mountains. It was a small green heaven of cottonwoods, weeping willows and Chinese umbrellas, an inviting spot that breathed coolness into the fiery fury of the desert in midsummer.

Hilary Logan, doctor of science, had bought the ranch in 1936, giving up his professorship at a School of Mines, to devote all of his time to experiments with sundry atomic processes, the rich fruit of which had been loganite, a metal stronger than tungsten-steel, lighter than unalloyed aluminum—almost as light as magnesium—a metal which would, if the formula had not been lost in the explosion of the laboratory, revolutionize many branches of industry and all branches of warfare.

At the turn in the road, when the ranch lights first came into view Sandra Page sat forward impatiently, bringing herself a dozen inches nearer an objective still more than five miles away.

He turned and looked at her. Their eyes met, and he was aware of the definite attraction that existed between them—and the hostility. Perhaps it was only awareness on his part. You could never tell about such things.

Lights twinkled and gleamed all about the ranch. Lanterns and flashlights darted here and there among the trees like will-o'-the-wisps. Beyond the cattle guard, off to the left of the main ranch entrance, cars were parked. There seemed to be hundreds of them. And beyond this area was the long, wide, shallow crater where, until tonight, had stood the adobe laboratory with its green tile roof. The lanterns and flashlights of a score of men were flickering in and about this crater.

Peter Storm parked his car and he and Sandra Page got out and walked toward the crater. Men and women in groups were discussing the explosion. Among the ranchers and the townspeople, Hilary Logan had had the reputation of an eccentric. Most of the people here had come in the same spirit of curiosity with which they will drive miles to see the results of an earthquake.

The sheriff's office had made an attempt at an investigation, although the deputies were making no attempt at keeping sightseers out of the crater. One deputy was standing at the edge of the shallow hole, with hands on hips, looking down into the jackstraw tangle of roof beams, fragments of torn metal, green tile, and small and large lumps of white adobe, and he was smoking a cigar.

The girl said softly: "I've just realized, for the first time, that he's really dead."

Peter Storm thought: "She's marvelous. She's swell —she's so damned clever."

The man in khaki turned and said with a chuckle: "I reckon they don't grow much deader, Miss."

Peter said: "Have you found enough of both bodies to identify them?"

"Not enough for one decent burial," the deputy answered. "The boys keep finding fingers and toes, and that's about all since they found Logan's head."

The girl was standing so close to Peter that he felt her shiver.

"It's my guess," the deputy went on, "that Ketzler was standing closer to whatever it was that blew up. It sure was some explosion."

"I suppose," Peter said quietly, "you'll never find out what caused it."

The deputy chuckled again. "We don't even know what was here. Just look at all this junk!"

"If it had been dynamite," Peter said, "would you know it?"

The deputy puffed at his cigar and said: "Well that's a question, friend. I've done a lot o' prospecting in my time and I've set off my share of powder. Now, if it was nitroglycerine, you might tell. Nitroglycerine blows down and powder blows up."

The girl was looking up at his face and in the moonlight she was pale. Peter, standing close beside her, thought she shivered again. He realized that he was attracted to her, a little afraid of her, and intrigued and puzzled by her. He saw, however, that she was no longer aware of him. She was completely absorbed in what the deputy was saying. The current of their mutual awareness had been broken—by her.

He said: "Let's try to find the foreman. Or a ranch hand."

Near the corral they found a slightly sinister, dark young man who seemed to swagger even when he stood with his cowboy boots planted apart, his thumbs hooked into the belt loops of his levis. His black eyes were yellow lightpoints above the glow of his hand-rolled cigarette.

No, he didn't know whether or not Mr. Ketzler had brought out any dynamite from town yesterday. He suggested that Tom Allan, the ranch foreman, might know. He put two fingers to his lips and gave a strange, wild, birdlike whistle.

[3.]

IN RESPONSE to the strange whistle of the sinister-looking young cowboy, a man with a smoking lantern sauntered out of the semi-dark. His blue eyes were inflamed, his pale brown hair was rumpled and his beef-red face was grim.

No, he knew nothing about Mr. Ketzler's eight cases of dynamite, but said dreamily, "That's plenty of powder."

"Plenty for what happened to that building and those two men?" Peter asked.

"Plenty," the red-eyed man affirmed.

"Is there any place where it might be stored?" Peter asked.

"I'd know about it," the foreman said firmly.

"Was there any use here for that much powder?" Peter insisted.

"I don't know what for."

"We wasn't aimin' to do any blasting," the cowboy drawled.

"Is anyone doing any prospecting in the mountains?" Sandra asked.

The two men stared at her face, pale in the rising moon. They stared so long in silence that Peter Storm guessed that the same strange loveliness in her voice that had attracted him in the Boulder Club had set their desert minds to wondering.

"No," the black-eyed one answered.

"Nobody goes to the mountains," the red-eyed man confirmed.

"That professor might," the cowboy muttered.

Tom Allan said scornfully: "What would a ratologist be doing with eight cases of powder?"

"A what?" the girl said quickly.

"Rats," the cowboy said contemptuously. "He's on a year's leave from an English college. He claims there's a hundred and eighteen varieties of rats around here—more kinds of rats than anywhere else, he says."

Peter Storm found something in the cowboy's voice that disturbed him. Or perhaps it was those pin-points of yellow light in his eyes, collected from all the lanterns or the stars. Something eerie. Or perhaps it wasn't the cowboy or his voice or his eyes, but the desert night.

A ghostly wind stirred the long plumes of a weeping willow. The bottom of the valley, beyond and far below the corral, was the color of bleached bone. And beside the moon, a dark cloud with a silver rim flickered ominously.

He felt the faint stirring of hope. He believed now that the blowing up of the laboratory had been a carefully planned job and that someone had the loganite formula. And if someone had it, he must somehow find out who.

"How long has he been here?" Peter asked.

"Just since yesterday," the foreman replied.

The cowboy said: "You were here this afternoon. You came in a big gray convertible with New York plates. You were the last one who saw Dr. Logan alive."

"What's his name?" Peter asked.

"John Medkin."

"A friend of Dr. Logan's?"

The cowboy shrugged. "I wouldn't know."

"Or of Mr. Ketzler's?" Peter said softly.

Sandra Page put in: "You didn't see him this afternoon, did you?"

Peter shook his head.

"He was out hunting rats all afternoon," the cowboy said. His eyes were half-closed and his mouth was sullen. He drawled: "I don't know anything about his friends."

"Or what happened to that dynamite?" Peter persisted.

The cowboy seemed to sway toward him. "I reckon I don't know anything about anything." His antagonism, Peter supposed, could be dismissed as typical of the reluctance of these desert boys to answer point-blank questions. They preferred to squat on their high heels, draw designs with twigs in the dust and discuss matters obliquely.

Peter glanced at the foreman. "Did he seem to be an old friend of Dr. Logan's?"

The foreman's inflamed eyes were growing narrow, too. "I wasn't there when they met. Dr. Logan put him in the cabin up by the pond, and the two of them spent most of last night drinking Scotch and telling stories."

"Was Mr. Ketzler with them?"

"No, sir."

"Did you see Mr. Ketzler and Professor Medkin talking together at any time?"

Tom Allan hesitated and said, "No."

Sandra Page was watching Peter from the corners of her eyes, and she seemed suddenly alert, as if she had sensed all the undercurrents he was sensing.

"Where's Ketzler's car?"

"Outside the main gate," the foreman said. "I'll show you."

"The keys ain't in it," the cowboy said.

"I know," Allan said. "I'll get a wreckin' bar."

As they started toward the main gate, Sandra Page said: "What's it doing outside the main gate?"

The cowboy muttered, "Sure. That's what I said."

"Did he usually leave it out there?" Peter asked.

"No, sir."

The cowboy accompanied them part way, then dropped behind and vanished in the gray light near the ranch house. The foreman took them to the workshop, where he secured an octagonal steel bar about two feet long, curved and fashioned into a claw at one end. They went on to the main gate, and crossed the cattle guard into the desert.

Simon Ketzler's maroon coupe was standing beside a narrow road which wound into a gravel wash between the points of two hills and vanished toward the mountains.

With the wrecking bar, the foreman pried open the lid of the locked luggage compartment. Except for a spare tire and a tool kit, it was empty.

Peter said: "When did he use this car last?"

"Yesterday."

"When he came in from town?"

"Yes, sir."

"You mean, he left it here and walked in?"

"Yes, sir."

"Did you see him unload anything?"

"No, sir."

"Is there a night watchman?" asked Sandra.

"No, ma'am, but Dr. Logan was often prowling around and sometimes he worked all night in the laboratory."

She said: "If Mr. Ketzler brought dynamite, he'd have had to unload it during the night, and you said Dr. Logan and Professor Medkin were up all night."

The foreman stared at her.

Peter said: "Where does this road go?"

"To our dump pile. It's a little box canyon."

"Did Mr. Ketzler ever leave his car here before?"

"No, sir."

"Do you know why he left it here all night and all day?"

The foreman hesitated. His lower lip was slightly projecting and his eyes were still fixed on Sandra Page's face.

"I asked him this morning if he'd run out of gas. He said no, he'd lost his glasses in town and he was afraid to go over the cattle guard, it's so narrow. Then I said if he'd give me his keys I'd run it in out of the sun, and he said he'd mislaid his keys."

"Very fishy," the girl said.

The inflamed eyes were moving slowly over her face. Peter wondered if he were telling the truth. He had the definite feeling again of undercurrents. Something seemed to flow out of the very night, and he knew that the desert moon, still low enough for the Joshua trees to cast long shadows, sometimes played fanciful tricks on summer nights.

The Joshuas began beyond the wash and grew thickly up the alluvial fan, and they grew in fantastic shapes, with arms and sometimes legs, and if you were lost on the desert, and frightened, you saw running men and dancers with long black hair.

The voice made him start. The man had come upon them so silently that Peter was not aware of him until he spoke, although later he was certain that he had felt his approach, had even sensed the heat of his body.

"Are you the gentleman who's been making inquiries about dynamite?" It was a hearty, clipped voice, with the slight accent and the clear enunciation that distinguishes the intellectual Englishman.

He was a big man, healthy and broad-shouldered and sunburned, with pale, shiny blue eyes. He was about thirty-six. He was blond and wore a neat blond mustache.

"This is Professor Medkin," the foreman said in a voice that sounded relieved.

Peter said: "My name is Storm, professor, and this is Sandra Page—Hilary Logan's niece. I'm an old friend of Dr. Logan's."

The big blond man reached out promptly for the girl's hand. He towered above her. And Peter had the definite impression that they knew each other, that there was some bond between them, or, perhaps it was that they were merely strongly aware of each other, and he wondered if she affected all men in the same way.

She was smiling up at the blond man and he was looking down into her eyes, making sympathetic murmurs about her loss. Peter became aware, with sharp displeasure, that Sandra Page and Professor Medkin approved of each other. Certainly there was a definite flicker of attraction between them. It annoyed Peter out of all proportion.

He felt a sudden and unreasonable antagonism toward this large, handsome, blond man, and when Professor Medkin turned to him, Peter was certain he had seen him somewhere before. The hand that shook his was large, hot, soft and strong.

Medkin said: "Yes, I've heard Dr. Logan speak of you, Mr. Storm. What a frightful tragedy it was."

The girl said: "Where were you when it happened, professor?"

And he answered, in his hearty, public school voice: "In a desert, Miss Page, looking for rats. I'm a mammologist on a year's leave from Cambridge, and I specialize in rodents. This desert is full of amazing specimens, you know. I was in the desert all day. I was on the way in—I should say about five miles away—when the explosion took place, and even at that distance the blast was so great that it frightened my horse and I had no end of trouble controlling him. I came riding in as fast as I could and found the laboratory in ruins."

Peter Storm became aware that the foreman had vanished. He had been standing near the girl, and now he was nowhere to be seen.

"I was utterly devastated," Medkin went on. "One of the best friends I ever had was Dr. Logan. I understand you were the last person to see him alive."

Peter said: "Yes, so they tell me." And he guessed that the cowboy had been talking to Professor Medkin. And he wondered why the foreman had suddenly vanished.

"As a matter of fact," Medkin said, "you are one of the very few men he ever allowed inside the laboratory. Tell me, did he seem apprehensive or worried?" His richly sunburned face had settled into the long lines of grave, sympathetic interest, but it seemed to Peter that his pale blue eyes were staring hard, and his impression was that this man was restraining a seething curiosity.

"No," Peter said.

The blond man shook his head sadly. "It was frightful," he said. And Peter warily watching him, wondered where he had seen him before and what the circumstances had been.

Medkin said very casually, "Have you any reason to suspect that Dr. Logan and Mr. Ketzler weren't killed by an accidental explosion?"

Peter wanted to take his time answering. He wanted to watch the mammologist's eyes. But Sandra Page broke in: "Mr. Storm found that Mr. Ketzler bought eight boxes of dynamite in Las Vegas yesterday and had them loaded in the back of his car. We just pried open the back and it isn't there. We've been trying to find what became of it, but no one seems to know anything about it."

The blond man looked at her a moment, then returned his pale blue eyes to Peter Storm's hard, brown, thoughtful face. His expression, Peter decided, was the appropriate one of astonishment, but his eyes were avid with repressed questions.

"That's very interesting," he said. "And quite mysterious. I'd like to have another look at that wreckage."

They crossed the cattle guard and started toward the crater. Medkin said: "But Ketzler was killed in that explosion!"

Sandra Page, looking up at him, nodded. "Yes. It doesn't make sense at all, does it? But he bought the dynamite and loaded it in the luggage compartment of his car, and he drove out here, and the dynamite has vanished, and they say there's hardly enough left of both of them for one decent burial."

The blond man was shaking his head. He was walking beside the girl with his hands clasped behind him. He wore a pale gray shirt and white duck trousers and white canvas Oxfords. He was looking down at Sandra Page with his head inclined attentively.

"Have you any theories at all, Miss Page?"

"He might have been working with someone else," the girl said, "and whoever it was double-crossed him."

"But isn't that a bit far-fetched, Miss Page? Why should there be a plot to kill an innocent and harmless scientist?"

Looking up at him steadily, she drawled, "It's really a mystery, isn't it, professor?"

They passed through a crowd of sightseers under a large black willow. For several seconds they were in the dense shadow cast by the tree. Emerging from it, Peter saw Sandra Page a few feet ahead of him, but not Professor Medkin. He looked behind him. He still did not see the tall blond man.

The girl stopped and turned. She said, with surprise, "Well, where's our little pal?"

The rest of the group under the tree moved out into the moonlight, but Professor Medkin was not among them, and he was not under the tree.

Sandra Page called: "Professor Medkin! Professor! Where are you?" But the blond man did not answer. She laughed softly and said, "Wasn't that cute, Mr. Storm? It's done with wires and lamp-black."

She had seized Peter's nearest hand, and for a moment he wasn't aware of it. Then he felt her warmth reaching up into his wrist, and he angrily freed his hand. She wasn't aware of it or of him.

She was smiling. "Did you see that cowboy vanish in a wisp of purple smoke? Did you notice the foreman sliding away on a moonbeam? Did you observe how neatly the professor transformed himself into a puff of steam? Shall I borrow a broomstick and go riding across the moon, just to round things out?"

Her eyes were huge and dark and glowing. "Well, Mr. Storm, where are we?"

"He is no professor," Peter said.

She said indifferently, "Perhaps you're right, but I think he's as baffled as we are."

Peter looked at her for several seconds before he said, "I think we're dealing with smart people." He was sure that this girl was one of them, that she fitted somewhere into this mystifying and somewhat ghostly pattern.

"Or bewildered people," she murmured.

He was looking past her at the Joshua trees beyond the cattle guard, and he thought for a moment that his imagination was tricking him. One of the ungainly desert trees had seemed to move. As he watched, it separated and part of it became a man who, crouching low, darted to another Joshua. He reappeared.

Aware of Peter Storm's sudden tenseness, the girl said: "What is it?"

"Another spook. See him?"

"No."

"Watch the Joshuas."

"I see a thousand spooks."

The mysterious figure came out into the moonlight. He was crouching, and he looked like a bent old man. Moonlight gleamed briefly on his bald head, then he scuttled from the shadows toward the maroon coupe.

Peter felt his heart compress, then it seemed to burst in his ears. He seized Sandra Page by the elbow with one hand. "Look," he cried, "it's Ketzler!"

She said amazed: "What are you talking about? It can't be!"

"It is!"

"Are you sure?"

Peter started to run. The starter of the maroon coupe whirred and growled as he neared the cattle guard. The engine purred before he was halfway across the bright rails.

The car moved forward, made a whispering turn in the gravel and went softly and swiftly down the road toward the highway.

The girl came running up, her heels ringing on the steel rails.

Peter said tersely, "Absolutely no question. He was hiding out."

She wailed: "Why are we standing here?"

He turned about and ran toward the mass of parked cars with Sandra at his heels. The gray convertible was blocked front and rear by cars. Peter slid behind the wheel and started the engine. The girl jumped in the other side and slammed the door.

Peter heard another car start, then the clang of the rails as it crossed the cattle guard, then the rising howl of its exhaust as it sped down the road toward the highway.

The girl cried: "Back out! Bump it out of the way!"

The gray convertible kicked up dust and gravel and rammed the car behind. It rocked and slid on locked wheels. Peter maneuvered until he was clear. People were running toward him. Sandra Page said wildly: "Don't mind a few fenders!"

He swung the convertible and sent it across the cattle guard and down the road into the dense yellow fog of dust churned up by the flight of the cars ahead. The girl cried: "Step on it, Storm!" But if he had not slowed, he would have gone off the road into rocks the size of skulls.

Sandra Page was leaning forward, trying to see through the white suffusion of the headlights in the billowing dust. She coughed. She said in a choked voice: "If that was Ketzler everything's completely cockeyed."

"Everything's cockeyed anyway."

"Ketzler got the formula, blew up the laboratory and hid in the Joshuas." Peter coughed. The dust was plating his eyes, his throat, his lungs. It was as fine as talcum and it tasted like ashes.

She cried: "Who was in that second car?"

"I'm sure of only one thing. Ketzler has that formula and I'm going to get it."

Sandra Page was holding a handkerchief over her mouth. "Have you a gun?"

"Yes."

When they reached the highway, no headlights or tail-lights were visible north or south. Both cars had vanished. Dusty tire tracks turned north onto the black pavement, and some turned south.

Sandra Page was so excited, so disappointed she was weeping. "Which way?"

Peter stopped the car, jumped out, squatted down and studied the curving dusty tracks in the flood of the headlights. He jumped back in again. He swung the big gray convertible south.

The girl cried: "Are you sure?"

"Yes."

"But he won't risk Las Vegas!"

"Why not? There are three roads out of there besides this one—one to Los Angeles, another to Salt Lake City, and another across Boulder Dam into Arizona."

The increasing roar of engine and wind made it necessary for her to speak close to his ear. "What's north?"

"Tonopah, Goldfield, Carson City and Reno. He could turn off seventy miles from here and double back into California by way of Death Valley Junction, but he didn't go north. He's too smart. Watch the road, too. Things may happen pretty fast."

The needle crept past ninety. Sandra Page yelled above the roar of the furnace-hot wind: "Horse or something on the left!"

Peter saw the green flicker of eyes, heard the clatter of a hoof as a dark shapeless object moved, swung wide to avoid it.

The girl was bending forward, with her face only an inch or two from the windshield, squinting her eyes against the white blur of the desert on either side.

She leaned back and said: "Doesn't this wash out Medkin?"

He answered: "If you prefer it that way."

She yelled: "Something dark on the right! Looks like a car without lights. See it?"

"Yes."

It was a car without lights, towing a trailer piled high with cordwood.

The gray convertible soared up and over a rise and the diamond-bright lights of Las Vegas appeared far ahead and below.

As they started down the long grade, the girl yelled: "Do you see a tail-light?"

"No. He may not be driving with lights. This moon is bright enough."

"He may be traveling faster than we are! You may be wrong. He may have headed north. What makes you think I prefer it any way?"

Peter flicked a glance at her. Her hair, or most of it,

had come free of the handkerchief he had lent her and was floating in a dark cloud.

"You had an idea that Ketzler was working with someone who double-crossed him. Does it fit Medkin?"

She cried angrily: "It doesn't fit anybody now! You're suspicious of Medkin."

"He's phony."

"You're naturally suspicious."

"Why are you trying to whitewash him?"

She shrieked: "I'm not!"

"I've seen him before."

A pair of headlights suddenly appeared out of a dip ahead and the road a half mile this side became flowing white fire.

Peter dropped to ninety, to pass the car.

The girl yelled: "Being sure you've seen people before is the secret of your charm."

Peter touched her elbow. She leaned back until her shoulder was against his. She put her ear close to his mouth. He shouted: "It's a wise man who knows when he's in the midst of his enemies. His name isn't Medkin, he isn't a a mammologist, and he isn't an old friend of your Uncle Hilary's."

A strand of her hair spread across his eyes and nose. He threw his head back to escape it. His eyes were watering. There was a hard pounding on the right side. The wheels on that side were off the road.

The road came back into focus, and he nursed the hammering wheels off the gravel shoulder.

Sandra Page was huddled beside him with her hands over her eyes. Her shoulder was hard against his. She removed her hands and yelled: "Anything over a hundred is too fast for epigrams."

She seemed to slump. Her shoulder was still pressed against his.

Peter tucked his chin down again. He was furious. He had wanted to make her talk, to betray herself; he hadn't meant to go off the road. And he had been furious at the flicker of attraction between her and the big blond man. He had been furious out of all proportion.

He told himself to try to be rational about it. Just why, he asked himself, was he furious? Possibly because he couldn't be sure. He believed, or he wanted to believe, that she was as strongly attracted to him as he was to her. Their personalities had clashed in the very moment their eyes met across the roulette table. And ever since, this attraction had been confused with hostility, with hostility outweighing attraction.

His judgment, he knew, had been sound. It had been necessary to keep her with him. She was a liar, she was treacherous; but she was less dangerous if he could watch her.

Still, he wished that she were not beside him now, because she fascinated him. It was as strange, as mystifying as all the other things that had happened tonight. He wanted to keep it off a romantic basis, yet it was as if he had been in love with this girl for a long time and had met her tonight after a long separation. And it was as if he had been listening for years for her particular voice and had recognized it unhesitatingly when he had heard it.

Then he recalled how the cowboy and the ranch foreman had stared at her in the moonlight the first time she
spoke, and he wondered again if her voice, her warm,
fresh personality affected all men as it affected him. It
might be that she was that rare exception to type that
appealed to all men.

Peter told himself that he was too practical, too
cynical to fall in love with a girl like Sandra Page. For
although she seemed to add up, as far as appearance and
personality went, to the sum-total of all the things he
liked in a girl, she was an industrial spy. She was worse
than a thief.

She was bending forward again, with her face close
to the windshield, her hair blowing about cloudily, con-
centrating on the road, doubtless thinking of how she
would double-cross him when they overtook Simon
Ketzler.

She cried: "Why are you going so slow?"

He hadn't meant to. It nicely illustrated just how
things were going. He was letting his feelings for a girl
who would doubtless cut his throat if it were necessary,
interfere with the most important case he had ever
tackled for Allied Metals.

He pushed the treadle to the floor. The soft and
sinister song of the engine deepened again.

A moment later Sandra Page yelled: "Tail-light!"

He saw it a split-second later. It was just rounding
the wide turn and traveling fast. It vanished where the
trees began on the outskirts of town.

Peter slowed to sixty-five for the turn. When he
reached the straightaway, the tail-light had vanished.

Beyond the railroad underpass, where the highway dead-ended into the Salt Lake Highway, he stopped. He counted four tail-lights on the grade north, and three vanishing in the direction of the bright glow of the business district.

He turned south. Sandra Page cried: "Why not north?"

"If I were Ketzler, I'd be heading for Boulder Dam."

"Why?"

"A hunch."

A highway patrol officer confirmed it. A maroon coupe had gone east a few minutes before on Fremont Street. Where Fremont ended, at the eastern edge of town, the road to Boulder City began.

Peter took it easy to the edge of town. Sandra Page had relaxed again. With her shoulders flat against the back of the seat, she turned her head and looked at him.

"If that's the car we're after, and if Ketzler's really in it, why should he be heading for the dam?"

"Does his name suggest anything?"

She thought about it a moment and said, "Germany?"

"I'd hate to see Hitler get loganite."

"So would I, Mr. Storm. Is there a tunnel from Boulder to Berlin?"

"If I were Ketzler," Peter answered, "I'd be heading for the Boulder City airport to charter a plane to New York. There's nothing out until eleven-one tomorrow morning. He was too early for the New York plane at the Las Vegas airport. I wouldn't hang around this neighborhood at all. I'd drive across the dam and over the Kingman cutoff to Kingman and on to Winslow and try to catch a plane there, or to Phoenix and try to make one there, and if I couldn't make either of them, I'd charter. Or, if I were prejudiced against flying, I'd turn south at the fork just beyond Railroad Pass and wait for the express train at Needles."

She was binding his handkerchief about her head again, tying it under her chin. She turned to look at him as she tucked in strands of brown hair. In the light from the street lamp, her face was white with excitement. She had lost the cornflowers.

She said mockingly: "You don't overlook anything, do you, Mr. Storm? Has it occurred to you that the taillight we saw on the bend might have been on the car that's following him?"

"You mean," Peter said, "that it mightn't be chasing him; it might be a convoy. You mean, it might be Medkin."

"Or the cowboy or the foreman or all three," she said. "It must have been running without lights until then. Would it have been if it were a convoy?"

"Nice point," he said.

"How much," she asked, "in hard cash, would loganite be worth to any country for war use?"

"Five or ten million dollars."

"And Ketzler is so smart and so thorough that he might have arranged for a convoy. So that, if we can pass the second car and overtake Ketzler, the second car would be upon us before we could get the formula, and we'd be very apt to be killed."

Peter glanced at her grinning. "Afraid?"

"No, Mr. Storm. Are you?"

"Yes, Miss Page."

"Were you afraid when I aimed that gun at you in your room?"

"Certainly."

She laughed. "I don't believe it. That telephone stunt was too cool. I believe you're made of pig-iron with brass and rawhide trimmings."

They left Las Vegas and were in the desert again. The moon was high, small and white. Beyond Railroad Pass heat lightning was still flashing in a dark cloud bank. The long grade was dramatized by a chain of headlights, each contributing to the danger of fast driving, by the heat mirage which multiplied every pair and overlaid the black surface with long puddles of melting white fire, making it almost impossible to see tail-lights ahead.

The heat seemed more oppressive on this side of the valley. As Peter increased speed and the hot wind cut into his face again, he said: "If you're thirsty, there's a full water bag hanging on the back."

Sandra Page was bending forward again, with her face close to the windshield. "I'm not thirsty. What form is the formula in? I mean, is it typed on a sheet of paper?"

"Probably," he said. He recalled that when he had asked Hilary Logan that question, the scientist had evaded it, had grinned slyly. It would have appealed to his sense of the dramatic, Peter believed, and his practical sense, too, to disguise it somehow.

He tucked his chin down again. The gray convertible took the long grade to Railroad Pass and the curve beyond it with Peter's right foot pressed to the floor. They overtook and passed only one car—an old sedan that was boiling.

Peter continued past the fork to the inspection station just over the line in the Boulder Dam recreational area. From the Federal inspector he learned that a man answering Simon Ketzler's description—bald, blue-eyed, pink-cheeked, about seventy—had driven through in a maroon coupe about four minutes ago.

Peter asked the inspector if another car had gone east shortly afterwards.

"Yes, sir."

"Driven by a big man in a gray shirt and white pants?"

"Yes, sir."

"Was he alone?"

"Yes, sir."

"What kind of a car was it?"

"I didn't notice the make. It was a big blue sedan."

Peter thanked him and drove on. Shifting to high, he said dryly, "Convoy?"

Sandra Page smiled at him. "You tell me, Mr. Storm. I'm always wrong."

"I only hope," Peter said, "I'm a better shot than Medkin."

"Are you a good shot?"

"Sometime I'll show you my medals."

[4.]

IN a suite on A deck of the westbound Italian liner, "City of Naples," Count Angelo Beretti was pacing back and forth with a radiogram from Rome in his hand. Count Beretti was a short, heavily-built man with gray hair, snapping black eyes and a gray military mustache. Even in chartreuse pajamas, his military bearing was unmistakable.

Count Beretti was furious and a little frightened. The radiogram from Italian official headquarters curtly wanted to know how it had come about that Count Beretti's visit to New York, supposed to be of the gravest importance and the greatest secrecy, had been mentioned in a New York newspaper.

Count Beretti was traveling to New York to keep a secret appointment with a man, one of whose many names was John Medkin, who had offered to sell the Italian Government the secret process for manufacturing a new metal of such remarkable properties that it would give Italy—if Count Beretti did not fumble his chance—a smashing advantage over all the nations at war.

There was no doubt in his mind as to the source of the leak. He was recalling with dismay how drunk he had got during an hilarious time with that charming blonde American girl last night.

The administration building and hangars of the Boulder City Airport were close to the road. Peter Storm stopped and made inquiries. No man answering Simon Ketzler's description had been seen.

He returned to the car, drove on through Boulder City and on across the great curved slab of floodlighted concrete which dammed the waters of the Colorado River in Black Canyon. The road on the Arizona side of Boulder Dam wound for miles among high mountains. The frequent curves made fast driving impossible.

Sandra Page urged him to drive faster. The tires screamed on a curve. Peter said: "Aren't you afraid of Medkin? He might take a shot at us if we pass him, you know."

"We won't pass him at this rate."

"We aren't two minutes behind him."

"Supposing he overtakes Ketzler first?"

"I'd prefer it that way."

"How about gas?"

"I'll have to stop in Kingman."

"I mean, their gas."

"They'll both have to stop somewhere."

She said impulsively: "I wish we could ask the police to help us. It would be so easy to head them off."

"It's strange," Peter said, "you haven't mentioned the police before. We'll go through Sulphide in a few minutes. We can stop there if you like, and you can phone ahead to the Kingman police."

When she didn't answer, he said: "Well, why not? You're the legal owner of the formula—remember? You're dying to get your hands on it so you can

destroy it and prevent war from becoming more horrible. Don't you remember?"

"You're driving too slow," she said.

"I'm driving faster than is safe," he said gently.
"Why didn't you have the police search me when you
were so sure I had the formula? Why didn't you take
that house detective into your confidence? Shall we stop
in Sulphide?"

She had turned her head so that he couldn't see her
face.

"No."

For the first time, her amazing resourcefulness wasn't
of any help to her.

"Shall I tell you why?"

When she didn't answer or turn her head, he said:
"Because you're not Hilary Logan's niece. I knew that
up in that hotel room. I know all about Hilary Logan,
because I had him well checked up. His only living
relative is his sister, Hannah Logan, an elderly school
teacher, who lives in Lebanon, Pennsylvania."

Peter became aware of a pungent smell in the air
that was like the smell of arnica. And the air was suddenly fresh and cooler. Somewhere in the mountains it
had rained lightly and released the arnica smell which
had always puzzled him.

He said: "I don't know who you are or who you're
working for. But I assume you don't want to notify
the police any more than I do."

She turned away from the windshield and looked at
him. Her face looked white and small, and her air was

humble. She even looked, he thought, as if she were frightened.

She said huskily: "What's your reason, Mr. Storm?"

Peter said bluntly: "What do you really know about that formula?"

"Frankly, very little."

"All right. The most important thing about it is that it's unpatentable. The reasons are technical. You'll have to take my word that it can't be covered with a process patent, or fenced with protective patents."

The girl said promptly: "I suspected that, of course."

"If the police should arrest Ketzler," Peter went on, "the formula would be anybody's property. Even if it weren't published, if it were to reach Hannah Logan, it would still be anybody's property—anybody who offered her the most money—Russia, Germany, Italy or Japan. My company wouldn't have a chance. Hannah Logan is a greedy old woman and she wouldn't hesitate to put money ahead of patriotism. My only chance, if I can get the formula, is to offer her a fair price for it— the same deal Hilary Logan accepted."

He drove a few miles along the twisting road before Sandra Page spoke. She dropped her shoulders back against the seat. She said: "Mr. Storm, you might as well know who I am. You're entitled to know, and there's nothing to be gained by lying. I was hired in New York by a man whose name I can't mention, a man who is one of the most important men in the British War Office. He offered me a fabulous amount of money to negotiate for that formula."

"Is Medkin in this?"

"Not to my knowledge. I never saw Medkin before in my life. You've got to believe me."

He turned his head a moment and glanced at her. Her eyes were large and dark. Her face looked white.

Turning back to watch the road, he said: "You've done this sort of thing before."

"I'd rather not discuss that, Mr. Storm."

He could tell nothing from her voice. If she was lying, she was, as usual, lying so well that it had all the sincerity of truth.

But he didn't believe her. He was sure she was still lying. Whether she was lying or not, she was still dangerous, still treacherous, still planning to double-cross him at the first opportunity.

He wondered why the pistol with which she had held him up in his hotel room hadn't been loaded.

She said with a note of pleading: "Our status is just the same as before. We both want the formula. I want it for the British Government. You want it for Allied Metals. Why can't we go on working together?"

Her voice had an hypnotic effect on Peter. He wanted to hear her talk. More than anything else, he wanted to hear her laugh. But his suspicion that she was working with Medkin was becoming a certainty. He believed that she was taking orders from Medkin; that the two of them had planned to rob Hilary Logan of the formula, but that Ketzler, working alone, had been too fast for them. And if it were true that she was working with Medkin, then she was completely ruthless, for she would certainly have known that Hilary Logan, once he was robbed of the formula, must be killed.

She said anxiously: "Our original agreement is still good, isn't it?"

He said curtly: "No. You're too clever and you're too risky."

"You'll need me if you overhaul Ketzler."

"I'm letting you off at Kingman," he declared brusquely.

She said nothing for a long while. The curving road suddenly emerged from the mountains and became a straightaway, running along a great mesa. But as far as Peter could see ahead, there was no tail-light.

He settled down and pushed the treadle to the floor. The moon, almost overhead, lighted up the desert brightly, but the lights of mining camps on the mountains on either side and to the south were bright against velvet black.

The big gray convertible devoured the black road and the needle passed ninety-five. The girl yelled above the roar of the parched hot wind: "Car without a tail-light!"

Peter had seen it. It was a prospector's small dusty pick-up truck loaded with picks, shovels, canvas, drums of water and gas. Peter swung off onto the left shoulder to pass it.

Sandra Page had slumped again. She shrieked above the roaring: "You can't handle it alone. You've got to let me help. Can't we make a deal?"

He shouted: "No!"

"I'll promise not to lie," she shrieked. "I'll promise not to double-cross you!"

"Then why," he shouted, "do you want to go along?"

"Look out for that rock!" It was in the middle of the road. But it wasn't a rock. It was a desert turtle. Peter swerved and avoided it.

"If I work with you on this," the girl yelled, "if I'm really some help, why can't your company make some deal with the British Government?"

They passed a car with one dim headlight. It was a touring car with the top down and it seemed to be full of people. Mexicans or Indians.

The hardest thing for him to understand was her complete hypocrisy. It was difficult to believe that a girl who seemed so honest, so impulsively honest, could be so dishonest. Her loveliness, her physical attractiveness, had nothing to do with this, but her warm coloring did, her eyes did, her mouth did, but, more than anything else, her voice did, and her laughter. They were all components of an impulsive, joyous, direct, honest nature, and this consistent contradiction in her baffled and angered him.

He shouted: "No thanks," and darted a glance at her face.

Her eyes were only a few inches from his. What he saw in them was not so much fear as hatred. It glared at him from huge eyes in that white face.

"You're off at Kingman," he shouted.

"If we overhaul them before Kingman—" she began.

She looked away from him and ahead. She shrieked: "Look!" It was a white-faced steer, heading into the road from the ditch on the right. Peter applied more throttle and swung left to avoid the steer.

"You're still getting out at Kingman."

The furious voice of the girl said: "You're just what I've always thought! You're a coward! And you're a blatant, cheap exhibitionist! You're a show-off!"

He thought for a moment she was going to slap him. He was entertained and annoyed and he was ready for it. But she didn't. She pushed her shoulder hard against his and put her mouth close to his ear.

"Mr. Storm, I'm terribly sorry for that. I forgot myself. What I think of you hasn't anything to do with this. Be a good egg. Let's stick together. I'm not afraid of anything. And I'm a good shot, too. Let me have my pistol. I have a filled clip in my purse."

He turned his head so that she could hear his answer. She cried: "What's that?"

He looked at the small, black, furry object in the path of the headlights. "Tarantula. Of course you want your pistol. Of course you want it in your hand, loaded, when we meet your pal Medkin. I'm pig-iron trimmed with brass and rawhide, you're solid loganite. If I'm a coward and a blatant, cheap exhibitionist—and I must say you're a sucker if you believe all you read in the papers—you're a cold-blooded thief who wouldn't hesitate at cold-blooded murder."

There was a loud rumbling sound on the right side.

"Get back on the road!" she yelled.

He got back on the road. She began to laugh. Not hysterically, or wildly, or eerily, but just as he had heard her laugh at the roulette table and in his hotel room. It was free, fresh, joyous laughter. It ended in a rapturous gurgle. It mystified Peter, but it didn't anger him. After thinking about it a moment, he decided that it strangely made sense.

"Storm," she yelled, "you're the funniest man I ever knew."

They were approaching the thinly-sprinkled lights of a town. Off to the left, down over the hill, was the old gold town of Chloride. The town ahead was the new silver town of Sulphide.

The road ahead was empty. Peter slowed to seventy-five. Dim lights in closed stores flicked past.

There was a sudden explosive rhythm beside them not unlike a burst from a tommy-gun. A man on a motorcycle forged up beside the convertible. Peter exchanged accelerator treadle for brake pedal. He pushed hard. Goggled eyes flashed at him as a jerk of the head motioned him to stop.

Sandra Page, one slim hand against her lips, cried: "This is awful! This is the last thing in the world we—"

"This," he interrupted, "is merely inconvenient."

He pulled off to the side of the road.

[5.]

AS PETER pulled the convertible to the side of the road, Sandra straightened up. The hand against her lips was trembling. He hoped she was preparing to spray the motor cop with charm, to soften him up with golden voice and warm loveliness and laughing blue eyes.

She said, "This isn't funny."

"Use your charm," Peter said. "It never fails."

"We can't tell him about Ketzler!"

"Good Lord, no," Peter drawled.

"I'll do my best," she sighed.

The man in uniform walked back from his vehicle. He pushed his goggles up on his forehead and looked at Peter. His face was young and desert-browned and dry-lined. His blue eyes were yellowed and uncompromising.

He said in a soft Arizona drawl: "I suppose you didn't see that sign out of town a ways that says our speed limit is twenty-five."

Sandra Page leaned across Peter and said sharply: "At this hour of night?"

He looked at her coldly. "At any hour of the day or night."

It was just like her, Peter reflected. The right kind of smile, the right words would have sent them off down the road in a matter of seconds. She had to choose this moment to be perverse. She was probably one of those people who hated cops.

"Let's see your driver's license."

Peter produced the small black leather case containing, among other valued items, his New York State driver's license.

The policeman held a flashlight to it. He glanced up with a quick hard grin. "Peter Storm, eh? Are you the guy who got into that jam in Reno?"

"Yes," the girl said promptly. "He's the guy."

"Drive down to where you see that green light."

"Just a moment," Miss Page said. "Won't you listen to any excuse?"

Peter looked at her thoughtfully. It was obvious that she was deliberately bungling things.

"I'm sorry, lady. I've heard them all."

"But, officer, look." When she paused, he played his flashlight in her face. "Don't you," she said with a coyness that Peter found peculiarly irritating, "extend the courtesies of the road to people who are—" She hesitated and shyly lowered her lashes—"who are eloping?"

The motor cop said heavily: "Are you eloping?"

She said softly, "Tell him all about us, dear."

"Yes," Peter said. "We're eloping. I'm afraid, in our excitement—you know how it is, officer—we weren't paying much attention to speed."

"I've heard that one until I'm sick of it," the officer said. "You just came through Las Vegas, didn't you?"

"Yes."

"Why didn't you get married there?"

"We thought," the girl said, "you had to file your intentions there three days beforehand."

"Did you think so too, Mr. Storm?"

"That's just what I thought."

The motorcycle policeman jeered: "After what you pulled off in Reno, you thought that. There is something very phony about this. Turn around and follow me down to that green light. And don't try anything funny, Storm. I know you're a dangerous guy. Well, so am I."

He returned to his motorcycle. As Peter started to follow him, Sandra Page said: "Isn't this lovely? If it hadn't been for your rotten reputation, we could have talked our way out of it. I hope you're proud of your reputation."

"You're not being any more devious," Peter said pleasantly, "than a rattlesnake stalking a rabbit. You put on that act deliberately. Why did you want me to be hauled in?"

She cried: "Well, why not? You were going to kick me out in Kingman. Why should I cooperate? I hope they give you sixty days on the road gang."

Peter grinned. "This town has a tougher reputation than I have. You'd better save your eloquence, smarty."

"If it weren't for your reputation," she retorted, "we wouldn't still be in it, sour-puss."

He stopped the convertible at the curb before the green light. The motor cop took them into the police station. Behind a counter with a grilled window a man was working at a ledger. He was in his shirt-sleeves and he was smoking a pipe. He was a hawk-nosed man with tired brown eyes and a black mustache. He wore gold-rimmed glasses.

"Sergeant," the motorcycle policeman said, "I just picked up these people doing eighty through town."

"Forty," Sandra Page said firmly.

"I heard it," the man behind the desk said. "It sounded closer to eighty than forty to me."

"It was forty," the girl said stubbornly.

The sergeant took off his glasses and peered at Peter Storm, then at Sandra Page. He looked at her a long time.

"This guy," the officer said, with something like triumph in his voice, "is Peter Storm."

The sergeant put his pipe down. "The fellow who got into that trouble in Reno?"

"It must be nice," the girl said, "to be so celebrated you're recognized wherever you go." She smiled at the sergeant. "He was mixed up in the Pendleton murder case, too."

Peter looked at her thoughtfully. She was so clever. This delay might ruin everything. Was she making matters difficult for revenge or for a more practical purpose? She was smiling up at him. There were gleams in her dark blue eyes.

"I think," the sergeant said, "the judge ought to know about this." He reached for the telephone.

"Wait a minute," Peter said. "What's the usual fine for speeding here? Let me pay it. I'm really in a great hurry to get to Kingman."

"He wants to buy a dog," the girl said.

The sergeant lowered thick black brows and picked

up the receiver. He called a number. He said a moment later, "Judge, Joe just picked up Peter Storm and a girl doing eighty through town."

The sergeant listened and said, "Yes, judge." He looked up. "He wants to know if you two are married."

"No," the girl said.

"I thought you said you were eloping," Joe drawled.

"That was just a gag," she said, and laughed.

Joe laughed, too. His teeth reminded Peter of a wolf's. The sergeant also laughed. He said: "Every other couple that we pick up says that. No," he said into the transmitter, "they aren't married, judge."

He hung up the receiver. "Judge Jeffers'll be right down." He picked up his pipe and relighted it. He considered Sandra Page for some time and said, "It don't pay to try to kid Judge Jeffers."

"Thanks," the girl said gayly. "Mr. Storm, you'll just have to control your sense of humor."

He took her firmly by the elbow and led her to a line of chairs backed against a wall. He sat her down and said, "All right, toots, you win. Stop throwing monkey wrenches, help me out of this, and I won't kick you out at Kingman."

She smiled at him, and her large blue eyes were glowing.

"I've changed my mind—toots," she mocked him. "I want to leave you at Kingman. I offered to help you. I offered to risk my life to help you. You wouldn't have me then, so you aren't having me now."

He glanced at his watch. Ten of the most precious minutes in his life had already gone since the motor cop had stopped them. Somewhere between here and Winslow, Medkin might even now be overtaking Ketzler. If he did, he'd get that formula.

He said, "I'll give you five thousand dollars if you'll help me out of this. I'll make it ten if you'll turn on all your charm and cleverness and get us out of here in anything less than ten minutes."

She gazed at him serenely. "That's bribery," she said. "I've a good mind to tell the judge about this." Then she began to laugh. With her face glowing, her dark blue eyes half-mooned, she laughed and laughed. The sergeant looked up from his ledger and peered at her over his glasses. He grinned and glanced at Joe who was lounging near the door smoking a hand-made brown cigarette. Joe leered.

"Here's the judge," Joe said.

Judge Jeffers was a thin, bony, irascible looking man of fifty-five, with bristling gray hair and the clear hard eyes of a hawk. He came bustling in. His neck, which was long, red and wrinkled, reminded Peter of a turkey's.

He glanced at the girl, then at Peter. Peter got up. The judge stared at him and said in a hard, crackling voice: "You Peter Storm?"

Peter said quietly, "Yes, judge."

"Who's this girl?"

"I beg your pardon, your honor. Judge Jeffers, may I present Miss Sandra Page?"

His politeness did not appear to soften Judge Jeffers. He said harshly: "Relative of yours?"

She said promptly: "I should say not, your honor."

He looked at her inquiringly. "Are you engaged to this man?"

"Indeed not!" And she laughed briefly, as if the question had struck her as absurd.

"Come into my office."

Peter glanced at his watch. Simon Ketzler was now twenty-three or -four minutes from here. About forty miles, at the rate he was traveling. Well beyond Kingman, roaring east, with Medkin just behind him, or overtaking him.

Judge Jeffers led the way into a small office furnished with worn and darkened golden oak. He turned on a bulb that hung over the desk. He said curtly: "Sit down, Miss Page."

He didn't invite Peter to sit down, and Peter was glad of it. There was a window open on the street. He was tempted to kick out the screen and make a dash for his car. But he knew that Judge Jeffers had merely to telephone to Kingman to have him stopped.

The judge was looking up at him with an expression of acute dislike. His eyes were shiny and hard and his mouth was thin.

"Was there any reasonable excuse for your driving through this town at eighty miles an hour?" he said.

The girl said promptly: "No, your honor."

He didn't glance at her. He kept his eyes on Peter. He settled back a little in his desk chair.

"Storm," he said slowly, "I've heard an awful lot about you. You're the kind of man I especially despise. You've been mixed up in a murder and you've broken up a home. You've brawled in the streets. You're a perfect example of the young man with so much money that he thinks he can get away with anything. You were born with a silver spoon in your mouth. You've been spoiled by over-indulgent parents. You're accustomed to being a privileged character. You're Peter Storm, the famous playboy. You're an important man, I suppose, on Broadway and Park Avenue."

He leaned forward a little farther. "But you're not on Park Avenue now, Storm. You're in a little frontier town called Sulphide, Arizona. Most newspaper readers never heard of it. But by tomorrow night they will, Mr. Storm!"

The venom in his voice, the malignant triumph in his eyes came as a surprise to Peter Storm. He had expected a judicial dressing-down, the heaviest fine the law would allow; nothing so ominous as this.

"Just a minute, please," he said.

Judge Jeffers pounded softly on his desk with one rigid finger. "Storm, you're the kind of man who's giving these Western States a bad reputation. You take advantage of our easy-going laws. The gambling and the free-and-easy ways of the divorcees in Nevada attract men like you. You're giving that State a bad name, but you and the wasters like you aren't going to do it to Arizona—not to Sulphide, Arizona, anyway."

He settled back, but his expression was no less pugnacious.

"The truth is, Storm," he went on in that hard, crackling voice, "this is just the case I've been waiting for. Young lady, are you a divorcee?"

"No, judge."

"Are you a resident of Nevada or Arizona?"

"No, judge."

"New York, too?"

"Yes, judge, but—"

He waved his hand. "All I wanted to know. In other words, Storm, you've driven out all the way from New York with a girl you aren't even engaged to."

"Oh, no," Peter said. "That isn't true."

"Isn't it?" the judge drawled. "I suppose it isn't true that you hired the lawyer to defend Carol Dunbar in that murder case."

Peter glanced at his watch. "I never denied it," he said.

"But you denied she was your mistress."

"I did, because it wasn't the truth."

"You hired the most successful criminal lawyer in New York to defend a red-handed murderess—"

Peter said soothingly, "She wasn't a murderess, your honor. She was acquitted, you'll remember."

"Why?" Judge Jeffers barked. "Because your lawyer was so smart he hung up the jury! Why did you hire him—out of the goodness of your heart?"

"I was sorry for the girl," Peter said. "I wanted to see her get a square deal. Now, about this matter to-night—"

"I see. And what happened in Reno a couple of days ago? You get mixed up with a married woman and when she runs off to Reno to get a divorce you follow her there and her husband objects and beats you up right in front of the courthouse."

"That's what the papers said," Peter interrupted. The trend this affair was taking was serious. The judge was righteous and malicious. Peter was thinking fast. Sandra was the solution, but Sandra would be of no help by her spiteful smile.

"I suppose," the judge said, "you went to Reno out of the goodness of your heart!"

"Her husband," Peter explained, "is a rat. She and I have been friends since we were children. I went to Reno to testify for her, and her husband got sore and picked the fight. He deserved what he got."

Judge Jeffers was shaking his head. "Storm, you're a bad egg. You're a notoriety seeker and you're dangerous. You have no respect for decency. You're outside the law, in a very curious way. Not the written law, but the law of decency. If I can't punish you for your real crimes, I'll punish you for something else."

The judge glared at Peter Storm. "I'm going to hold you for speeding. In the morning, I'm going to phone the United States District Attorney, in Phoenix, and I'm going to press Mann Act charges against you, and I'm going to make them stick."

He stopped talking and looked at Peter expectantly. Peter said, "You can't do that."

"Can't I?" the judge cackled.

Sandra Page was gazing at Peter with a faint, mysterious smile. She turned her large blue eyes and said: "I'm so sorry about all this, your honor. I can go now, can't I?"

Judge Jeffers leaned forward and said indignantly: "What makes you think you can go now? You've been traveling with him, haven't you? You crossed State lines with him, didn't you? And you're not married to him!"

She clasped her cheek with her hands. She stared at him wildly. She gasped, "Why—why—"

"I am holding you, young woman, on immorality charges."

She started to rise. She sank back again, as if she were suddenly faint. Her face was luminously white. Her eyes were blurred with shock. She panted: "But you can't do that! I only met this—this man this evening!"

"Is that so?" the judge said heavily. "You've both come from New York City, according to the look of things. You've apparently driven out here all the way together, crossing all the State lines."

"That isn't true!" she wailed. "I came to Las Vegas by plane. This evening. I can prove it!"

He gazed at her a moment, then picked up a pen and pulled a lined yellow pad toward him. "All right," he said, "we'll check up."

She cried in panic. "Oh, no!"

Judge Jeffers seemed to be enjoying her distress. He was faintly smiling. "Why not?"

"My—my father's a minister!"

"Oh," he said, "so your father's a minister. Where?"

She hesitated, staring at him with trembling lips and moist eyes. "Cohasset, New York." She said rapidly, with tremulous pleading, "It's a tiny little place. Everybody adores him. It would utterly shatter him."

Judge Jeffers scrawled something on the pad. She wailed: "You're not going to wire him?"

Muscles hardened along the ridge of Judge Jeffers' jaw. "It's time," he said grimly, "he learned about the kind of things you're up to. Maybe it isn't too late to save you."

She fluttered her hands with hopelessness and desperation. "But don't you see? It would ruin his life! Why should he be punished for what I do?"

Judge Jeffers settled back in his chair again. There was a relentless look about him.

"You should have thought about that before you started traveling around with this man. And you should have thought of this man's reputation before you started crossing State lines with him. You knew what his reputation was, didn't you?"

"Yes, but—"

"You knew how scandalous his reputation was," the judge went on remorselessly. "In the eyes of the law, Miss Page, and in the eyes of decent-thinking people, you are not an innocent woman. You are over twenty-one, aren't you?"

"Yes, but—"

"And you knew how scandalous his reputation was. No decent woman goes driving wildly about the country at this hour of the night with a man like Peter Storm."

"Just a minute—" Peter began.

"There is nothing," Judge Jeffers said firmly, "you can say to influence me."

The sergeant came to the doorway and said: "Excuse me, judge. That Mexican we locked up this afternoon says he's awful sick. Do you want to take a look at him?"

The judge said, "Yes. Keep an eye on this pair. We're holding them both."

Judge Jeffers went bustling out. The sergeant lounged in the doorway, puffing at his pipe. He looked at Peter, who was frowning and thoughtful, and shrugged. He looked at the girl, pale and frightened, and sighed.

"You're a mighty nice-lookin' couple to get into all this trouble."

The girl looked up at him miserably.

"The judge," the sergeant went on, "is a just man, but sometimes he's a pretty hard man, and he's got prejudices. I'll tell you one thing—he ain't bluffing. Now you," he said to Sandra Page, "it ain't you he's gunning for. It's Storm. And if you're going to try to wiggle out of this, there's several things you want to take into account. One's his son. His son's a wild one, too. He's in Hollywood, in pictures, and they haven't spoken for four years. He can't get anywhere with immorality charges against you. He just wants to throw a scare into you. He'll hold you as a material witness."

The girl was staring up at him, wet-eyed, as if she were not hearing a word he said.

"You know how the Mann Act is," the sergeant said.

"It's for criminals," the girl blurted. "We aren't criminals."

"It's broken ten thousand times a day," the sergeant said, "and it don't amount to anything unless somebody wants to get mean and press it. That's what he aims to do—and don't think he won't. You can't buy him off and you can't talk him out of it. You two folks are stuck unless you figure out something pretty quick."

"But what can we do?" the girl cried. "He's absolutely heartless!"

The sergeant glanced back over his shoulder and said, in a lower voice: "I'll tip you off to something else. The judge is the biggest booster Sulphide has. He's sore because we've been left off some of the new road maps. He's crazy about publicity. Maybe he's just making goats out of you two to get some publicity for Sulphide, maybe not. But it's something for you to think about, and a couple of clever-looking people like you should be able to figure out something."

Sandra Page was bending forward with her elbow on her knees, and looking up at him disconsolately.

"For instance?" Peter said.

"Well, why didn't you stick to your story that you were on your way to Kingman to get married? You're a mighty nice-looking couple and you'd look nice standing up together."

"It's too late for that," Peter said.

"If it was true, it wouldn't be," the sergeant argued. "It's the only way you two'll get out. I know. I know the judge. All he wants is something to happen that will get Sulphide on the front pages."

"But it isn't true," the girl said.

The sergeant nodded. "Yes, ma'am," he drawled. "But it might be."

Peter walked slowly toward him. His green eyes were

bright and very alert. "Buddy," he said, "you've given me an idea."

Miss Page glanced up at him quickly.

"If you two," the sergeant said, pausing to puff three times at his gurgling pipe, "were to let the judge marry you—"

"Yes," Peter said.

The girl looked at him incredulously. "You don't mean that seriously!" she said huskily. "You don't mean that you seriously mean to ask that man to—"

"Exactly," Peter said. "I don't enjoy the prospect of the publicity we'll get if he presses these charges any more than you do. Unfortunately, it just happens I've been represented in the news as a notorious character."

He saw that she was trembling. Her fists were clenched at her sides. Her chin was up.

"So," she said, "simply because of your reeking reputation, I'm to be dragged over all the front pages, and my father will be shamed out of his church and out of Cohasset."

"I have a swell mother," Peter said, "who lives in Boston. She won't like it any better than your father will. You should have thought of this, Miss Page, when you were thinking up such clever things to say to that cop."

She cried: "Don't you dare blame it on me! It's your terrible reputation and nothing else! I'm nothing but the innocent victim."

"It seems to me," the sergeant said, puffing at his pipe, "you were pretty sassy when Joe brought you in here."

She whirled on him. "And why not? We were brought in here because of this man's rotten reputation. And I'm going to be smeared all over the front pages because of it!"

"And meanwhile," Peter said quietly, "the man we wanted to see about the dog is getting farther and farther away."

She stared at him wildly. "But I'm in love with another man. I'm practically engaged to him. This would ruin everything!"

"If you two were to let Judge Jeffers marry you," the sergeant pointed out, "it would save your reputation. You could get a divorce right away, and marry this other fellow."

She stared at him, then she turned and stared at Peter. Her chin and her mouth were trembling. Her eyes were full of tears. He felt terribly sorry for her. No matter how unscrupulous she was, no matter how hypocritical, no matter how ruthless, she was certainly in a desperate position now. Her eyes were two blue blurs of woe.

She said to the sergeant: "Will you leave us alone a moment?"

He said, "Why, sure! But you'd better think fast, young lady. He'll be back any moment now." He went out, pulling the door shut after him.

[6.]

SANDRA walked slowly toward Peter with her fists on her hips. She looked at him and said: "You think this is terribly funny, don't you?"

"No," he said. "I think it's very tragic."

"No, you don't. You think it's a perfect panic. You haven't anything to lose. You haven't a reputation. You kicked it overboard long ago. But I have. I'm a decent person. I'm in love with a decent man, and it happens that he's horribly jealous. If I don't marry you, my reputation will be ruined. And if I do, I'll lose the man I'm in love with."

"I know," Peter said, "and I'm terribly sorry."

"What good does being sorry do?" she cried. "Why weren't you sorry years ago before you started being what you are?"

He said gently: "There's isn't a thing about those stories—the Pendleton murder and this Reno mess—that's any truer than the interpretation will be of what happened here tonight."

She stared at him a moment longer, with her lower lip thrust out. Then all the fight seemed to go out of her. Her eyes filled with fresh tears and her lower lip trembled and she suddenly caught it between her teeth.

"Let me try to think," she whimpered. "Stop talking."

She turned and walked slowly to the window with her

hand to her throat. She looked out of the window for perhaps twenty seconds. She suddenly turned. Her eyes were clear. Her mouth was firm again. She was pale and she looked composed.

The door opened. Judge Jeffers came bustling in.

The girl said with decision, "All right, Mr. Storm. I'll do it."

Peter, who had known that she really had no choice, walked toward the judge with his hand outstretched. He said quietly, "Judge Jeffers, you've done me the greatest favor anybody has ever done for me in my life."

Judge Jeffers backed away a step. He looked down at Peter's hand, then at his face. He looked suspicious and startled. He was so startled that when Peter took another step, reached for his hand, grasped it and warmly shook it, he did not protest.

Smiling, Peter said: "You see, judge, Miss Page promised two months ago to marry me. She flew out to Las Vegas to join me. She's wanted to reform me, to put me on my feet and pull me together and keep me out of these messes."

The judge darted a suspicious glance at Sandra Page. He returned his cold, hawk-like eyes to Peter's lean brown face.

"But when she heard about this Reno trouble," Peter said, "it was too much even for her. We quarreled, and she said she wouldn't marry me if I were the last man on earth. So I agreed to drive her to Needles to catch the express—it makes a service stop there at a little after two o'clock."

"Why didn't you go by way of Searchlight?" the judge interrupted.

"I heard the road was bad. So I told her I'd drive her to Needles to catch that train, and I started out for Kingman hoping by the time we got there, I'd have persuaded her to change her mind."

He shook Judge Jeffers' hand vigorously again. "Now, you've done the trick! You've done everything I failed to do. You've made her see she's got to marry me to keep me out of trouble."

The judge still looked as if he were amazed and skeptical. Peter glanced at Sandra Page. She smiled a sickly, demure smile. He went over to her and took her in his arms. He smiled over her head at Judge Jeffers.

"You see now, judge, why I'm so grateful. I'd be lost without her. I don't know what I'd do if she didn't stand by me."

He felt her tremble with repugnance at his touch. He bent down and kissed her hair above her left ear and whispered: "Speak up, you dope!"

She smiled sweetly at the judge and said: "Don't you think it would be sweet if you married us instead of arresting us?"

The judge said, "Why, this sort of catches me by surprise. Do you really mean this? Do you two really want to get married?"

Peter tightened his arms a little and Sandra Page said: "More than anything in the world."

He contemplated them a moment longer, then said, with decision: "All right! I'll marry you."

Peter removed his arms from the trembling girl. He

glanced at his watch. Fifty minutes had elapsed since Joe had stopped them.

"Have you got a ring?"

"No, judge."

"Well, Mrs. Scott, the town clerk, runs a little jewelry store. We'll get her out of bed for the license and ring. I'll get my wife, too. Sergeant!"

"Yes, judge?"

"These people are getting married!"

The sergeant took his pipe out of his mouth. "Well, that's fine, judge. They certainly are a fine looking couple."

"Call up Mrs. Scott and Mrs. Jeffers and tell them to come right down here."

Judge Jeffers was smiling now. His face was flushed and his eyes were sparkling. He seemed to have undergone a complete reversal of character.

He seized Peter's hand unexpectedly and shook it and said: "Storm, I want to congratulate you. Maybe the newspapers have been a little bit hard on you. Whether they have or not, I don't know, but I do know something about human nature. And I have an idea this young lady is going to steer you right."

He laughed. "Miss Page," he said, "any time your husband doesn't toe the straight and narrow, just let me know and I'll issue a bench warrant and we'll straighten him out mighty fast. You want Sergeant Murphy for your best man, Storm?"

"I'd be delighted."

"Miss Page, would you like my wife for your matron of honor?"

"I'd love it," she said.

"You might ask Joe to give you away," Peter suggested.

"That would be very appropriate," she said demurely.

The judge beamed. "Well, that's dandy. Now let me tell you what I've decided to do about the newspapers. This story can't be kept bottled up. I'm going to call up Kingman right after the ceremony, and see that the papers get the story right. I'll tell them you two drove here especially to get married. You wanted to be married in Sulphide, Arizona, because it's the last of the old frontier towns of the real West."

He called over his shoulder: "Sergeant, did you get Mrs. Scott?"

"Yes, judge; she's on the way down. She'll stop at the town hall and bring down the license book and she'll stop at her store and pick up a tray of rings."

"How about my wife?"

"I've got her on the phone now."

"Tell her to bring along a bunch of her white zinnias for a bridal bouquet."

Peter Storm glanced at his watch. One hour and three minutes had elapsed since Joe had stopped him. Simon Ketzler, if he had maintained his terrific speed, was now more than halfway to Winslow or Phoenix. Peter's chances of overtaking the killer, or the killers, of Hilary Logan and securing the formula for loganite were diminishing with each passing minute.

The sergeant said: "Storm, would you like to wash up?"

"Thanks."

Peter looked at his face for a long time in the wash-
room mirror. It was a hard brown face, lean but com-
pact, and with its slanting brows, its green eyes and its
rakish smile, it was the face of a trouble-maker.

Looking at his face, he thought: "The damned thing
is a mask. I'm not like that. I'm not a satyr. I'm not a
polite racketeer. I'm not that dangerous."

His face was, he felt, as contradictory as was Sandra
Page's, with its look of fresh young innocence. A face,
he reflected, is usually the sum-total of all the things
you've done, all the mistakes you've made, and of all the
things you want to be and do. That was why a young
face had so little character—the sum-total was still too
small. That was why the face of the girl he was about
to marry was still so innocent—none of the things she'd
done were recorded.

In his suite on the "City of Naples," Count Beretti
was giving a room steward a coded radiogram to be
despatched to an address on Fifty-eighth Street, New
York. The addressee was a man one of whose many
aliases was John Medkin. The message contained this
intelligence:

Disregard previous plan of meeting. Regret am no
longer incognito. Will proceed immediately on arrival
New York to your apartment. Acknowledge.

Peter Storm glanced at his watch. "With this ring,"
he said soberly, "I thee wed."

It was a silver ring, made, Mrs. Scott said, of the
first silver that had come from the Lucky Girl Mine, a

mine which, if it had not put Sulphide, Arizona, on the map, had placed it in a position for Peter Storm to put it on the map. It was silver filigree, intricate with orange blossoms and leaves—a narrow and beautiful band.

He placed it on Sandra's finger.

In the voice of fatality, Judge Jeffers said, "I pronounce you man and wife."

Peter took his bride in his arms and kissed her. She was trembling. She was, it seemed to him, green, she was so pale.

Mrs. Scott, a pretty, freckled woman of forty, was wiping her eyes. Mrs. Jeffers, who had been staring continuously at Storm with birdlike curiosity, now smiled tremulously. The judge, the sergeant and the motor cop kissed the bride.

Peter glanced at his watch again. Just one hour and thirty-four minutes had elapsed since Joe had stopped him on the highway.

They went out onto the sidewalk and Peter opened the door of the convertible for Sandra. She got in and arranged her bridal bouquet in her lap and smiled wanly at Mrs. Jeffers.

Peter said: "I think we'd better be getting along. And thank you—all of you!"

"It was so sweet of you," Sandra said in her lovely golden voice.

Mrs. Scott looked at Peter a moment, then smiled. "Good-bye! Good luck! Come back!"

Peter slipped behind the wheel. He waved his hand and started the car, and he took away with him a memory of the birdlike curiosity in the eyes of the judge's wife, and her tremulous smile.

Thirty seconds later Sulphide, Arizona, was a thin sprinkling of diamond-bright lights behind them.

The speedometer was quivering at ninety when Sandra Storm shouted, "Would you mind not driving so fast?" She was huddled in her corner as far away from him as she could get. "I can't stand it."

He dropped the needle back to sixty.

She said: "What a horrible ordeal it was."

"I'm sorry," Peter said.

"For heaven's sake," she wailed, "stop saying you're sorry. It's the most hypocritical of all bromides. It usually means, 'I'm not sorry, and to the devil with it,' or, 'I'm sorry you caught me at it.' You aren't sorry. What does marriage mean to a man like you? Just another sensation! Just another cheap thrill! More headlines! More publicity!"

"And what," Peter inquired, "does marriage mean to a girl like you?"

She said promptly: "All right, I'll tell you. But it won't mean anything to you. A man like you can't understand what marriage means to me. For years, I've thought of marriage as a wonderful adventure with a man I'd be mad about—and no matter how discouraged or hopeless he ever felt, I'd have laughter for him. Silly, isn't it?"

"Very silly," Peter said.

"I've always thought a girl who could laugh things off would be a wonderful asset to any man. But this is something I can't laugh off. Would you like to hear the story of my life, Mr. Storm?"

"Go right ahead."

"All right! I had a grandfather and a grandmother who lived to be ninety and died within a few weeks of each other. You wouldn't understand why, but I'll tell you about it, anyway. That was her idea, too. In fact, that's where I got mine—that a laughing girl has something that, no matter what happens, makes life worth living for any man. She died first.

"After the funeral, he took me for a walk, and he said, 'Sandy, the only reason I've lived so long is that I couldn't bear the thought of leaving her laughter behind.' But that kind of sentiment is beyond your grasp, Mr. Storm."

"Is Sandy your nickname?"

"To those I like."

"Sandy Storm," he said. "That's cute. I like it."

"I don't like anything about it."

"I was about to observe," Peter said, "that, like all imitations, you seem all right until a real test comes along. When things go your way, you can laugh. But when you're in a really tough spot, when things look really dark for you, Sandy, you're a cry-baby and a quitter. You're like all people who brag about their sense of humor. It works only when the sun is out."

She said quickly: "I told you you wouldn't understand. If I were in love with you, it would be different. A man like you would have stopped even my grandmother."

"Don't you think the irony of it is funny?"

"You can drive faster if you wish. I'm all right again. You've lost Ketzler, anyway."

"Not yet."

"But you can't possibly overhaul him now," she said with impatience. "And Medkin will have caught him anyway."

"Then I'll have only him to deal with."

"But he'll simply vanish!"

"There are only a few ways to vanish," Peter said, "and I know them all."

"You might have tried one of them in that police station."

"It isn't," Storm said, "as if he were a common murderer, merely looking for a place to hide out. He has something in his possession worth millions of dollars, and he's in a great hurry to get it to the market."

She had been holding her bridal bouquet of white zinnias in her lap. She tossed them out of the car. Peter plucked the white zinnia out of his buttonhole and tossed it out of the car. He felt suddenly depressed.

The heat, it seemed to him, had increased. Usually, after midnight, the desert began to cool off. There was the oppressive feeling of a thunderstorm in the air. Off to the left, in the east, the dark cloudbank was growing, and now and then the moon was covered by a scudding cloud.

He realized that this girl's attraction for him was heightened because she was the first girl he had met who did not think that because of his rather colorful and scandalous escapades he was glamorous. Although he didn't consider himself an exciting personality because of his adventures, he discovered that he wanted very much for Sandra to think so.

Actually, his colorful newspaper past was about the only thing he'd ever had to be proud of, as far as other people were concerned. Most men, he reflected, have accomplishments in their business or professions to be proud of; anyone who has any sort of publicity resulting from his achievements is able to be publicly proud of recognition.

He thought: "I'm in a business, or a profession, where my achievements, if any, must be unknown. None of my accomplishments can ever be published—everything I do must be done more or less in the dark, or I'm worthless to the company. Therefore I have no really solid triumph of my own creating to make me proud of myself."

Worse than that, pepole would give him no credit, even if his achievements as confidential agent of Allied Metals were published. He had inherited, at his father's death, a large interest in Allied Metals. He was, according to the company's books, a millionaire, and people either envied him for it, or despised him because of it. And the girl he had married, instead of being pleased at marrying millions, was heartily disgusted.

He wished he knew just who Sandra was. And he wished he knew how dangerous she was. He had dealt with so many people who had used much the same tactics as hers. And yet, in a sense, Sandra was totally unlike those others.

She had deliberately delayed him with her rudeness

to the motorcop. If she weren't working with Medkin, why had she done it?

He shouted above the roar of wind: "What did you do before you went in for this sort of thing?"

"What sort of thing?"

"Industrial spying."

She gasped, as if with indignation, looked at him speculatively a moment, and yelled: "You mean, after I stopped being trigger man for Jimmy the Stinger's mob?"

"That's terribly funny," Peter shouted, checking speed for a cottontail on the side of the road, "but why the mystery? Who are you?"

WHEN Peter shouted: "Who are you?" to the girl beside him in the speeding car, she put her lips to his ear. "I've often asked myself that. More times I've looked into the mirror and said, 'Sandra, you minx, who—' "

"Okay," he said.

She slid closer to him. "What about Lynne Van Pell?"

He hadn't thought about that highly emotional young woman in hours. He didn't want to think about her now.

The road was beginning to twist again. He reduced speed.

"Well, what about Lynne Van Pell?"

"Aren't you in love with her and engaged to her?"

"No."

"But the papers were full of it less than a week ago. Didn't she say in an interview that you and she were engaged?"

Peter said, "I'm not responsible for what Lynne Van Pell says or does."

The girl laughed. She said derisively: "Don't the people in cafe society ever mean what they say?"

"I wouldn't know."

"You ought to. You're one of its gayest flowers. Lynne Van Pell will love this."

Peter glanced at her. "What about the man you're in love with and practically engaged to? Who is he?"

"I'd prefer not to talk about him."

Peter drove a mile or so before he said, "You can get a divorce and marry him. If he's any kind of a man, no matter how jealous he is, you can explain everything to him."

She said bitterly, "No, I can't. You've attended to that. With your horrible reputation, a divorce within any reasonable length of time would make just as ugly a story as the one we—we escaped by marrying."

"Perhaps you'll fall in love with me."

"If you really meant that, Mr. Storm, I think I'd soon be able to laugh again."

"The important thing," he said, "is what the judge said. You should have thought about my reputation before you started driving wildly about the country with me."

"I didn't think I'd be dragged into one of your scandals. I didn't think my father would be dragged into it."

Peter said, with astonishment: "Weren't you lying about that?"

"Certainly not!" she said indignantly.

"Is he really a preacher in a town in New York State called Cohasset?"

"He is."

"That's amazing," Peter said. "I didn't know you ever told the truth about anything. I thought it was against your principles."

She looked at his dark profile and began to laugh.

"Storm," she said, "there's one thing I admire about you, and that's your boyish whimsicality."

The lights of Kingman were just ahead. The gray convertible rolled down a grade and into a wide dusty street. Peter drove into the center of town. It looked deserted. He drove on to the transcontinental highway, Route 66, to an all-night filling station.

A motorcycle policeman came out of a side street and followed. He had curly red hair, freckles, and a permanent grin. He dismounted and came over when Peter pulled in and told the filling station attendant to fill the tank.

He said: "Are you Mr. Storm?"

Peter said warmly, "Yes."

The red-headed motor cop pulled off his gauntlets and held out his right hand. "Congratulations, Mr. Storm! And every happiness to you, Mrs. Storm." He beamed at them.

"Judge Jeffers must have been pretty busy," Mrs. Storm said.

The red-headed young man laughed. "He's a busy man. Are you staying overnight?"

"No," Peter said. "We're looking for a man who came through here an hour and a half ago in a maroon coupe."

The red-headed man chuckled. "He came through all right! He was doing about eighty. I was going to knock him off, then I figured, oh, what the hell, maybe he had a reason. There was a big blue sedan a couple of minutes behind him."

"Which way did they go?"

"West. And the rate they're traveling, they'll be in Barstow by now."

Peter thanked him and paid for the gas. He pointed the gray convertible westward on Route 66. The girl said: "What's west?"

"Needles—Barstow—Victorville—San Bernardino—Pasadena—Los Angeles."

"So what, Mr. Storm?"

"If you're determined not to get a divorce, you'd better start calling me something else."

"I'll call you Storm. That's quaint."

"It's possible," he said, "that Ketzler realized he was being followed. He seems to know these roads. He may have been scared. Or he may have reasoned that Medkin would assume he had turned east at Kingman. Or he may have planned to turn south at Topock or Needles and work to Phoenix by way of Parker, Salome and Wickenburg. And there's still the other possibility Medkin didn't stop to make inquiries. He seemed to know where Ketzler was going."

"The convoy theory?"

He said with exasperation: "If you would only talk!"

"If I knew," she said crisply, "I'd have talked long ago."

There were too many curves for fast driving. Peter said, "There's going to be a cloudburst. Smell it?"

"All I smell is heat."

"Those clouds back there mean business."

"Why not stop and put the top up? We've lost Ketzler. Why are we following him? Why are we in such a hurry? I hate cars with tops down. My hair is in a snarl."

"We'll stop at the river," he said. "Your hair is beautiful."

He reduced speed for a left curve. Just beyond the curve, on the left, was a car well off the pavement on the gravel shoulder.

It was a maroon coupe. Its headlights and tail-light were on.

A split-second after he saw it, Sandra seized his arm and cried, "What's that?"

Peter jammed on the brakes. The convertible was sharply slowing, but the stopped coupe seemed to be rushing toward it.

She said huskily, "Be careful!"

He intended to be. He did not know whether Simon Ketzler would be there, or Medkin, or both or neither. He had no intention of stepping out of the car and getting himself shot.

He pulled off the road fifty feet behind the maroon coupe. He turned off the lights, then the ignition. He waited and listened. He heard nothing but the ticking sounds of hot metal in the roaring silence of the desert.

Sandra whispered: "Give me that pistol."

"You're going to stay right here," Peter said. "I may need your pistol. Give me that clip."

She looked rebellious. She hesitated. Then she fumbled in her purse, found the clip and gave it to him. He snapped it into the butt of the pistol, pulled back the breech mechanism to inject a shell into the chamber, and dropped the pistol into his coat pocket.

"You stay here," he repeated, and looking cautiously about him, opened the door and got out. He stopped and listened but he heard nothing but the ticking of the engine as it gave off heat. A thicket of Joshuas grew to the edge of the ditch.

He walked cautiously toward the coupe, aware that Sandra, disregarding his injunction, was following him. Near the open door a man was sprawled on his back.

The girl asked in a wavery voice. "Is it Ketzler? Is he dead?"

"Yes, shot through the head." They were silent a moment pondering over the mystery of the slain man, then Peter suddenly drew his automatic.

"What is it?" asked Sandra staring with him into the shadows.

"I thought I heard someone."

Sandra had knelt to see if a spark of life remained in Hilary Logan's aged assistant. Now she rose. "I feel sick," she said. She went back to the convertible, sat on the running board and put her hands over her cheeks.

"There's whisky in the glove compartment," said Peter lowering the pistol, "I guess I was imagining things. Don't be alarmed."

"I'll be all right in a moment."

It was evident that Simon Ketzler's killer had made an exhaustive search. A black gladstone and an old brown valise had been emptied and slashed or ripped to shreds. Clothing and toilet articles were scattered about in the ditch. The upholstery of the coupe had been slashed. Horsehair and cotton stuffing had been pulled out by handfuls. The dead man's pockets were inside out. Near his head was a black billfold and near his right hand was a nickel-plated revolver. Peter examined it. It had not been used.

Peter examined the billfold. It contained one hundred and forty dollars in ten-dollar bills.

He heard the girl get up from the running board and the faint crunching sounds of her sandals as she walked slowly toward him across the thin desert crust.

She said faintly: "I have a very poor digestion for this sort of thing. I suppose it was Medkin."

"Who else?"

"He made a pretty thorough job of it."

Peter picked up the dead man's coat which was lying near the body. He held it up for the girl to see. The lining had been ripped or slashed.

She said: "He must have been here a long time to do all this."

"The question is," Peter said, "did he find the formula or was he scared off?"

Then he saw the platinum watch chain. It was lying a few inches along the ground, the other end disappearing into the dead man's pants pocket.

Peter pulled it out. With it came a small bunch of keys. A small ornament glittering near the other end was a Phi Beta Kappa key.

It was a watch chain and the watch was missing. It had been, Peter was certain, Hilary Logan's watch. He had noticed the chain in the afternoon because Dr. Logan had absent-mindedly played with the Phi Beta Kappa key while he was talking to him, and he had been fondling the key when Peter had asked him what form the formula was in. Dr. Logan's fingers had strayed absently along the chain to his watch pocket.

And Peter had realized at the time that it would have appealed to Hilary Logan's sense of the dramatic, and to his practical sense, too, to record the formula in some way that was not obvious. Peter was sure now that his suspicion had been well-founded. If the formula was not actually somehow concealed in the watch, then it was engraved on one of the inner surfaces.

Sandra cried: "The watch is missing!" She knelt beside him and examined the chain. She said excitedly: "Storm! This loop has been pried or pulled open!"

Peter thought: "Clever girl."

"It must have been Dr. Logan's watch," Sandra said. "What do you think, Storm?"

Peter shook his head and said, "I think it's highly improbable."

She looked at him doubtfully. "If Medkin had wanted to rob him of everything valuable, he would have taken that billfold. Why did he take only the watch?"

"How," Peter asked, "do you know that he took only the watch?"

She still looked doubtful. "It's obvious, Storm, but it certainly wasn't to Medkin. It took him a long time to figure it out. Look at these footprints!"

The thin dry crust of the desert was broken as if by many milling feet. Peter was on his knees. He got up and looked about him. He saw footprints proceeding in a straight line toward the Joshua trees.

He followed them about two hundred feet into the desert when he made another discovery. Off to the right, some distance ahead, the moon gleamed in a scimitar shape on bright metal. Then, for the second time that night, a Joshua tree gave birth to a man. He was tall. He wore a pale shirt and white trousers.

Peter stepped behind a Joshua as he pulled out his automatic pistol. He said, "Medkin, stay there. And put your hands up."

The man took one step backward and lifted his right hand. There was a spurt of dirty red flame where his lifted hand was, instantly followed by a thunderous crash. Then there was instant blackness and an astral part of Peter Storm for an indefinite time roamed in strange places.

A knock occurred at the door of Count Angelo Beretti's suite on the New York bound Italian liner, "City of Naples." He opened it. The charming American girl with whom he had dined, danced and drunk was standing on deck, immaculate and fresh and lovely in white flannel slacks.

She cried gayly: "Good morning, Count!"

He stared at her coldly. "What do you want?"

She pouted. The morning sunlight gleamed in her hair. Her brown eyes were clear and very alert. "Why, Count! Are you angry?"

"I want nothing to do with you," Count Beretti said stiffly. "You violated a confidence."

She said with dismay: "But you knew I'm a reporter! I told you so, don't you remember? My paper's delighted that I scooped everyone else. Now, of course, they want to know why you're going to New York. Please don't be angry."

Count Beretti thought of his appointment with Scott Higgins that was supposed to be so secret. And he wondered how much he had told this impudent girl. Did she or did she not know why he was going to New York?

He had been so worried about it he had not slept all night. He glared at her out of blood-shot, haggard eyes.

Ordinarily the courtliest of men, Count Beretti glared at the girl a moment longer, then slammed the door in her face.

[8.]

A VOICE far away cried: "Storm! Storm!" And Peter
Storm opened heavy lids against which stars were press-
ing down. He was lying flat on his back and a face was
dim above him.

Cool water spilled over his head and the stars and
moon were pink through a liquid film.

"Storm!"

He looked up into Sandra's shadowed face and saw
the square water bag in her hands against the moon.

He blinked and mumbled, "Scott Higgins."

"Lie still," the girl said. "What did you say? Higgins?"

Peter assembled his scattered thoughts. "No. I didn't
say anything. Did I say anything? There are bells in
my head, Sandy. Medkin. Where did he go?"

"He got into a car hidden back here and went crash-
ing out of the desert and went cannon-balling down the
road west."

Peter tried to sit up. Something in his head felt like a
great sharp-edged weight banging about. He groaned
and fell back.

"Take it easy, Storm," she said tremulously. "If I
were a nice girl, I'd bind up the gash in your head with
strips of my petticoat. But I don't wear a petticoat.
And my slip is satin and satin's too slithery."

"Get one of his shirts."

"All right."

She was back in a moment, tearing the white cloth into strips.

He said: "Is it much of a gash?"

"No. I think it's called a crease. It's what they do to rambunctious mavericks, isn't it?"

"Shavetails," he said, and fingered the sticky wound that ran through his hair well up on the right side. "Only he didn't mean to crease me. He plays for keeps, that fellow."

"Don't worry," she said, "his bullet only scratched you." She washed out the wound and bound it up with strips of Simon Ketzler's white shirt.

Peter tried to sit up again, and again fell back.

"This," she said, "would be a nice time to tell me all about your medals. Did he beat you to the draw, Mr. Earp?"

Peter said, "There's a calliope in my head now."

He tried to sit up again. She pushed him back. "Wait till the parade passes."

"Did you see him?"

"No. I'd just started to follow you when I heard the shot, then the car."

Peter was thinking fast. The moment before Medkin had shot, Peter had placed him. His real name was Scott Higgins, and he had been pointed out to Peter by a friend in the British Intelligence as a gentleman adventurer, a soldier of fortune with a very colorful and checkered background. He had operated in strange places all over the world—in Java, China and Persia. He was a man who would do dirty jobs for anybody, for a price. Scott Higgins, Peter knew, was a daring and clever man, and a dangerous opponent in a game where the stakes were as high as the value of loganite.

Sandra was looking at Peter curiously. "Have you figured out just what happened here?"

"Isn't it pretty obvious?"

"I always bow to your greater logic, Storm."

"I'd say that Medkin drove Ketzler off the road and shot him at once, then made a quick search but didn't find the formula. Then I think he drove his car into the desert, where it couldn't be seen from the road, so that he could take his time and be able to make a quick getaway if anyone stopped. Will you help me up? This chase has only begun. I'm full of pinwheels."

She helped him to his feet. He started to fall. He put an arm about her shoulders and she put an arm about his waist. The stars, the moon and the fantastic Joshuas slowly wheeled.

"Now your left foot," she said.

"What kind of a driver are you?"

"The kind that hugs the left on all blind curves and blows the horn like mad."

She helped him into the car and slid behind the wheel. She backed into the road and started west. She drove like an angel. Peter found the pint of Scotch in the compartment and offered the bottle to her.

She said, "I think I need that now." She took a drink and gave him the bottle. He took a long drink and put the bottle back.

The headlights of a car coming from the west suddenly appeared around a curve. The car passed. Peter turned and watched it. It was stopping beside the maroon coupe. It was a gray sedan.

"Did it stop?" Sandra said.

"Yes."

"We must have been the first ones who stopped since Medkin overhauled him. How come?"

"There isn't much traffic this time of night, and people in the desert are afraid of cars that are stopped."

They were approaching the bridge over the Colorado River when a searchlight gleamed along the rails that paralleled the highway. The deep honking note of a streamliner's whistle pierced the roar of wind and engine.

The streamliner passed them. They crossed the bridge and presently entered Needles.

"The station's just ahead," Peter said. "Pull in by those two cars."

She pulled in beside a station wagon. The other car was a large blue sedan. Sandra got out and opened the front door on the driver's side and looked at the identification slip on the steering post.

"Storm! It's Hilary Logan's car! Didn't you say the train stopped here?"

"Yes."

"Then we've lost him for keeps—unless you want to notify the police at the next stop."

"Let's check up."

They went into the station. From the station agent they learned that a man answering Medkin's description —tall, blond, mustached, wearing a pale gray shirt and white pants—had made inquiries just before the train came in, and had been informed that the streamliner did not make a regular stop at Needles, but only a service stop. The tall blond man had gone out into the switchyard.

"Did he want to buy a ticket?" Peter asked.

"Yes, sir. To New York."

"Would they have let him aboard?"

"Possibly."

Sandra looked at Peter. "So now what?"

He took her by the elbow and led her to a bench near a telephone booth. He sat her down.

"Smoke a cigarette while I do some phoning."

She was looking up at him, wondering about him. "Storm," she said, "with that bandage, you're terrific. All you need is a cutlass in your hand. Well, what are you going to do about Medkin?"

He looked at her thoughtfully. "Fly to Chicago and meet him when he gets off the train. We can get a plane out of Boulder City tomorrow morning at eleven. We'll spend the night in Kingman."

"Storm," she said, "you're a very relentless man. I'd hate to have you for an enemy."

Peter grinned. "You have, my dear."

He went into the booth and called the Boulder City airport. He knew that the streamliner reached Albuquerque at two this afternoon. It was now two-forty-five. He could make it by plane in four or five hours, depending on the plane and the weather. He should have ample time in which to get rid of Sandra, fly to Albuquerque and intercept Scott Higgins.

When the Boulder City airport answered, he put his mouth close to the mouthpiece and spoke softly. He said he wanted to charter a plane at once to Albuquerque.

"How's the weather?"

"It's not at all good east, Mr. Storm. Flight Four reported very strong cross winds and lightning storms and we're afraid of a cold front over the entire southern Rocky Mountain area. I can give you a definite report in twenty minutes, but I'm sure there's no chance of your getting through. Where can I reach you?"

"I'll phone you from Kingman. What have you for charter?"

"A six-place job that's just had a complete thousand-hour overhaul."

"How soon can you have it ready?"

"Give me an hour, Mr. Storm."

"All right. I'll want it to pick me up at the old Kingman airport. I'll phone within an hour."

Peter next called the Comanche Hotel, in Las Vegas. He instructed the desk clerk to charter a car and to have Miss Sandra Page's luggage, in Room 217, and his belongings sent to him at once at the Arizona Hotel, in Kingman.

"If you have a couple of spare suitcases, pack my things in them. Send the bill for all of it to my New York address."

When he left the booth, Sandra was sitting back on the bench with her eyes closed. He walked slowly toward her. Her linen dress was rumpled. Her white sandals were brown with desert dust. Her hands were limp in her lap, and her wedding ring looked as new and shiny as stainless steel. Her lips were chapped from the hot dry wind, and her nose was shiny.

None of it made any difference. No matter how tired or rumpled she was, it didn't make any difference. She had nothing to worry about.

Looking at her, watching her breast slowly rise and fall, he suddenly felt irritable. Here, he reflected, he was married to this girl who appealed to him more than any girl he had ever known. He knew absolutely nothing about her. She had doubtless been hired for this job because she affected men just the way she was affecting him.

"Nuts," he said.

She opened her eyes. They were deep blue and misty. She smiled drowsily. "Storm," she said, "has that logical mind found something discouraging?"

He said: "You will probably never know."

"I don't like that look in your eyes. Do I look like a tramp?"

"You'll get by."

She was gazing up at him curiously. "So will you, Storm. What's news?"

"I called the Boulder City airport and made reservations to Chicago. Then I called the Comanche and told them to send your things to the Arizona Hotel, in Kingman."

"Storm," she murmured, "you're magnificent. You think of everything. You're not planning to get rid of me, are you?"

"Of course not."

"Are you going to let me go with you when you meet Medkin in Chicago?"

"If you wish."

"Aren't you afraid I might double-cross you?"

"No, Sandy. You won't double-cross me."

They went out to the car. The moon was gone and there were no stars. The heat was greater, and there was an oppressive closeness in the air. Peter put the top up.

They were crossing the Colorado River bridge when Sandra said: "Are you going to notify the Kingman police about Ketzler?"

"No."

"Are you forgetting that a highway patrol officer in Las Vegas, a Federal inspector at the Boulder station, and that red-headed reception committee in Kingman will recall that we made inquiries about a maroon coupe?"

"They won't recall it until after we're gone." He said curiously: "Does it make any difference to you, honestly, whether we catch up with Medkin or not?"

"No. I lost all interest in this game in Sulphide. I haven't your relentlessness, Storm. I'm tired. All I can think of is bed."

"You're a liar, Mrs. Storm."

"All right," she said, "I'm a liar."

The sandstorm struck when they were halfway up the winding grade from the Colorado River bridge. The air was suddenly fogged with fine brown sand. Tumbleweed and fragments of desert brush flew across their vision. The road became dim. The air became hotter. The heavy car lurched as the gusts increased. Sand was runnelling across the road in yellow streams like water.

Peter shouted above the uproar: "A good sandstorm can scrub off all the paint and turn the windshield into ground glass."

"Is this a good one?"

"No. Smell the rain? It's raining somewhere near us."

There was a sudden sulphurous glare off to the right.

Peter said: "I think this is the edge of our cold front."

The girl cried: "The coupe's gone! Ketzler's gone!"

Peter had just recognized the spot. Some of Simon Ketzler's clothing was still scattered along the ditch and being snatched up by the wind.

Brook Van Pell returned to his house on Sixty-first Street, walking through the dawn to sober up. He was shaky, as he always was after he had given in to one of his drunken rages. He felt weak and somewhat ill.

His butler let him in. There had been no telephone calls for him.

"There was a call from Kingman, Arizona, about an hour ago, but it was for Miss Van Pell."

"Who was it?"

"I don't know, sir."

"Where is she?"

"In her room, with the door locked, sir. She left orders that she was to be disturbed by no one."

Brook Van Pell told him to go to bed. He went up to his library and began to walk up and down. It was now almost seven o'clock.

His worries came swarming back. Why hadn't Sandra

telephoned? She had told him she would telephone him immediately on her arrival in Las Vegas.

He wanted a drink. He badly needed a drink to steady his nerves, but he dared not start drinking again. He must be sober if Sandra called.

KINGMAN was a ghostly town thinly seen through sheets of driving sand.

Peter drove to the ·Arizona Hotel. No one was in the lobby but the desk clerk, who stared curiously at Sandra, and suspiciously at the bandage about Peter's head.

He suddenly grinned. "Aren't you Mr. Peter Storm?" He glanced again at Sandra and his face became red with excitement. "Then you must be Mrs. Storm!"

Sandra smiled wanly and Peter said: "We want accommodations for the night."

"Yes, sir! I can let· you have a nice quiet room with tub and shower."

"We want two rooms," Peter said.

The clerk jerked his head up and stared at him. His face became brighter red.

"Con-connecting rooms?" he stammered.

"Yes," Sandra said coolly.

"I'll have the boy bring your things right in, Mr. Storm."

"They aren't here yet," Peter said. "They're coming over from Las Vegas by car."

"I'll have them sent right up," the flustered clerk said.

"Before we go up," Sandra said, "I want to telephone my father. I want to tell him about things before someone else does."

She crossed the lobby to the row of telephone booths and entered one. The light came on as she closed the door.

Peter knew that it was risky to permit her to telephone anyone. She would obviously mention that Peter knew that Medkin was aboard the streamliner, and the man she warned would, in turn, warn Medkin by telegraph. Peter had tried to minimize the danger by telling her that his plan was to intercept Medkin at Chicago. He couldn't restrain her by force from using the telephone. There was actually no way to stop her. This was an added hazard, but there was nothing he could do about it.

Peter lighted a cigarette and the desk clerk said, "Have you been in an accident, Mr. Storm?"

Peter said dryly, "A slight one."

"It's a bad night for accidents, Mr. Storm."

"A singularly bad one," Peter agreed.

He walked to the end of the lobby and looked out. The sand in the air was still so thick he could hardly see across the street. He returned to the row of phone booths and entered the one next to Sandra's. He heard her voice, low and pleading, but he could not make out what she was saying.

He called the Boulder City airport. The field manager said: "It's as bad as I thought, Mr. Storm. Everything's closed down between here and Amarillo, but I'm quite sure it will clear in a few hours. Where can I reach you?"

Peter told him and hung up. He heard Sandra's voice, high with a tense and repressed emotion:

"But—darling—"

She might be, Peter reasoned, talking to her father, and she might not even have a father.

He heard her say: "Darling, you've been drinking, haven't you? No. No, it isn't so simple. He was there this afternoon. He was the last person who saw Logan alive. An hour after he'd gone, the laboratory blew up. I was sure he had the formula, so I climbed the fire escape into his hotel room and went through his luggage, and he caught me at it and I've been with him since. What? Yes. We went right out to the ranch. Yes. I saw Scott Higgins. We talked to him. Then we saw Ketzler get away. What?"

Her voice sounded hysterical.

"Yes, darling. No. Yes, it was. Scott Higgins got away first and caught Ketzler the other side of here and escaped. He killed him. Yes. He is now on the train and Storm intends to fly to Chicago and meet him. We almost caught him in the desert where he killed Ketzler. He shot Storm in the head, but the bullet just grazed him. Storm recognized him as Scott Higgins.

"What? No, Higgins got away and went to Needles and caught a train. He tried to buy a ticket to New York. No, darling, we were stopped for speeding in a little town called Sulphide. Darling, please stop stopping me. Storm is outside waiting for me and he's terribly suspicious. The police were going to hold Storm on the Mann Act and me on immorality charges. We—we were married." Her voice had faltered. There was such a long silence that, for a time, Peter believed that the man at the other end had hung up. Then he heard her sobbing. Then:

"But, dearest, there was nothing else to do. I had to consider dad. It would have ruined him. He would have lost his church. What? Oh, darling, how can you say such things? I do not love him. I detest him. I despise him."

There was another long silence. Peter's head was pounding so that his eyes felt as if they were jumping out of their sockets. He felt sick. He had never heard her use a tone like this one. It was the meek, humble tone of a girl talking to a man with whom she was desperately in love. It made him sick and it made him furious. And he knew that his jealousy was ridiculous. She had told him that she was in love with another man, practically engaged to him.

She was saying: "There was nothing else to be done. It doesn't mean anything, darling. I'll get out of it as soon as I decently can. Oh, please don't say such things. You know I adore you. What?"

Another long silence. Then: "In Kingman. Yes. At the Arizona Hotel. No. We have connecting rooms. If I'm to keep my eye on him—What? No, he kissed me just when we were married. I had to kiss him. People always have to kiss each other when they're married. It was utterly meaningless. No, he hasn't. No, I'm not afraid of him. He won't—What?"

Another long silence. Then: "Yes, darling. Of course. If you say I'm a clever girl, then I'm a clever girl. I'll do my best and keep you posted. Darling, I miss you horribly. I simply ache for you. I—"

Peter left the booth. He couldn't stand any more of it. His head was splitting and he felt sick and disgusted. He lighted a cigarette and saw two men, one short and plump, one tall and lean, talking to the desk clerk. They turned and stared at him and started toward him. As they did so, the door of the booth opened and Sandra came out. She was holding a handkerchief to her nose and her eyes were red.

The short man said: "My name's Ben Cassel, Mr. Storm. And this is Jim Croyle. We're newspaper men."

Shaking their hands, Peter said wearily, "Well, that's just swell. Boys, this is Mrs. Storm. Darling, these gentlemen—"

"They're reporters," she said coldly. He knew her well enough now to know she was furious.

The reporters were staring at his bandage. "What happened, Mr. Storm?"

"A slight accident," Peter said.

"Just a simple little gunshot wound," Sandra said.

The reporters laughed. Peter glanced at her. "Don't forget, darling, what happened in Sulphide."

"You needn't remind me," she said. "I'll never forget."

"Judge Jeffers," the fat man said, "tells us you ran away to Sulphide to get married because it's one of the last of the old frontier towns."

Peter nodded.

"As a matter of fact," Croyle said, "it's less than ten years old, but we'll let the judge get away with it. How long have you and Mrs. Storm known each other?"

"Only a couple of months."

"Met in New York, I suppose?"

"That's right."

"And she flew out here to marry you?"

"Yes."

The thin man said: "What's Lynne Van Pell going to say?"

Peter murmured: "Gentlemen! Gentlemen!"

"But you were reported engaged to her. She practically confirmed it. Weren't you planning to marry her?"

Peter said, "No."

"But she seems to think you were, Mr. Storm," the fat man said. "We phoned her in New York the moment Judge Jeffers phoned us. She accused me of playing a practical joke on her. She said it was ridiculous. When I insisted it was true, she lost her temper and called me a lot of names and hung up on me. She sounded to me like a very emotional girl."

"Lynne Van Pell," Sandra said pleasantly, "has discovered the secret of perpetual emotion."

The fat man said: "Can we quote you on that, Mrs. Storm?"

"By all means!"

Peter said, "Sandy, do you know Lynne?"

"Slightly. And I think she's an awful little heel."

The thin man said "And how about Carol Dunbar, Mr. Storm?"

Sandra jeered: "Good! They're going to drag in that murder case, too! And all about how you hired Carol Dunbar's lawyer out of the goodness of your heart!"

Peter said plaintively: "Listen, boys. Can't you leave Miss Dunbar and Miss Van Pell out of this?"

"And the married woman he was so gallant about in Reno?" Sandra said. "What was her name, darling?"

"Grace Thorpe," the fat man said. "What about the story that you were going to marry her as soon as the smoke cleared?"

"The truth is," Sandra said, "Mr. Storm is planning to start a harem."

Peter glanced at her and wondered if she were deliberately trying to make this story worse for a practical reason, or whether she was merely feeling sadistic because of her recent telephone conversation with the man she was in love with.

"The truth is," he said, "we're a pair of very tired people. And we're just a bit edgy, boys. What we really want you to say is that we're very, very happy now we're finally married."

The reporters glanced quickly at Sandra. She smiled. "Very, very happy," she confirmed. "But awfully sleepy. Is that all?"

"Well, not quite, Mrs. Storm," the fat man said. He grinned and added, "You ought to know that we aren't quite through."

Peter said suspiciously: "Why should she know?"

The fat man said: "Isn't she Sandra Page, the New York reporter?"

"Gentlemen," Sandra said, "my husband will answer all questions."

"Is there any mystery about it?" Peter said.

"Haven't you done general reporting on various New York papers?" Cassel asked.

"My life is an open book," Sandra answered. "Yes, I did general reporting on a lot of New York papers."

Peter wondered if this was the answer. Was she, after all, only a reporter who had been sent west to get a story about him? It didn't quite hold water. It didn't check with some of the things she had said in the phone booth. But it alarmed him. If she were a reporter and planned to write a piece about what had happened tonight, his career as undercover agent for Allied Metals was ended.

"Didn't your aunt, Mrs. Agatha Chadwick," the thin man asked, "present you to society in 1935 at a big party?"

"Yes."

"Weren't you pretty active as a debutante?"

"Not nearly so active as debutantes are now. That was in the pre-glamour girl era, Mr. Croyle." She was watching Peter with large innocent eyes.

"She was known," Peter said, "in the jargon of the day, as a supersmoothie."

The fat man laughed and said, "She's still super."

"And," Peter said, "still a smoothie."

The reporters laughed and the thin man said: "Do you plan to keep on with newspaper work, Mrs. Storm?"

"Perhaps—if my husband will let me."

"Will you let her, Mr. Storm?"

"Until we start having children," Peter answered.

He saw the hotel doors open. A tired-looking man came in with a suitcase in each hand and one under each arm. A bellboy who had been loitering behind the reporters went to meet him.

The man and the bellboy went to the desk, and the clerk called over: "Mr. Storm, this is your luggage from Las Vegas."

"Send it up," Peter said. "Boys, you'll have to excuse us now. It's been a very upsetting night and we're worn out."

The bellboy showed the Storms to their suite, Rooms 204 and 205. There was a short hall between the two rooms and off this hall was the bathroom.

The bellboy had taken them into Room 204. He said: "Where shall I put the bags, sir?"

"Here." Peter tipped him. When the bellboy was gone, Peter locked the door.

Sandra had gone to a table on which stood a lamp. Light from the lamp glowed up into her face. She looked young and innocent. Her face was a mixture of tan and scarlet and her dark blue eyes had a smudged look because of the thickness of her lashes.

Looking at him steadily, she said: "Is this your room or mine?" Her voice was low and husky. He had never seen her eyes so large or so dark.

He said lazily: "Does it make any difference?"

"Will you take my things into the other one?"

"Of course. But we have some things to talk about."

"Can't they wait until morning?" She wasn't looking at him. Her eyes were darting about the room. She was trembling.

He carried her suitcases into the adjoining room. She followed him. When he put the suitcases down, she said with an air of determination: "You know, I don't really know the first thing about you, except what I've read in the papers. You—you haven't a very pleasant reputation. And as long as we're apt to be living for—for a little while under rather strange, rather embarrassing circumstances—"

"I understand," Peter stopped her.

"Do you?" she said quickly. "I'd like to have a very definite understanding. I hope you realize that to me, it's a very difficult situation. I hope—" She stopped. Her eyes fluttered away from his face.

And he realized that she was badly frightened. What he did not realize was that, with the bandage at a rakish angle about his head, his dark face, his sultry green eyes, his lazy and deliberate smile, he looked very menacing.

Her eyes, enormous and dark, returned to his face with pleading. "I hope," she said with an air of breathlessness, "you don't intend to try to take advantage of it."

Her hands were stiffly at her sides. He saw a pulse beating fast in her throat. She undid the handkerchief and shook out her hair. It was only something to do. She was suddenly blushing.

"After all," he said in a lazy, insinuating voice, "there's a key on this side of this door. All you have to do is turn it. And people who are really frightened prop chairs under doorknobs."

She looked at him as if she were about to burst into tears. She cried: "You know we both want these connecting doors left open! That's the whole point! You know I don't trust you out of my sight any more than you trust me!"

Peter grinned. "Oh, so that's the point."

"Isn't that why we're living on this ridiculous basis?"

He said, "I don't know, Sandy. I don't know why we're living on this ridiculous basis. Hasn't it something to do with publicity?"

"If I weren't a fool," she said promptly, "I wouldn't be here at all."

They looked at each other with deep and prolonged speculation and suspicion, then she smiled tentatively. "Let's have a cigarette, Storm, and stop being fools."

He held out a package. She took two and lighted them and gave him one. Her hands were shaking. She laughed softly and said, "You're a liberal education."

"How," Peter said, "is your father?"

She lifted her head quickly. "All right."

"How did he take the news?"

"Very badly. He didn't mind my having got married. What burned him alive was my marrying you. It seems your reputation is known even in Cohasset."

"By the way," Peter said, "I was in the next booth. I was eavesdropping."

She sat down suddenly on the bed and ran her hands into her hair at the temples. She was looking at his feet.

"I know it," she said wearily. "I saw you go out."

"But you didn't know it until you saw me go out."

"No."

"That was the man you're in love with."

She nodded without looking up.

"Also the man you're working for—the representative of the British War Office. Two things interested me very much. The first was that I've been right all along on Scott Higgins—that you're working with him."

Sandra looked up quickly. "You haven't been right. I'm not working with him."

"The other thing is that you don't tell lies to the man you're in love with. I'm wrapping that up in rose petals for the future. Who is this fellow?"

[10.]

SANDRA faced Peter with a gleam in her eyes when he demanded the name of the man she was in love with. "I won't tell you," she said.

"You're not representing any War Office or anything like it. You were lying about that, too," he accused her.

"I'm afraid," she said wearily, "I'm just an all 'round liar."

"Is it a gang?"

She half-closed her eyes. "Certainly. I'm a moll."

"You're a reporter."

"Is there," she said with quick defiance, "anything shameful about that?"

"You are," he said, "the most amazing, the most contradictory girl I ever knew. You're beautiful. You have the sweetest voice I ever heard. You have the air of being the most sincere, most direct person that ever lived. You fairly reek of decency and honesty and the right kind of upbringing. Yet you're as bold as a tabloid photographer, you're as dispassionate as a judge passing sentence on a chicken thief, you're as sly as a coyote, you're as unscrupulous as a Japanese spy, you're as untruthful as a German propagandist . . . and all the time, damn you, you look as if a West Indian daiquiri wouldn't melt in your mouth! How did you get this way?"

Her mouth was demure. "I fell in with the wrong kind of people when I was five."

"What paper are you on?"

"I'm not on any. I've been on most of the New York papers. I even covered some of the trial of your mistress, Carol Dunbar, for a Brooklyn daily."

Peter said quietly: "Please don't make that mistake again. She is not my mistress. She never was my mistress."

Sandra lifted her hands and waggled her fingers at him. "Please, Storm, please. I'm sorry. But you do get yourself into such awful messes. Just consider how this one will look in today's papers. Millionaire boy friend of Carol Dunbar, who was acquitted of murdering Max Pendleton, theatrical producer, weds New York newswoman! Glamour Gal Lynne Van Pell furious over broken engagement to Park Avenue playboy! Threatens reprisal! Grace Thorpe, Reno divorcee, indignantly insists Storm promised to marry her! Newlyweds now involved in desert mystery murder!" She looked at him wonderingly. "Storm, how do you do it?"

Peter was careful not to betray the anger he felt. He said, "Please, Mrs. Storm. I try my best not to be conspicuous."

Sandra waved her hand airily. "And you aren't any more conspicuous than a headless body walking along Broadway."

He looked at her a moment, with his head forward, his jaw forward, his fists clenched. She seemed suddenly aware of his menacing attitude. She took a step back and stared.

Then she began to laugh. Not hysterically or with the slightest strain. It was laughter from a gay, free soul. "Storm," she said, "you look like a Roman gladiator. All you need is a lion."

"And you," he said, "would make a wonderful Christian slave if I only had some oil to make a wick of you."

"I'm going to take a shower," she said. "And I'm trusting to your honor that you won't give me grounds for a case of desertion while I'm doing it."

He grinned at her and went into his room. He waited until he heard the soft roar of the shower. He picked up the telephone and, when the desk clerk answered, said: "Put a stop on this phone, also the phone in 205."

The desk clerk said discreetly, "I understand, Mr. Storm."

"Do you?" Peter said. "When word comes from the airport that a plane can get through, don't telephone but send a bellboy to 204 with the message written. The door will be ajar. He is to walk in and give me the message and say nothing. Is that clear?"

"Yes, sir."

"Mrs. Storm is very tired and I don't want her disturbed."

He hung up the phone. The sound of the shower stopped presently. A few minutes later, his wife came out. She came to the doorway of his room. She wore a sapphire-blue terry-cloth bathrobe over white satin pajamas, and sapphire-blue terry-cloth mules with high heels. Her face was fresh and pink from the shower and her eyes were glowing.

"If you use that shower," she said, "watch out for the upper part of the spray. There's one jet with a diabolical sense of humor. First it shot me in the eye, then it soaked my hair."

He said lazily: "I married you because I knew you'd mother me."

She was gazing at him thoughtfully, with a faint line between her remarkably clear blue eyes. There was laughter all about her mouth, although she wasn't smiling.

"Don't waste any thoughts on me, Storm. I'm not worth it."

He looked at her steadily a moment longer, and said, "Go to the devil."

She seemed surprised, then she laughed softly and said: "In your strange way, you're all right. Good night."

She went into her room. Peter lifted to the bed the two suitcases in which someone at the hotel in Las Vegas had packed his things. He opened them and listened. He heard Sandra getting into bed, and he heard her sigh of content as she stretched out in it.

He looked out and saw a portion of Kingman over rooftops and a portion of sky pale with dawn. The sandstorm had blown itself out. The air was still. He glanced at his watch. It was 4:45. He felt uneasy. If word did not come from the Boulder airport by six, he would drive to Phoenix and charter a plane there. He did not want to be here when the police decided they wanted to question him about the man in the maroon coupe.

He took one of the suitcases into the bathroom and shaved and showered. He removed the bandage and examined, in the mirror, the wound made by Scott Higgins' bullet. It was about four inches long and shallow. It didn't amount to anything. He cleaned it with absorbent cotton soaked in witch hazel. He put on fresh clothing, then went out and waited for the bellboy.

The shower had awakened him, but it had also relaxed him. He wanted to lie down, but he dared not even sit down. His eyes had a dry, burning feeling, and his bones ached for sleep. He recalled that he had had no dinner. He was past hunger. There was only a great emptiness and a dull demand.

He wanted a cigarette. "When I'm dying, I hope there'll be cigarettes handy."

He picked up the pack on the dresser. It was empty. He looked quickly through his pockets. He looked frantically through his suitcases. He was out of cigarettes. He was tempted to go into the girl's room, but he did not want to waken her.

He went back to the window and watched the coming of the desert morning. He felt grouchy. No dinner. No cigarettes. A nasty new crop of publicity blooming all over the front pages. Possible involvement in a desert murder case. And, asleep in the next room, a girl he was crazy about, who, if he came within ten inches of her, would hit him with the first thing she could lay her hands on.

He looked at his watch. 5:30.

His unhappy thoughts drifted to Lynne Van Pell. Her sultry dark eyes. Her thin vital figure. Her arrogance. Her selfishness. Her cruelty. Her passionate tempers.

What would Lynne do when he reached New York? She might do anything. She was absolutely unpredictable. He had drifted into a relationship there that was hard to understand now. Parties and openings and prizefights and night spots.

But there hadn't been anything definite. There had been no crossing of a definite line. There had even been none of what was once called "an understanding." Lynne had confiscated him for herself as greedily as she confiscated anything she wanted and took the future for granted.

Except for a tracery of wine-red clouds low on the eastern horizon, the sky was a clear green-blue which deepened to a soft robin's egg blue as brightness increased. The first flat clear rays of the sun were fingering the tops of the taller buildings when the bellboy knocked. It was getting close to six.

Peter, with a finger at his lips, let him in and took the slip of yellow paper and the telegram out of his hand.

He read the message:

"Mr. Storm: Boulder City airport just phoned. Weather is now all clear to Albuquerque. Plane is leaving at once for Kingman airport and should be there before you are."

He opened the telegram and read:

IS THERE ANY TRUTH IN THIS ABSURD RUMOR THAT YOU HAVE JUST BEEN MARRIED? I REFUSE TO BELIEVE IT. TELEPHONE ME AT ONCE. I ADORE YOU.

LYNNE.

Peter pointed to his two suitcases and whispered: "Put these in my car. Can you go to the airport with me and drive my car back?"

"Yes, sir."

When the boy had gone with the suitcases, Peter uncapped his fountain pen and wrote a note.

"So long, Sandy. You were sleeping so prettily I didn't have the heart to disturb you.

"Storm."

He tiptoed into the connecting hall and listened. Her breathing was rhythmical. He tiptoed on into her room. She was lying on her back, her head slightly turned. Her face was flushed and faintly moist with sleep.

He looked at her tumbled hair with its strong red lights on the pillow and at her lashes curving along her cheeks. Her lips were slightly parted. They were still chapped from the hot wind of last night.

One of her wrists was lying across her forehead. The palm of her hand was up and the fingers were pink and slightly curled. Her other hand was lying across her breast, rising and falling as she breathed. And each time it rose her silver wedding ring caught a gleam of light.

He turned away and left the note on a table in plain sight, and tiptoed out. He hung a 'Do Not Disturb' sign on the doorknob of her room, went downstairs and paid the bill. He left instructions that his wife was not to be called and went out to his car.

The cabin plane was waiting on the field with its propeller lazily twisting when Peter drove up. He should reach Albuquerque by eleven. With three hours to wait for the express, he would go to the best restaurant in town and answer that dull gnawing with a thick steak, mashed potatoes and something particularly rich and heavy for dessert.

The bellboy was placing his suitcases in the plane when a small black sedan drove onto the field.

A short, thickset, weather-browned man in khaki with a bullet belt about his waist and a revolver in a black holster at his hip got out and came around the tail. He had a long, lipless, turtle mouth and he wore a gold badge on the left pocket of his shirt.

He said: "Mr. Storm, Sheriff Johnston wants to have a little talk with you about a fellow that was found dead beside the road down near Topock last night. When Dr. Whitaker got there he says he saw your car leaving there, going west. We just want to check up on a few things."

"Tell the sheriff," Peter said pleasantly, "that I just left for New York on urgent business. And tell him that if he'll write out the questions and send them to me, I'll answer them fully by airmail."

The fine desert wrinkles about the deputy sheriff's turtle mouth became more pronounced. "I'm sorry, Mr. Storm, but I have a warrant for your arrest."

Peter said quietly: "What charge?"

"Suspicion of murder."

11

SHERIFF JOHNSTON was waiting for Peter in his office in Kingman; a tall, lanky man of fifty with pale gray eyes and a soft southwestern drawl that resembled the whine of a spent bullet.

He said: "I hate to delay you, Storm. I know you're on your honeymoon and I know how anyone appreciates privacy at such a time, but the fact is, you're the only witness we have in this case. And Sheriff Ward, of Las Vegas, is sending over a man to ask some questions about the explosion that killed Dr. Logan."

"Then why did that warrant read 'suspicion of murder'?" Peter asked.

"Technically," the sheriff answered, "you are under suspicion. Where is Mrs. Storm?"

Peter glanced at his watch, which said 7:20. "Let's get the preliminaries over with," he said amiably. "She's sleeping. If you need her later, we'll wake her up."

That was his problem—to talk his way out of here in two hours without having to call in Sandra.

The sheriff's gray eyes were slightly narrowed. "Were you going without her?"

Peter looked surprised. "No. I always look over a plane when I charter it, and I'm even fussier about the pilot. I'm afraid I can't be of much help. Did you know that the man who killed Ketzler shot at me, too?"

The sheriff glanced at the adhesive tape on the side of Peter's head. "That's just what I want to know about."

"I'd have reported it," Peter went on, "if I'd recognized him, or seen him clearly. But there was a cloud over the moon, and a sandstorm was blowing up."

"Supposing you tell me just what happened."

Peter complied, selecting his words with care. He knew that desert sheriffs, in dealing with desert murders, are the best detectives in the world, because their methods are those of the stalking Indian.

He said that he had gone to the Three Tree Ranch last night to investigate the explosion, that he had seen a man who resembled Dr. Logan's assistant, Simon Ketzler, furtively climb into a maroon coupe and drive off.

"We were pretty close behind him as far as Sulphide. We were delayed there an hour and a half getting married."

Sheriff Johnston was nodding. He smiled faintly. "Yes, I know about that."

"We found the maroon coupe off the road near Topock," Peter went on, "with Ketzler lying dead beside it. I followed some footprints into the Joshuas. I saw a car off to the right. It was a blue sedan. A man stepped out from a Joshua and shot at me. I was unconscious for several minutes."

"Was he tall? Short? Fat? Thin?"

"It was too dark to say. He was just a dim figure of a man."

"Where was Mrs. Storm?"

"Back at the road. She didn't see him, either. She said

she heard the shot, then the sound of a car. A blue sedan came charging out into the road and went west."

"Did she see the license plates?"

"No."

"In other words," the sheriff said, "this man in the blue sedan killed Ketzler and stuck around an hour and a half, and when you got there, tried to kill you. What was he doing there all that time?"

Peter shrugged. "Naturally, I don't know."

"He tore out the upholstery," Sheriff Johnston went on, "and he practically tore Ketzler's clothes off his body. He was looking for something. His idea wasn't revenge, and it wasn't money, because we found a billfold of Ketzler's full of money. What do you suppose he was looking for?"

"I wondered about that, too," Peter said, "but I was much more curious about the man himself. He evidently followed Ketzler out of the ranch before I did."

The sheriff nodded. "Yes. The maroon coupe, the blue sedan and your convertible were seen a few minutes apart by a highway patrol officer in Las Vegas and a Federal inspector at the Boulder Dam station. A motorcop here said the coupe and the sedan went through a couple of minutes apart, and that you followed an hour and a half later. Apparently the only person who saw the man in the blue sedan was the Federal inspector at Boulder. He says he was a red-headed man dressed in white."

Peter wondered if the sheriff was lying. He decided that he wasn't, and felt tremendously relieved. He tried to recall his conversation with the inspector. He was sure he had said pale gray shirt and white pants and that there had been no reference to the color of Scott Higgins' hair, which was brass-blond.

"It wasn't the man I thought it was," Peter said. "The man I had in mind hasn't red hair."

"Who was the man you had in mind?"

"I was a little suspicious of the ranch foreman and a cowboy there. But the foreman has light brown hair and the cowboy is dark."

The sheriff looked up at him. He had been drawing designs of cactus on a sheet of paper. "Where did you go when you left Ketzler dead beside the road?"

"Mrs. Storm drove toward Needles. I was almost unconscious. We parked off the road a while just this side of Topock, then the sandstorm came up and we decided to come back here."

The sheriff looked at him speculatively, and said, "Did you by any chance happen to meet a man at the ranch named Medkin?"

Peter said, with control: "Yes. A big blond fellow. A mammologist. He was there studying desert rodents."

"He has disappeared," the sheriff said.

Peter raised his eyebrows. "I wonder," he said, "if you might be interested in saving a human life. I wonder if I might have a cup of coffee."

Th sheriff said: "Haven't you had breakfast?"

"I haven't," Peter said gravely, "eaten since yesterday noon."

The sheriff said vigorously: "We'll let the taxpayers blow you to breakfast. What would you like?"

"Ham and eggs and toast and coffee," Peter said. He

wasn't really hungry. The sheriff's relentless questioning had taken away his appetite. But he wanted a moment to think.

The sheriff went out and left him alone.

Peter thought: "I've got to out-think him. I've got to be out of this office by ten o'clock. And there's something that will get me out if I can remember what it was."

Sheriff Johnston returned with three telegraph envelopes in his hand. He said: "Breakfast will be along in a moment," and gave the telegrams to Peter. "These were sent over from the hotel. There are some reporters outside, and I understand there's a plane load of them flying up from Los Angeles. We'll have them in later. Suppose you pull up your chair and we'll talk while you eat."

The sheriff, Peter realized, was on something of a spot. The newspapers were interested in this case. And his political career might very well depend on his handling of it.

Peter moved the chair to the desk and opened the telegrams. The first was from the president of Allied Metals, in Pittsburgh.

WHAT'S THIS ALL ABOUT? PHONE ME AT ONCE.

DAN RYAN.

The other telegrams were from New York.

PLEASE COMMUNICATE WITH ME IMMEDIATELY ON ARRIVAL NEW YORK URGENT.

CAROL.

WHY HAVEN'T YOU PHONED? WHY DID YOU HAVE YOUR ROOM PHONE STOPPED? HAVE BEEN TRYING FRANTICALLY TO REACH YOU. ALL THE MORNING PAPERS SAY YOU AND SANDRA PAGE ARE MARRIED. IT'S TOO UTTERLY FANTASTIC FOR ME TO BELIEVE. SHE IS CRAZY MAD ABOUT MY BROTHER. I MUST SEE YOU AT ONCE DARLING. SHALL I FLY OUT? WIRE OR PHONE INSTANTLY.   LYNNE.

Peter folded the telegrams and put them in his coat pocket. He knew that Lynne was given to exaggerations, but it was quite possible that the man Sandra had phoned last night was Brook Van Pell, and if this were true, then the mystery, or a portion of it, had been cleared up and replaced with another quite as tantalizing.

If Brook Van Pell was the man with whom Sandra was in love, then he must be the man for whom she was working. And if this were true, how had Brook Van Pell learned about loganite? Of secondary importance but of equal interest was Brook Van Pell's activity in this particular field. Brook Van Pell was a corporation lawyer, and a very successful one.

How, Peter wanted to know, had Van Pell learned about the existence of loganite? He tried to recall what he knew about the man. He knew him only slightly. He know that Van Pell had persuaded Carol Dunbar to return to New York from Pittsburgh, where Peter had got a job for her as a stenographer for Allied Metals shortly after her trial for the murder of Max Pendleton.

According to rumors Peter had heard, Carol Dunbar was now Van Pell's mistress.

The telegram from Carol was disturbing. He hated to think that Carol had betrayed his trust in her, had learned about loganite and told Van Pell about it, but he knew that she was—and had been for years—hopelessly in love with Brook Van Pell. And he had learned that girls who are hopelessly in love are not to be trusted.

Her telegram, he reasoned, indicated that she was somehow involved. If she had learned about loganite while working as secretary for Jake Tinch, the chief metallurgist at Allied Metals, and if she had inadvertently betrayed the secret to Brook Van Pell, then she was probably a very worried girl now.

And if all this were sound reasoning, then he himself was indirectly responsible for the leak.

The more Peter thought about it, the less he liked the look of things. He believed, in the light of this new information, that Sandra did not realize the seriousness of the job Van Pell had given her. He was convinced that she was much more innocent than the circumstances indicated. And he reasoned that she knew nothing about Carol Dunbar.

Granted that the leak was his own fault, the surest way to repair the damage, the surest way to solve the problems involved, was for him to overtake Scott Higgins and secure the loganite formula before that wily individual could reach New York.

He answered Sheriff Johnston's questions with the

thoughtful, deliberate air of a man who wishes to be helpful. His breakfast came. He ate it slowly.

The man from the Las Vegas sheriff's office arrived at nine-fifteen. Deputy Sheriff Niles was a gaunt, white-haired man with white stubble on his chin and jaws and an air of grim determination.

Sleepless, quite exhausted by Sheriff Johnston's questioning, Peter, for the first time, felt somewhat desperate. To these determined men, his time meant nothing. When he had been introduced, Deputy Sheriff Niles said: "There are some things we'd like to have light on, Mr. Storm. First of all, what was your connection with Dr. Logan?"

"He was just an old friend," Peter said.

"You mean, you dropped in yesterday on a friendly visit on your way down from Reno?"

"Yes. On my way down to meet the young lady I married."

"You're in a rather peculiar position, Mr. Storm. You were not only the last man who saw Dr. Logan alive, but you're the only man who had any kind of contact with the man who killed the man who killed Dr. Logan."

"Except the Federal inspector at the Boulder Station," Peter mentioned.

"That," Deputy Niles said with a thin-lipped air, "was hardly a contact. What made you suspect that Dr. Logan's laboratory might have been dynamited?"

"When I talked with Dr. Logan and Ketzler in the laboratory," Peter answered, "they weren't working on any experiment. Their paraphernalia had been dismantled and they were preparing to pour some concrete forms for the foundation for a new set-up. There was no reason for the explosion. I asked the only man in Las Vegas who sells dynamite if he'd sold any recently to anyone at the ranch, and he said Simon Ketzler had bought eight cases, with caps and a coil of fuse, the day before.

"I went back to the ranch and questioned one of your men, and the foreman, and a cowboy; and a visiting mammologist named John Medkin, who was there studying desert rodents. I understand he has disappeared."

"Yes. Leaving all his things behind. How well did you know Ketzler?"

"I met him yesterday afternoon for the first time."

Deputy Niles questioned him about the man in the blue sedan. He looked steadily at Peter with the expression of a man who doesn't believe a word he hears, and Sheriff Johnston was obviously skeptical. There was something about these two brown, steady-eyed men as relentless as their desert sun.

Peter glanced at his watch. 9:45.

"Don't you assume," Deputy Niles said in his soft, slow voice, "that Ketzler killed Dr. Logan for something of value, and this man in the blue sedan also knew about it and followed Ketzler and caught him and killed him and got it?"

Peter said thoughtfully: "That sounds reasonable." There was a burning sensation in his eyes.

"Wasn't Dr. Logan experimenting with precious

metals? Mightn't he have had a store of gold in his laboratory?"

"He didn't mention it to me."

Deputy Niles was leisurely lighting a cigar. "Didn't he tell you about his experiments?"

"All he said," Peter answered, "was that he was using high frequency currents in changing the molecular structure of metals."

Sheriff Johnston said: "It's hard for us to believe that this man in the blue sedan fired that shot at you and that neither you nor your wife saw him."

"He was among the Joshuas," Peter said, "and the moon was behind a cloud."

"Yet there was enough light for him to see you well enough to shoot you in the head."

"All I saw," Peter said, "was a dim figure, then the flash of his gun. That blue sedan must have left tracks. A comparison between its tire marks and those of my car should certainly confirm what I'm saying."

The sheriff was shaking his head. "I sent a man down there to check up on that. The sandstorm completely obliterated those tracks."

Peter suddenly sat up. Something had magically produced that elusive item in his mind.

He said slowly: "Sheriff, what you're really getting at is that I had ample time and opportunity to kill Ketzler, rip the upholstery out of his car and find whatever it was I was looking for."

Sheriff Johnston was looking at him suspiciously. Deputy Niles was suddenly tense.

"Ketzler," he said, "fired that shot that wounded you!"

"But there wasn't," Peter said gently, "a used shell in Ketzler's gun. I looked."

"You didn't know, of course," the sheriff said ironically, "that there was a half-full box of shells among Ketzler's things."

"No," Peter said. "What you're really getting at is that you want to make an arrest and that I'll do if you can't find the man in the blue sedan."

He got up. "Because of my reputation," he went on, "for getting into serious kinds of trouble, I am the man who killed Ketzler." He paused. He dropped his hands to the desk. "Sheriff, if I can prove conclusively that the man in the blue sedan killed Ketzler before I got there, you'll let us go, won't you?"

Sheriff Johnston, looking at him speculatively, hesitated. He nodded. "Sure! Go ahead and prove it."

Peter glanced at his watch. 10:42. The door opened and a thin, bony, peevish-looking man of fifty-five came in. His gray hair was bristling and his hawk-like eyes were inflamed. Judge Jeffers had evidently not had enough sleep.

He said in his hard, crackling voice: "Well, Mr. Storm! I didn't expect to see you again under these circumstances."

Peter said wearily, "Good morning, judge. I seem to be in a little more trouble."

"Yes, yes, yes," the judge said testily. "Why didn't you tell the truth last night and you mightn't be in all this trouble?" He glared at Peter, and Peter thought,

"If this old vulture hadn't popped in, I'd have been out of here in half an hour."

The judge said righteously: "Young man, you're a dangerous character. You thought you were being mighty clever last night. Well, I'm glad your sins have caught up with you at last."

"That's the rub," Peter said. "They're somebody else's sins."

Judge Jeffers stared at him with his lower lip thrust out. "Why," he barked, "didn't you tell me you were chasing this Simon Ketzler? My men would have gone right down that road with you and helped you catch him!"

"I doubt that," Peter said. "You didn't believe anything I said anyway. Besides, I didn't think it was Ketzler."

"More lies!" the judge snorted. "You told me you ran off with that girl to try to persuade her to change her mind and marry you."

"Exactly," Peter said. "And that was why Ketzler was so unimportant. When I saw him get into that maroon coupe, I knew it couldn't be Ketzler. It was too fantastic. Like everybody else, I thought he'd been killed in the explosion. But I seized the opportunity to take the young lady for a long drive, hoping she'd cool off and see things my way. When we reached Sulphide, I said nothing to the police about it, because I was sure it wasn't Ketzler and I didn't want to make a fool of myself."

"Why did you chase Ketzler after you left Sulphide?" the judge demanded.

"We talked it over," Peter answered, "and decided that the man in the maroon coupe was in too much of a hurry to be innocent, whoever he was. He must have averaged ninety all the way from the ranch to Kingman. And we were curious about the fellow who was chasing him."

Peter paused. There was a gleam in Judge Jeffers' eyes. "Storm," he said, "you're the fastest liar in the state of Arizona."

"You're doing me a great injustice," Peter said sadly. "Sheriff Johnston claims that I had the time and the opportunity to kill Ketzler. They've agreed that all I have to do to be released is to prove I didn't."

Judge Jeffers looked at him shrewdly. "Can you prove it?"

"I can try," Peter said pleasantly. "Sheriff, who found Ketzler's body and reported it to you?"

The sheriff hesitated. "Dr. Whitaker."

"Of Kingman?"

"Yes."

"Please tell him he's wanted here urgently."

Sheriff Johnston hesitated again. He glanced at Deputy Niles, then shrugged and reached for the telephone. He called a number. He said presently, "Tell Dr. Whitaker that Sheriff Johnston is calling." Then: "Have him come to my office as soon as you can reach him."

He hung up and said to Peter: "He's out on calls. His office girl will try to locate him."

Peter glanced at his watch. 12:59, or 1:59 Mountain

Time. The streamliner was just pulling into Albuquerque.

Dr. Whitaker arrived at one-fifteen. He was a gentle, mild-mannered man of sixty.

Sheriff Johnston said: "Doc, it's about that dead man you found near Topock last night. This young fellow is mixed up in the case. Mr. Storm—Dr. Whitaker."

Dr. Whitaker shook Peter's hand and said, "You're the young fellow who got married last night."

Peter said, "Doctor, weren't you driving a gray sedan?"

"Yes."

"When you stopped beside the maroon coupe last night, did you notice what time it was?"

"Yes. It must have been about two-ten, because the streamliner came through a minute or two afterward."

Peter hesitated and ran his hand nervously through his hair. "Can you say how long Ketzler had been dead?"

The doctor nodded. "Yes, of course. One stage of rigor mortis had occurred, which meant he had been dead approximately one hour."

"Just a minute," Judge Jeffers broke in. "Doc, can you pin it down as close as that when a man's been dead such a little while?"

"Definitely," Dr. Whitaker answered. "Rigor mortis begins at the extremities and works inward. One hour after death, there is a definite stage of rigor mortis. But, Sheriff, I told all this to Saunders last night when I reported that dead man."

"You told him," Peter said sternly, "that Ketzler

had been dead an hour? Sheriff, I resent this very much. You've known it all the time. Judge, what time did Mrs. Storm and I leave Sulphide?"

Judge Jeffers smiled dubiously. "About one-thirty."

"Ketzler," Peter said, "was being killed about the time we were being married. Sheriff, if you'll accept Judge Jeffers as our alibi witness, we'll be on our way. You've been running a bluff."

Sheriff Johnston grinned slowly. "I could hold you for obstructing justice. You and your wife are the only witnesses we have, and I'm convinced you're holding out on us." His voice became slower and lazier. "Will you wire me if anything occurs to you later?"

"Gladly, I'll wire you at once."

"All right. You can go. Do you want to see these reporters first?"

"Let Judge Jeffers talk to them," Peter said. He had observed an appreciative gleam in the judge's eyes. He thought: "He's a strange old duck. I really think he's glad I got out of this mess."

The judge's eyes gleamed with pride as he said. "I'll be delighted to talk to the reporters for you, Mr. Storm."

Deputy Niles looked disappointed and displeased. "Where can we reach you if we need you?"

Peter gave them his New York address and hurried from the room.

He took a taxicab to the airport, stopping on the way to telephone the hotel. The clerk said that Mrs. Storm had not yet come downstairs, although she had had breakfast served in her room awhile ago.

"Have reporters been trying to see her?"

"Yes, sir. But she put a stop on her phone and said she is seeing no one. Shall I ask her if she'll talk to you?"

"It won't be necessary," Peter said. "When she comes downstairs, tell her I called and said that a laughing girl is a wonderful asset to any man. Mrs. Storm will understand."

12

IT was almost three when Peter reached the airport. The plane he had chartered was still waiting. He told the pilot he had changed his plans and wanted to go to La Junta, Colorado.

The express, Peter knew, stopped at La Junta at 9:20. He intended to carry out his original plan. He would board the train and give Scott Higgins his choice of surrendering the formula or being turned over to the police. The police would, it was certain, catch him eventually, anyway.

It was eight forty-six when Peter alighted from the plane at La Junta Airport. He told the pilot to have the plane serviced and to wait. He took a cab to the Santa Fe station.

With a little more than twenty minutes to wait for the train, he bought a paper. The two right-hand columns and a large part of an inside page were devoted to a somewhat garbled account of the explosion which had killed Dr. Hilary Logan on his ranch near Las Vegas, Nevada, and the roadside mystery killing of Dr. Logan's assistant. But most of the space was taken up with the story of Peter Storm's and Sandra Page's elopement to Sulphide, and Peter's examination by Sheriff Johnston.

There was the usual version of his participation in

the defense of Carol Dunbar in her trial for the murder
of Max Pendleton, the theatrical producer, and a
wholly inaccurate account of his recent brawl on the
courthouse steps in Reno with Grace Thorpe's husband.
And a statement by "Glitter Girl Lynne Van Pell,"
who branded the earlier reports of Peter Storm's marriage as "absurd and crazy" and had refused to talk to
the press thereafter.

And almost at the end of the story was a reference
to the mysterious blue sedan which had figured in the
killing of Simon Ketzler. It had been found, abandoned
at the Santa Fe station in Needles, California. But there
was no mention of the ticket agent. And there was no
intimation that the police or the reporters suspected the
real reason for Dr. Logan's death, or Ketzler's.

The streamliner's searchlight suddenly appeared
around the curve, and the gleaming stainless steel train
pulled into the station.

Peter found the train conductor and asked him if a
tall, blond, mustached man wearing a pale gray shirt
and white trousers had boarded the express last night at
Needles.

"Yes, sir."

"What car is he in?"

"He got off at Albuquerque."

Peter thanked him. He was disappointed, but not
greatly surprised. If Scott Higgins was taking orders
from Brook Van Pell, as Peter was now certain he was,
it was logical that Van Pell would have wired him as
soon as he had learned from Sandra that Peter knew

Higgins was on board the train. The streamliner had stopped at Albuquerque at two o'clock.

Peter went to the telephone office and put through a call to the ticket office at the Albuquerque airport. He asked the man who answered if Flight Two had left Albuquerque on schedule, at two-fifty-seven, and was told that it had.

"Did you take a passenger—a tall, blond man of about forty with a mustache and a slight English accent? Six feet two; weight about a hundred and ninety."

"Yes, sir. Mr. Eric Donaldson."

"Did he buy space to New York?"

"Yes, sir."

Peter thanked him, then called the Kansas City Airport and ascertained that a Mr. Eric Donaldson had been aboard when Flight Two, on time, had cleared for St. Louis.

Peter phoned the St. Louis airport and was informed that Mr. Eric Donaldson had been aboard when Flight Two left for Indianapolis at 10:42 P. M.

He had dinner. At eleven-thirty, or twelve-thirty, Central Time, he phoned the Indianapolis airport and was told that Flight Two, now a sky sleeper, had left on schedule at 12:15, and that Mr. Eric Donaldson was aboard, occupying Lower Four.

Peter was now sure that Scott Higgins intended to remain aboard Flight Two the rest of the way into New York, arriving about 5:30.

He put in a call for Dan Ryan, at his residence in Pittsburgh.

When he said, "Dan, it's Pete Storm," the president

of the Allied Metals Corporation betrayed the extent
to which his nerves had been stretched during the past
twenty-four hours by barking: "Have you got it?"

"No, but you're soon going to have it."

"What's going on? Where are you?"

"I'm in La Junta, Colorado. There's been a leak. The
explosion was an inside job. Dr. Logan's assistant, Ketzler, blew him up and ran off with the formula. He was
tracked down and killed by a man named Scott Higgins, alias John Medkin, working for a New York corporation lawyer named Van Pell. Higgins is now on the
plane due in Pittsburgh at 3:34 your time. He's traveling under the name of Eric Donaldson.

"Take two of your men to the airport and grab him.
The formula is in a platinum pocket watch. Get it
before he can get rid of it. This man is very dangerous
and may be armed. Warn your men to be careful."

"Who's this girl?" Dan Ryan barked.

"All that'll keep. I have a plane under charter and
I'll fly to Amarillo, Texas, and make connections that'll
put me in Pittsbugh by half-past two this afternoon.
I'll phone you from Amarillo. Take this man Higgins
to your house and keep him under guard until I get
there. Is that perfectly plain?"

"Okay, Pete. The mill we've been building for handling loganite will be done in a week. The powers that be
have sent men here, and they're impatient for us to
get started."

"We'll be started," Peter promised him, "within a
week."

Peter returned to the airport. His plane had been serviced. He slept all the way to Amarillo. Landing there, he first attended to his reservation on Flight Four, which would stop at Amarillo at 5:06 A. M. Then he phoned Dan Ryan.

The president of Allied Metals said: "Your man gave us the run-around. He got off Flight Two at Columbus. Does that mean we've lost it?"

"No," Peter said. "It merely means I'll be going to New York instead of Pittsburgh. Where is Jim Severance?"

"In Baltimore."

"Can you reach him?"

"Yes."

"Tell him to go to Washington first thing in the morning, and get me all possible information on Scott Higgins, alias Prof. John Medkin. The F. B. I. may have a file on him. Tell Jim to send report air mail special delivery to my apartment. I'll phone you tonight."

Peter next called the airport at Columbus. After a wait he was told that Mr. Eric Donaldson had left Flight Two there and had immediately chartered a small plane to New York. The man to whom Peter talked was puzzled.

"Mr. Donaldson's plane won't reach the Newark airport until at least an hour after Flight Two."

Peter could have told him that the plane Mr. Donaldson had chartered wouldn't reach the Newark airport at all. Scott Higgins' strategy was clever and it was also obvious. There were a dozen small airports within a short radius of New York, not to mention a thousand cornfields, pastures and golf courses, any one of which a small plane could get into. He had selected the cleverest way of reaching New York without detection.

Peter, determined to outwit the wily Medkin, now put through a call to Ben Macklin, one of his two legmen, in New York.

He said to Macklin: "Ben, I want you to keep an eye on Brook Van Pell, the corporation lawyer." Peter gave him Van Pell's address, and said, "Get up to his house immediately. He'll be leaving shortly. Be prepared to follow him into the country somewhere. I don't know where. He will meet a man who is flying from Columbus, Ohio. The fellow he is meeting is a big, handsome blond man with a mustache and a slight English accent. He's six feet two and weighs about one hundred and ninety. I'll reach Newark late this afternoon. Be at my apartment at five o'clock."

Ben Macklin said: "Okay, Mr. Storm. Do I take Eddie Dolan?"

Eddie Dolan was Peter's other legman. "No. I have another chore for Eddie."

Peter's last long distance call was to the Arizona Hotel, in Kingman. The desk clerk said that Mrs. Storm had left the hotel at seven that evening in a taxicab for Las Vegas. She had made a reservation on the plane that left the Las Vegas airport eastbound at about halfpast eight."

"Did she leave any message?"

"Yes, Mr. Storm. She left a note and told me to read it to you if you called. It says: 'When dirtier tricks are played, the blatant exhibitionist will play them. I adore you just as much as ever. Sandy.'"

When Peter left the phone booth, his face was slightly flushed. Sandra had unerringly said the one thing that would annoy him. Because she loathed publicity so, he wired the city editor of every New York newspaper, inviting them all to have photographers and reporters meet the plane when it brought Mrs. Peter Storm into Newark.

Peter then wired Eddie Dolan, instructing him to meet the plane and to trail Mrs. Storm.

As she rode along the Pulaski Skyway from the Newark air terminal, Sandra Page Storm tried to compose herself. She smoked and tried to assure herself that everything would, with a little time, work out all right. Someone must have notified the press that she was coming in on this plane, and she supposed it had been Peter Storm.

The size of the mob of reporters and news photographers had shattered her morale. She had tried to be gracious and to keep smiling. And all the time, all she could think of was to get away from them, to get into New York, and to put her problems into the capable hands of Brook Van Pell.

Brook would, of course, have a solution. A simple, clever solution. For her father's sake, she must avoid anything resembling scandal. She could not live in the same apartment with the attractive, purposeful man she had married. That was, she told herself again and again, utterly out of the question. Yet, with all this publicity, her picture in all the papers, how could she live away from Peter Storm without causing a scandal?

It was to Sandra, an insoluble problem, but she was sure—and she felt happier and more relaxed every time she told herself so—that Brook would find a way. Adoring her as he did, the last thing he would want for her would be either alternative—a scandal, or her living in Peter's apartment.

She had phoned Brook from the airport, and he was waiting for her in the lobby of their favorite cocktail lounge, the Pelican—tall and straight and dark-skinned from his polo—just, as she told herself, as she recalled him, as if it had been months since she'd seen him, instead of days.

Sandra was so happy to see him that her eyes filled with tears. Blinded with them, she groped for him and went into the circle of his strong arms. He kissed her and said, "Darling, darling, it's been awful, hasn't it?"

She said, in a breaking voice, "Darling, it's been ghastly." She wanted to laugh. She knew she must look a sight. He had her hand tucked tight under his elbow, and at the feeling of his strength, she felt much better. All the awfulness she had been through was worth it now. With him, she wasn't uncertain or afraid. Everything would work out all right. His presence said so. His very calm and strength verified it.

They went to their favorite booth, and she sat across from him and gazed at his face, smiling through her tears, adoring him. His gray eyes, in his dark, lean, good-looking face were grave and gentle and solicitous, and his smile made all she had suffered triply worth it.

He hated women who wept. He had said so often. Sandra opened her purse and repaired the damage as best she could. Her eyes were red, the lids swollen, and she knew she looked a wreck. But she was too excited, too nervous at seeing him again, to do justice to the repair job.

Brook Van Pell was bending toward her, looking at her with the busy, hungry eyes of a lover.

She said tremulously, "Darling, have we got the formula?"

13

IN answer to Sandra's eager question, Van Pell bent toward her with his elbows on the cloth, and smilingly shook his head. "Not yet, but we will. Scott Higgins double-crossed me. At least, he thinks he did. Shall I tell you how smart I was?"

She said with a wild little laugh: "Just talk. Just let me hear you talk, I don't care what you say."

"You are so lovely, Sandra. You are so beautiful."

Sandra nodded. "That's very nice talk."

"Did I ever say your voice is like a violin and temple bells and all the other lovely sounds there are?"

She laughed weakly. "I don't know, darling. Did you?"

The waiter came for their order. When he had gone, Brook said: "First of all, I want to hear about Storm."

Sandra said: "It's a long story, Brook."

"I want to hear it all."

"You shall—every smallest detail." She told him about Peter Storm, beginning with their encounter at the roulette table in the Boulder Club, in Las Vegas, ending with Peter's desertion of her in Kingman. Van Pell was especially interested in the marriage into which Judge Jeffers had forced them. He questioned her about that, and about the hours she had spent with Peter Storm in their hotel rooms, in Kingman.

Brook Van Pell said: "It's an amazing situation. Didn't he try at any time to make advances?"

"No, Brook."

"Didn't he even try to kiss you?"

Sandra shook her head. "Only when we were married."

"Not even in your room?"

"No."

"That's odd."

"Why?"

"He has a pretty bad reputation, you know. And you're a very attractive girl. I don't doubt that you're the most attractive girl Storm has ever known."

"He was really very decent," Sandra said. She could feel her heart beating more and more rapidly. She knew that Brook was jealous, and she had been dreading their discussion of this topic. She had been afraid that he might be difficult, that he might not believe the truth about Peter Storm's decency.

She went on, making her voice steady: "He didn't once touch me. He didn't try to. We had connecting rooms, with a hall between. I took a bath and came out and said goodnight to him and there was a look in his eyes, and I said, 'Don't waste any thoughts on me," and he said, 'Go to the devil'."

Van Pell seemed startled and amused. "Did he say that?"

"Yes, darling. Then I went into my room and took off my dressing gown and got into bed, and I was asleep in fifteen seconds. That was the last I saw of him. He must have come into my room in the morning just before he left, for there was a note on my table. When I woke up, he was packed and gone."

"Didn't he try to kiss you good night?"

"No, darling."

Brook Van Pell, with elbows on table, shoulders hunched up, was gazing at her speculatively. His eyes were dreamy, as if he were visualizing that entire scene in the Kingman hotel as Sandra described it.

He seemed to shake himself a little, then he said: "Do you like him?"

"I detest him!"

Van Pell laughed softly. "Not really!"

"Of course!"

"A great many women think he's damned attractive."

"I'm not one of them," Sandra said stoutly. "What difference does a thing like this make to him? He loves notoriety. To him, it was just another thrill."

Brook Van Pell's eyes were lively with amusement. Sandra's heart suddenly stopped beating so rapidly. She knew now that Brook believed her. He wasn't going to be jealous or angry. She was so relieved that her face became hot, then icy cold.

He said, with his slow smile: "He must have been terribly disappointed in you. And you really dislike him?"

"I do. And—darling, what am I going to do? If I divorced him immediately, it would just about kill father. With all the publicity we're having, it would be a front page scandal. And if we separated, and Storm lived in his apartment and I lived in mine, it would be almost the same."

Sandra spread her fingers on the tablecloth. "Darling,

that was the thing I most wanted to ask you about. What am I going to do? I can't live at Storm's apartment."

Van Pell said gently: "You'll have to be patient, my sweet."

She cried: "I was sure you'd have a solution! It's the only thing that kept me from flying to pieces—being sure you'd know how to solve it."

"I understand, darling. Let's put it on the shelf for just a moment and finish up these other odds and ends. Let me tell you about Scott Higgins. I told you he tried to double-cross me."

"That," Sandra said, "was why you sent me to Las Vegas—because you were afraid he might."

"Yes, and if it hadn't been for you, I'd have lost him. I selected him for that job because he's accustomed to putting over difficult, big deals. I'm going to see to it that that man is punished. I sent him to Las Vegas, in good faith, to offer Dr. Logan the most generous terms for loganite. Higgins has double-crossed me all 'round. I suspected he was up to tricks when you phoned me from Kingman. You also gave me an idea what his plans might be.

"When you told me the train he had taken, I wired him at Winslow, told him that Storm was hot on his trail, and advised him to leave the train at Albuquerque and take a plane that left there forty-five minutes later, which he did. I checked up on him by telephoning every airport where his plane stopped. He wired me from Indianapolis, asking me to meet him with a bodyguard when his plane reached Newark at five-thirty this morning."

Brook Van Pell was chuckling. His air was that of a man immensely pleased with himself. His gray eyes had a glow.

"Of course, I didn't take any stock in that. Scott Higgins is smart. He's one of the smartest men at this sort of thing I ever knew. When I phoned the airport at Columbus I learned two things. One, that Storm was also checking up on him, the other, that Higgins had left the plane there and chartered a private plane to New York. I realized that he planned to fly here and land in a field or at any one of fifteen or twenty of the small airports that are fairly close in to New York."

Sandra said: "So you lost him."

Van Pell chuckled. "My dear, did you know that there are only about a dozen ways into Manhattan by automobile?"

"It hadn't occurred to me," Sandra said. She was seeing Brook Van Pell more clearly than she had ever seen him before. And doing a thing she had never done before. In a detached way, she was analyzing him. Having watched Peter Storm at such close quarters, and having spent so much time analyzing him, her perceptions were sharpened. Where Peter was warm-blooded and purposeful and relentless, Brook was cool and driving. It seemed to come down to a matter of comparative blood temperatures.

"It hadn't to me, either," Brook went on, "until it was suddenly dumped in my lap as a problem— if a man were coming into Manhattan by automobile, just how could anyone go about spotting him?"

"How could you be sure," Sandra answered, "that he was coming into Manhattan by automobile?" She was, she realized, seeing Brook for the first time without his glamour, as she might have seen him, she thought, after, say, six months or a year of marriage.

"After all," she said, "there are lots of other ways into New York—buses and trains and subways and ferries."

"The kind of man who would charter a plane," Van Pell replied, "is the kind of man who would charter an automobile. I gambled on that."

He was so proud of his plan for trapping Scott Higgins that he smiled. Her admiration for his driving qualities, her love for him remained as strong as ever. It was simply that the romantic haze through which she had seen him before she knew Peter Storm was no longer there. She was glad of it. In place of the attractive, wholly charming, flawless man she had known before she went West was an individual with strength and with weaknesses to all of which she would now busy herself adjusting.

He bent toward her, still with that boyish proud smile.

"Darling, I posted men at every point where a man might come into Manhattan by automobile — the bridges, the ferries and the vehicular tunnel." Van Pell straightened up. "I must confess it mightn't have worked during the rush hour.

"Luckily for me, he came into Manhattan at seven-

twenty in the morning, over the Spuyten Duyvil Bridge.
The men I had posted there recognized him instantly
from the photographs I'd shown them and the description I'd given them. Luckily—again—Higgins is a man
of very distinctive appearance, easy to describe, easy to
recognize in a crowd. They followed him to a brownstone apartment in the Fifties. I never knew before
where he hung out."

Sandra said eagerly, "Then you've seen him?"

"Sandra, Higgins is a very clever fellow. Before I
could get dressed and out of the house, my man phoned
me again. Higgins had left his apartment in riding
clothes. My trailer trailed him. He went to a Central
Park riding academy and got a horse and took a ride in
the park. A three-hour ride. Just to make sure he was
Higgins, I drove over and took a peek at him. It was
Higgins. And while he was riding, another of my men
searched his apartment. He went over it with a fine-
tooth comb, but he didn't find the watch. Therefore,
Higgins had the watch with him—still has."

"Unless," Sandra said, "he gave it to someone before
he came into the city."

The dark-skinned, gray-eyed man across the table
from her was gently shaking his head. "No, my pet.
Higgins has the watch, and he is being very astute."

"Look, darling," Sandra said with quick impatience.
"Isn't it about time for everybody to stop being so
clever? Isn't it about time for some red-blooded action?
Where is Higgins now?"

"In a movie. He didn't go home from his ride. He

went to luncheon in his riding clothes, and since then
he's been going to movie shows."

"Why," Sandra said recklessly, "don't you take a
few men and just grab him?"

Van Pell chuckled. "No, Sandra. That's why he's
mingling with crowds. He's playing it safe. Any attempt to gang up on him might involve the police."

"But what's he doing?"

"Playing safe and waiting. Killing time."

"Why?"

Brook Van Pell bent forward, looking at her out of
the tops of his eyes. Then he glanced quickly about him,
as if to make sure that what he was about to say would
not be overheard. As an added precaution, when he
spoke again, he whispered.

"It's like this, Sandra. I've checked up thoroughly on
Higgins. I think—in fact, I'm dead sure I know where
he intends to sell loganite. I've learned that practically
all the jobs he's done have been for Italy. Of course
you know how important loganite would be to any of
the nations either at war or on the fringe of it. I have
checked up on the Italians now in this country who are
important enough to trust with this job. I found there
aren't any. Then I saw an item in a newspaper saying
that Count Angelo Beretti is on his way here from Italy.
Have you ever heard of Count Beretti?"

"No, Brook."

"He's a big shot and he's coming here on a mission
of great importance. And there's no question in my
mind that his mission is to buy loganite from Scott
Higgins for Italy."

Van Pell gazed at her steadily a moment, then went on, still in a whisper: "His ship, the 'City of Naples,' docks here at ten o'clock tonight. Count Beretti will go through customs without examination, because he will be traveling on a diplomatic passport. He may go to a hotel, but my guess is he'll go immediately to Scott Higgins' apartment. He should reach there by ten-thirty. Scott Higgins will be waiting for him, and he won't be expecting anyone else. He won't for example, be expecting me."

Sandra was nibbling nervously at her lower lip. She was pale. "Darling, that man is dangerous. He hadn't the slightest hesitation in shooting Storm the other night. Storm is a good shot and he was prepared for him. Higgins was as fast as a rattlesnake."

Van Pell chuckled. "Don't worry, darling. I'll catch him completely by surprise. The point is, he'll be expecting Count Beretti, not me. Or anyone else."

Sandra was frowning. "But, darling, how can you be so sure of all this? Perhaps he'll meet the ship. Perhaps he'll meet Beretti at some agreed upon place."

Van Pell was nodding. "I've considered all the possibilities. And I'm prepared for them."

Sandra said tremulously, "Well, I hope so, Brook. But he is dangerous, and you can't be too careful. Darling, I love you so. I don't want you to take any chances."

He reached across the table and took her hand. "I won't, my sweet. I never take chances."

The warmth of his hand gave her assurance and courage. She said, sighing, "All right, Brook. Now tell me what to do about this awful mess I'm in."

He narrowed his eyes and looked at her meditatively. "It's a tough one, honey. I've been turning it over in my mind."

She cried: "There must be some easy solution, Brook! I've been depending on you for it!"

He tilted his head a little and raised one eyebrow a little. It was his most whimsical, most charming pose. "After all, Sandra, you can't go to a hospital with appendicitis, and you can't visit your father in Cohasset. Happy brides of forty-eight hours' standing simply don't do those things, certainly not when every gossip columnist has his eye to the keyhole and his ear to the ground."

He laughed and said: "They're very acrobatic, these fellows. At least, they have ears like these clever gadgets that anti-aircraft batteries use to locate approaching planes. And they amplify a whisper into a thunder."

Sandra stared at him with growing consternation. She said thinly: "Brook, do you mean you're letting me down? Do you mean I've got to go and live in Peter Storm's apartment?"

He said hastily: "Darling, don't misconstrue me. Do you suppose I want you to go and live in his apartment?"

Almost in tears, Sandra said: "But what am I to do? You're the one person I can turn to. You've got to think of some way."

"I'm trying, darling. But it's difficult. Look. Let me try to make something clear to you that I may have slighted before." He looked at her a moment, then said vigorously, in his resonant voice: "I don't have to tell you how tough this war will be before it's done. This country is rapidly preparing a great war machine. Expecting a nation with a great war machine not to use it is just like expecting a child to whom you have given a fascinating toy not to play with it.

"Our real safety is to develop a war machine able to smash them all. With loganite, we can do it. That's why, Sandra, I intend to put my entire fortune behind loganite. I'm planning factories and mills. If this country ever needs it, I want to be able to supply loganite in every conceivable form."

Van Pell sat back. His eyes were glowing. His lips had become thin, and his voice crisp.

"That's why I want loganite. That's why I'll take any chance to get my hands on that formula, on that watch. And that's why, actually, I'm still worried. I mean, about Storm."

Sandra gasped: "Storm! But he's out of it!"

"I'm not so sure. He is a very clever and very relentless young man. And I'd hate to see his company have loganite."

"Why? They'd manufacture it for this country. He said so."

Van Pell smiled slowly. "Did he? Did he happen to mention that Allied Metals is about to be investigated? Did he mention that Allied Metals is suspected of having pro-German sympathies?"

"No!" Sandra gasped. She wanted to say, "I don't believe it!" But she was too shocked. And perhaps it was true. Once you were involved in this sort of intrigue, the most incredible things seemed to happen. And she knew that Brook would not lie to her.

He bent toward her. "Darling," he said, and his voice was again gentle: "I love you. The one thing I really want is to marry you. Nothing else matters. And the thought of your going back to Peter Storm's apartment, even for the shortest time, makes me feel ill. But someone must keep the closest watch on him."

Sandra caught her lower lip in her teeth. Her heart was pounding again. She looked at him dully and said: "I see. What you've really been working around to is that you want someone to spy on Storm, and no one will do but me."

Van Pell said quickly: "I hate you to put it that way, darling. My way of looking at it is this: There are times when, it seems to me, patriotism must come before anything. You know I'm no flag-waver, but I know you'll agree with me that this is a critical time for every nation. I'd sacrifice anything. I'd sacrifice my life, if necessary, to make sure that loganite got into this country's hands."

She looked at him searchingly. His gray eyes were glowing with his sentiments. He was one of the most cynical men she had ever known. She had never heard him use the word patriotism before, although he had often fascinated her with his shrewd analyses of propaganda.

She said, "Brook, I wonder if you realize quite what you're asking me to do. It isn't my pride, or my horror of scandal nearly so much as my real fear of Storm.

You know that he's dangerous with women. You know that, no matter what precautions I take, we'll be living on a basis of the greatest intimacy. And one thing I haven't told you is that he's in love with me."

Van Pell said quickly: "I naturally assumed that. No man could be near you and not fall in love with you."

It sounded, Sandra thought, like nothing but cheap and purposeful flattery.

"If I'm to watch him properly," Sandra went on in a flat voice, "it means that I'll practically have to occupy the same room with him. Will you like that?"

He was staring at her. "Sandra," he said quietly, "my only reason for suggesting it was that I was sure you could manage things. Darling, listen to me, you're tired now. And you're confused. The one thing you're forgetting is that no matter how headstrong he is, you'll be absolutely safe as long as he knows you detest him."

14

FLIGHT FOUR reached the Newark air terminal on schedule at 4:29. Peter, wary of reporters, attended to his luggage, then went to a phone booth, called his apartment, and asked his man Henry if Ben Macklin had called.

"No, Mr. Storm. The only calls have been from newspapers. I've been telling them all I don't know where you are."

"Keep on not knowing. Has there been a special delivery air mail letter from Washington or Baltimore?"

"No, sir. There have been a lot of telegrams. I opened all of them. The only one that sounds important is from Mr. Ryan, in Pittsburgh. Shall I read it?"

"Yes."

"It says, 'Contacted Severance in Baltimore. He will secure information you desire and forward it special delivery air mail.' "

"Okay, Henry."

Peter's next call was to Carol Dunbar. When she heard his voice, she cried weakly, "Oh, Peter!" and then he heard the sounds of her sobbing.

Uncomfortably, he waited. She presently said: "Darling, I'm in perfectly awful shape. You'll have to bear with me. First of all, did you get the formula?"

"No, Carol."

"You mean, things are just hopeless?"

"I don't say that, but things are certainly not under control."

"You weren't planning to come here, were you?"

"I will if you need me," Peter said.

"I do need you, darling, but I don't want you to come here. I think Brook is having me watched. I don't know. I've been having hysterics for two days. I had a doctor and he left me some sedatives. Oh, darling, things are such an awful mess. And it's all my fault. After all the things you've done for me, and the little I've ever been able to do for you, it just kills me to realize that I'm the cause of all this trouble."

Peter said sternly: "Carol, that isn't true."

"Peter," she said in a tired voice, "I know what I'm talking about. I'm responsible. A couple of weeks ago, Brook and I went to Atlantic City for a week-end. We did a lot of drinking and I somehow told him about loganite. I don't even remember what I said. But next morning when I was sober, he talked about it. He was terribly excited. I don't even remember what I told him then. Peter, I can't explain the hold that man has had on me."

She stopped. Peter heard her sigh. She went on: It was one of the reasons I was so glad to get away from here after the trial and take that job with Allied Metals. I knew if I just didn't see him, it would be all right. Then when he came to Pittsburgh in the spring and wanted me to come back to New York—well, I just did. I don't know why."

"How," Peter interrupted her, "did you find out about loganite?"

"You knew I was transferred to the metallurgical department," she answered. "I was Jake Tinch's secretary for five months. I handled most of the correspondence with Dr. Logan."

"Well, stop worrying about it," Peter said. "There were other leaks. The real trouble was caused by Dr. Logan's assistant. You had nothing to do with that."

She cried: "You're just trying to make me feel better! I've never caused you anything but trouble. And you've always been so decent. I'd be in prison or I'd be dead if it hadn't been for you! And all you got out of it was the nastiest kind of notoriety—the papers intimating I was your mistress! And every time they mention your name, they still intimate it."

"We don't care," Peter said.

"I do," Carol said indignantly. "There's never been anything between us. You're the decentest person I ever knew. That's why I feel so sick about it. If I could only be a little bit helpful to you!"

"You have been," Peter said. "You've been swell."

Carol was silent for a moment. Then: "Darling, what about this marriage of yours? Wasn't it rather sudden?"

Peter told her briefly what the circumstances of his marriage had been. He concluded: "The town of Sulphide, Arizona, needed some publicity, or the judge thought it did, and I just happened to be handy."

"You knew she was interested in Brook, didn't you?"

"Yes."

"Is she mixed up in this?"

"In a way."

"What are you going to do about it?"

Peter said carelessly: "Oh, we'll be divorced when the smoke blows away."

"Are you in love with her?"

He hesitated. "Well," he said, "you know my perverse nature. I was the little boy who always wanted the apple that was out of reach."

Carol cried: "You poor lamb! I'm sorry. And of course this awful stuff about us had to be dished up all over again. Isn't there any hope of your working it out?"

"No. She's in love with him."

"I wonder," Carol said, "what it is about that man. He's as cold as ice. He's utterly selfish. He's unjust and he's cruel. She'll get over him."

"And I," Peter said, "will get over her."

"Will you?" Carol said. "I've always had the idea that when you met the girl who had what you wanted you'd never get over it."

Peter laughed. Carol said impulsively: "Oh, why can't I be of some use to you! Let me think. All I can tell you is that he's planning to sell loganite, if he gets his hands on it, to the highest bidder. He hinted that one night when he was terribly tight. Russia or Italy or Germany or Japan. He doesn't dare try to sell it to this Government. But that isn't helpful."

"Were there any details?"

"No. That's all he said, and he was vague about that.

He doesn't trust me. He doesn't trust anybody. Have you seen Lynne?"

"Not yet."

"You will, darling. Did you see what she said in the papers?"

"Some of it."

"That you and she were practically engaged?"

Peter said, "That isn't true. There was never anything."

"Well, she's mad about you and she may cause trouble. Brook said so. He said she was simply burned up. And these Van Pells are dangerous people. He's horribly jealous of you, you know. Whenever he gets drunk, he insists that you and I lived together. He always insists that I've just phoned you or just written or wired you. He seems to suspect there's nothing I wouldn't do for you." Carol laughed. "I'm afraid he's right. Night before last he beat me up so badly that I've had to stay in bed ever since."

Peter said in a shocked voice: "Oh, Carol, no."

She said lightly, "Oh, it isn't the first time, but this was the worst. I'm black and blue all over. He used his fists, and he hit me with everything in the room but the ceiling. He said if he found I'd seen you or communicated with you in any way, he'd do worse than that."

Peter said gently: "Look, Carol, I've just had an absolutely unexpected royalty check on some oil wells I'd forgotten about. It's about five thousand dollars. I want you to take it and—"

She sharply stopped him: "No, you don't, Mr. Storm! I'm not letting you help me any more."

"But you can't put up with this, Carol. After all, I've got plenty of money and it isn't a bit of good. And we're friends."

"Darling," she stopped him, "I'm going to tell you a secret. I'm washed up with Brook. It's all over. I've been in touch with my sister, in San Francisco. She's found a good secretarial job for me in a steamship office. I may even be sent to Honolulu or Samoa. And I'm leaving tonight—in two hours—and I'm leaving no forwarding address."

Peter said, with relief: "I think that's the smartest thing you can do, Carol. Is there anything I can do?"

"Not a thing, darling. I'm going to stand on my own feet. Goodbye, and I hope you get some of the wonderful breaks you deserve. I don't think Sandra's good enough for you. I don't think any woman is, but then, I'm prejudiced."

Leaving the booth, Peter suspected that he would never see Carol again.

When Ben Macklin came into Peter Storm's study, he looked uneasy, and his air of world weariness, always prominent, was pronounced. Peter Storm's legman was a good looking young man of twenty-seven with the bold black eyes and the assured manner of a vaudeville actor.

His usual vigor was lacking. His handclasp was flabby and he did not meet Peter's eyes. He was smoking a black cigar.

He said: "Mr. Storm, I'd like to get something straight. When I read in the papers that you and this young lady had been married, I was tickled to death, because it sounded like the real article. The fact is, it was a kind of a shotgun marriage, wasn't it?"

Peter said gently: "Go on, Ben."

"Well," Ben said, "I've just heard an earful. Your wife and Brook Van Pell have just spent the afternoon at the Pelican, and I figured at first that she was giving you the run-around, then I figured your marriage must be a phony, because she is certainly crazy about that guy. She cried when she met him, she was so happy, and she hung onto his arm when they went in as if she was afraid he might melt and run down a crack. It was an awful shock to me, Mr. Storm, because up to then, I thought everything was on the up-and-up, and I never saw a nicer looking girl."

"Let's have it," Peter said.

"Well, I did what you said, Mr. Storm. I went up to Van Pell's house right after you phoned from Amarillo. He didn't leave the house till about ten. He drove into Central Park, stayed there about five minutes, then back to his house, and stayed there until mid-afternoon, when he went down in his town car to meet your wife at the Pelican. Eddie Dolan came in right after Mrs. Storm did. She and Van Pell went to a table near a window, so Eddie and I sat at the next one. Your wife—"

Ben stopped. He was sitting on the arm of a chair, and he still looked uneasy. "Mr. Storm," he said impulsively, "I hate to say these things, because I can't tell you how tickled I was when I read in the papers that you'd gone and done it, and I knew you wouldn't have picked anybody but a winner.

"I knew she wouldn't be any dizzy blonde, or any

hot-headed brunette, and when I saw Mrs. Storm, I said to myself, 'Boy, did he do it!' And when she began pouring it out on Van Pell, I was so sore I could have socked her. And so was Eddie. Excuse me, Mr. Storm, but are you in love with that dame?"

Peter had walked to the window. He had his back to it. His green eyes were half-closed. He looked thoughtful and a trifle tired. He had been prepared for this. He had assumed that Sandra would fly to Van Pell the instant she reached New York. He knew that she was in love with Van Pell, but all his discounting didn't make the fact any more palatable. When you're in love, in a case like this, he reflected, you don't think; all you do is wish.

"Does it matter?" he said carelessly.

Ben looked at him shrewdly and said, "Okay, boss. Well, all she wanted to know was how could she wiggle out of coming here to live, and how could she do it so there wouldn't be a scandal. There was more to that, but I'll pick it up later, and if that Van Pell isn't a heel, then I never saw a heel. He stalled her on that one.

"Mr. Storm, that guy's smoother than boarding house gravy. He cross-questioned her on what happened in that Kingman hotel until she was almost hysterical. Did you kiss her? Did you make any passes at her? Did you try to kiss her goodnight? And he asked her in three different ways what she thought about you."

Peter grinned slightly and said, "I know the answer to that one. She said she detests me."

Ben Macklin looked uncomfortablably at the floor. "That was the word she used, Mr. Storm. How could a clever looking girl like her spend all that time with a swell guy like you, and be treated the way you treated her, and then say she detests you?"

"Ben, I'm afraid," Peter answered, "you're becoming a sentimentalist. Was a man named Higgins mentioned?"

"Yes, but I can't give you anything very useful. Van Pell talked about him most of the time in a whisper. Eddie and I had our ears sticking out like the wings of a bomber, but he was talking too soft and we had to talk too and pretend to pay no attention. Van Pell said he had a deal on with Higgins to buy a formula from a Dr. Logan, but that Higgins had double-crossed him, had got this formula, which is in a watch, by killing that guy Ketzler, and that Higgins tried to sneak into New York this morning in a car from wherever he landed in the plane he chartered, but Van Pell outfoxed him by having every automobile approach to New York watched, and his men at the Spuyten Duyvil Bridge spotted him and trailed him to his apartment."

"Where is it?" Peter interrupted.

Ben Macklin said sadly: "Mr. Storm, that guy is too slick. He didn't even tell your wife. All he said was, his men had trailed Higgins to an apartment in the Fifties."

"East or West?"

"He didn't say. I tell you, Mr. Storm, that fellow is so suspicious that if he could divide himself in half, he wouldn't trust one half out of the other half's sight. Well, this Higgins outfoxed him by going for a three-hour horseback ride in the park. That was why Van Pell went to the park this morning, but I didn't see

Higgins when I tailed him there. He said he did, so he did. Since then, Higgins has been going to movies and mingling in crowds, so he'd be safe if anybody started any rough stuff."

Ben stopped and raised his hands in a hopeless gesture. He puffed fiercely at his cigar and said: "The rest of it was whispers—just whispers. I caught a couple of words, but they don't mean anything to me. They may to you. One was Italian. Eddie and I caught it several times. And several times he said something about a ship. And tonight. Can you put ship, Italian and tonight together to spell anything?"

Peter grinned. "I'll try."

"Well, after all this whispering, they started talking natural again. She kept asking him what to do about you. Then he went into a song and dance about patriotism," Ben Macklin said, making a grimace, "that made me sick to my stomach. And he said that he would lay down his life, if he had to, to get loganite for the glorious U. S. A. He told her that Allied Metals was under suspicion of having pro-German sympathies and that there was going to be an investigation. There's no truth in that, is there?"

"Certainly not."

"Well, then he worked it around to where she had to come and live here, to keep an eye on you, because he was suspicious of you, and wanted a spy here. And she said, jumping up from her chair, 'I wonder if you realize what you're asking me to do. You know Storm is dangerous with women, and he's in love with me.'

"He grabbed her wrist and then he soft-soaped her

a little and she said 'I suppose you know it would mean I'd practically have to occupy the same room with him," and he said he was sure she could manage you, and he said she was upset and that all she had to do to keep you away, if you started making love to her, was to mention how she detests you."

Peter was standing at the window, with his back to his legman, looking down at the swift steel flood of Park Avenue traffic. He turned about, smiled at Ben and said: "My wife is too smart to be fooled by anyone who isn't as smart as he is. It's very interesting, Ben. What else did he say about loganite?"

"That he was going to put his fortune into manufacturing it so this country's war machine could smash all the others. And she thinks he sent Higgins out there to buy loganite, and that Higgins double-crossed him. Her job was to watch him and report to Van Pell if he started anything that looked funny."

"The man's a genius," Peter said. "Keep an eye on him and learn all his tricks, and you'll be a genius, too."

"I doubt it," Ben said sourly. "First, you have to have quicksilver in your veins. That guy has a look in his eyes. I think he's crazy, or on the edge of it. Well, right after that, they went out. They went to his house in the limousine. He got out and your wife said good-bye and stayed in the car and went into Central Park. She got out by the zoo. She is now sitting on a bench near the reptile house, crying her eyes out, and Eddie is keeping an eye on her. I guess she likes snakes."

Peter's colored man-servant, Henry, came into the room and said: "Mrs. Storm is here, sir."

Peter said: "Ben, you'll find Eddie downstairs. Tell him to watch Van Pell. Have him keep in touch with me. You'd better go home and get some sleep and relieve Eddie at midnight. Henry, has that airmail letter come from Washington?"

"No, sir."

[15.]

GOING up in the elevator, Sandra had tried to compose herself, to put her thoughts in order. She had spent an hour in the park, trying to think things out, but she had been unable to think at all clearly. Through all of the things that Brook had said, the thought persisted that he should, if he really loved her, put her above everything else. Yet she had been deeply moved by his patriotism. And she realized that the reason she had never known that side of him was that she had never investigated it.

Her eyes were red from crying, but she didn't care. She felt that, in spite of all his arguments, Brook had done the wrong thing in deciding that she was to come here. No matter how important loganite was to him, no matter how patriotic his motives were, he should have considered the danger to her, of living at close quarters with a man like Peter Storm. But when the suspicion obtruded itself, that no man could love a girl very much if he would urge her to live on such a basis with another man, she put it out of her mind as unworthy.

She walked down the hall to the door of Peter Storm's tower apartment and pressed the button. The door was opened by a tall, broad-shouldered Negro of about forty.

He held the door open only a few inches and looked at her steadily. Before she could speak, he said, "Are you a reporter?"

She said: "I am Mrs. Storm. Please tell Mr. Storm I'm here.

He opened the door wide, but his expression didn't change. He quickly said, "Yes, Mrs. Storm. Will you come in, please."

Sandra thought, glancing at him as he stepped aside for her to enter, that he looked like a man who knows a great deal and never talks about it. Any man who worked for Peter Storm, Sandra reflected, would have to know a great deal and never talk about it.

He said, "Will you sit in here, Mrs. Storm, while I tell Mr. Storm you're here?"

It was Peter Storm's living room. On three sides were windows with French doors that opened onto terraces. From the windows she could see, over the rooftops, all of lower New York, boats moving on the East River, and, faintly misted, Hell Gate Bridge.

It was a comforting room. There was something secure, something steadying about it. For the first time today, she felt peaceful, and she was surprised, for she had expected, once she entered Peter Storm's apartment, to feel at least jittery.

She loved the room. The walls gleamed softly with a dull gold Chinese paper in which there was a faint geometric design. The floor was covered with a thick green rug. There were no curtains at the windows. Instead, on either side of each group, were tall rubber plants which shouldn't have been effective, but were. Over the fireplace, set flush in the wall, was the portrait of a Chinese mandarin in a robe of orange, green and red, and it harmonized perfectly with the room.

Facing the large central windows, opposite the mantel, were four comfortable chairs around a low table on which stood a small bronze figure of a dancing nymph, so slim, so graceful, so lovely that it seemed alive.

Sandra reflected: "The most amazing, the most bizarre things must have taken place in this room."

A red lacquer cabinet was the most important piece in the room. It stood on straight black teakwood legs. All its beauty was in its color and its slightly raised intricate design. Hidden lights glowed on a collection of miniature horses. There were horses in all attitudes, carved in ivory, jade, lapis lazuli and a variety of woods and metals. And Sandra recalled having heard that the collecting of miniature horses was Peter Storm's hobby, that he had made long trips and paid fabulous sums for some of these charming specimens.

She thought: "I suppose he's a lot of things. He can't be completely disreputable. He's too clever. It would be too dull."

It occurred to her that, though she had spent a great many hours with him, he had betrayed nothing of himself to her but his driving relentlessness, and she thought: "He's probably many-sided. And it would take years to learn them all. Only an unusual person of remarkably good taste and culture could have created this room."

And she found that her ultimate feeling about it was one of mild resentment. With everything so confused,

it was easier if all her entries in the account of Peter
Storm were in red ink.

His voice behind her said: "And I haven't a single
etching to show you."

She turned about, with her heart jumping. He looked
brown and lazy and amiable. His green eyes were
amused. Their assured sparkle, the v-shaped lines on his
forehead—all of him displeased her. It occurred to her
that, except where she was concerned, he was probably
the most impervious man she had ever known. Warm
but impervious. Brook Van Pell was cold, but he wasn't
nearly so impervious as this man.

His amused green eyes, the way his skin glowed, with
its dark tan, and the slight curl of his hair about his
forehead suddenly irritated her. He was so vital. He was
so attractive. Her feeling of relaxation, her curious
feeling that this place was a refuge from all her storm-
ing troubles, was instantly gone.

Watching him, as he approached her, she was frightened. Her heart was thudding in her throat. She had
an impulse to run out of the apartment, to escape and
to hide. She knew, from that look in his eyes, that he
would be persistent. He would persist until he had reduced her to a wreck, because, when he wanted anything, he was relentless.

Peter went toward her slowly, trying not to let her
see that he felt sorry for her. He thought she looked
pathetic. She had been crying, and she showed it. She
wore the identical dress he had seen carefully laid out
upon the chair beside her bed, when he had gone into

her room in Kingman yesterday morning and left the note.

In spite of the fact that her make-up was gone, that her spirits were low, that she was pale and tired and had been crying, she still was either beautiful or it didn't matter. He had never before seen her when she was pathetic. He had never seen her helpless and appealing.

He wanted to take her in his arms and comfort her.

Sandra could not control the quivering of her lower lip when she said, "Storm, you-you've got to take me in. I've got to live here."

The fragrance of the perfume she used seemed to fill the room.

He said gravely: "How about this man you're in love with?"

"My father comes first," Sandra said. "I can explain it to the man I'm in love with, but not to my father."

Because he knew what was going on in her mind, her disappointment in Brook Van Pell, how upset she really was, Peter impulsively put out his hand to take her elbow. She squirmed away. She lifted her head. She was, suddenly, no longer a pathetic, limp girl. She was gallant and fearless. She was doing the amazing thing he had seen her do in the desert—taking herself in hand, concealing her real feelings, preparing to be clever and charming in order to get what she wanted.

She said quickly: "You don't have to be sorry. I'm not sad. I'm furious." She was making a gallant attempt at being her light-hearted self. She said brightly: "Storm, you can't abandon me. You took me for better or for worse—after bullying me into it. You made sacred pledges and promises and vows."

"Are you sure," Peter asked maliciously, "that this man you're in love with won't mind your living with me?"

All of her light-heartedness was gone again. She was gazing at him with hot resentment.

"What difference does that make now?"

"Have you," Peter gravely asked, "talked it over with him?"

She looked at him steadily. "Why do you ask that?"

Peter shrugged. "I think, if I were the man, I'd want a pretty elaborate explanation. I'd hate to see the girl I loved going to live in another man's apartment. But," Peter said amiably, "perhaps he's just broad-minded."

Sandra was growing angry. Her color was better and her eyes were bluer than before.

"You'll have to forgive me," she said, "for forgetting how clever you are. If you were in love with a girl who had my problem, what would you do about it?"

Peter frowned. "Just what is your problem?"

"To begin with," Sandra answered, "you've given me so much publicity that I can't move without being flash-bulbed. Either I live here or there'll be a scandal. So how would you solve it?"

"If I were the man you love," Peter answered, "I'd tell you to hole up in your father's house in Cohasset, then I'd come up here and tell me to announce to anyone who inquired that you were here but were seeing no one. A highly-publicized bride is entitled to her seclusion. The world would understand and sympathize."

"But you wouldn't co-operate!" Sandra said indignantly.

"If I were the man you love, I'd make me co-operate. Why doesn't he?"

She was biting her lip and glaring. "Perhaps he's just as sick of the situation as I am, and just doesn't care!"

"In that case," Peter said gravely, "he can't be much of a man. Did you tell him I'm in love with you?"

"What difference does that make?"

"Sandy," he said gently, "are you sure this man really loves you?"

She gazed at him, hating him with her cornflower-blue eyes. "You think this situation is terribly funny."

Peter slowly shook his head. "I'm only trying to put myself in his place—letting the girl I love go to live with a man who loves her and who has every legal right to love her. I'm trying to imagine myself being so broad-minded. And I'm trying to imagine what I'd be thinking and how I'd feel."

"Perhaps," Sandra said scornfully, "he trusts me."

"To use your favorite expression," Peter answered, "what difference does that make?"

Sandra was eyeing him defiantly. "Storm," she said, "are you trying to scare me away?"

He shook his head. "No, Sandy. You see, this seems like a fairly spacious apartment, but it actually isn't. There is only one guest room and it connects with my bedroom."

It seemed to Peter that her eyes were larger and suddenly darker. She said with a breathless air: "It seems to me we had a similar arrangement in the hotel in Kingman."

"But this isn't Kingman, Sandy. It's my apartment. And I'm in love with you. Why should you think, because I didn't bother you in Kingman, that you can walk into this apartment and live here alone with me and assume that I'll do nothing about it?"

She looked at him steadily a moment and then said calmly: "Because I detest you."

"But I love you, Sandy," he said, putting his hands on her shoulders. "I don't believe I've ever been really in love before. Anyway, I've never had so many emotions stirred up at once by any one girl—admiration and respect and a desire to be terribly helpful."

She said scornfully: "If you feel it so deeply, then why don't you do something about it?"

16

AS Peter started toward her, Sandra started away. She cried with alarm: "You know what I meant!" But he caught her shoulders and spun her into his arms. He held her arms tight. She struggled a moment, then stopped. She said nothing. At first, she did not try to avoid his lips. He kissed her. She did not try to escape it. Her lips were soft and warm and completely unresponsive.

Suddenly she twisted her head, but he followed her mouth with his, hungry for even this slight satisfaction, and kissed her hard and long. He kissed her until she began to struggle again, and then he let her go.

Her face was crimson and her eyes were enormous. She wiped her mouth slowly with the back of her hand. She said: "I suppose I deserved that."

Peter said: "Sandy, I can't help loving you. I'm crazy about you."

"Maybe," she said scornfully, "you'll learn I meant what I said."

"Maybe," Peter said angrily, "you'll learn I don't put much stock in words."

She stared at him a moment longer. "I don't suppose it occurs to you that you're being contemptible. After all, with circumstances forcing me here, I'm practically at your mercy. I have to listen to what you say, and I can't strike back. I don't mind that. But I should think you'd loathe yourself for touching a girl who detests you, and for crossing a line that a decent man wouldn't dream of crossing. You know I'm in love with another man. You know it makes my skin shrink when you touch me. I should think you'd respect that."

Peter took a deep breath, lifted his shoulders and let them fall as he said quietly: "Okay, Sandy, we'll try to work something out, but I'm in love with you and I'm not making any promises."

The Negro came into the room and said, "Pardon me, Mr. Storm, Miss Van Pell is here."

"Here?" Peter exclaimed.

"Yes, sir."

"Very well. Take her into my study. Where are your things?"

Sandra said breathlessly: "Coming over by cab."

"Put them in the guest room when they come," he told Henry. "Has that air mail letter come?"

"No, Mr. Storm."

Peter said to Sandra: "You'll want a maid. Shall I attend to it or will you?"

"I've already attended to it. She'll be here in the morning. Is there a place for her?"

"We'll make a place. Henry doesn't sleep here. The servant's room is full of things. We'll have it cleared out for her tomorrow. Perhaps we'd better take a larger apartment. Shall we dine here or go out?"

"I'd rather dine here. Henry, have you made any plans for dinner?"

"No, Mrs. Storm."

"We'll have something simple. Steak and potatoes and a green vegetable."

Peter said admiringly: "Sandy, how did you know?"

"Instinct," she said.

Lynne Van Pell was standing at the window of his study looking down at Park Avenue when Peter went in. At the sound of his footsteps she whirled about and stood perfectly motionless, staring at him. She was a slim, nervous, clever-looking girl, with a thin face and a wide, thin-lipped, vividly red mouth. Her face, except for feverish spots at her cheekbones, was pale. And her large amber eyes had a wild look.

She stood staring at him as he came down the room toward her. She was smoking a cigarette. She always held a cigarette close down in the notch formed by her forefinger and middle finger because, she had once explained to Peter, if you hold a cigarette that way while in bed, it can't fall and set the bed afire if you should fall asleep.

She said huskily, "Hello, darling," and looked him over carefully. "You look marvelous. Marriage seems to agree with you."

"Thanks," he said cautiously, and felt slightly apprehensive. She was the most willful, most erratic, most unpredictable girl he had ever known. Lynne, he reflected uneasily, was the kind of a girl who might shoot a man.

She was keeping herself under remarkable control. It wasn't like her. Ordinarily, she was never still. She had nervous, slender hands, and she was always making quick movements with them. She was very vivid and alive. Her calm now was ominous.

In the same husky voice she said: "I'm glad you're looking so well. I haven't slept a wink in two nights. I can't eat. I've smoked a thousand cigarettes. And I'm tight." She seated herself, with that dangerous air of relaxation, on the arm of a chair. She smiled. "By the way, darling, why did you marry that girl?"

His green eyes shifted about her face and steadied. "Because I'm in love with her."

He had never seen her so geared up. But she was always geared up. She'd burn out, he reflected, in another ten years.

"You're a liar," Lynne said huskily. "You're in love with me and you have been for over a year."

"All right," he said gently, "let's look at it. I am not in love with you, Lynne, and I haven't been."

She said with that false air of serenity: "You're still lying. I've seen the way you've looked at me. I know what's been in your mind. You can't fool me. I know men. I've been looked at by thousands of men." Her voice was still controlled. "I've had dozens of men in love with me. Some of them said so, and some of them didn't. You're one of the ones who didn't, but I knew what was going on. I knew you were crazy about me. That's why I fell in love with you."

Her hands were beginning to move now. She couldn't keep herself bottled.

"And I'll tell you something else. Dozens of men have been in love with me and have tried to do things about it. One of the reasons I fell in love with you was that, even when you were craziest about me, I mean, those moments, you didn't try to do anything about it. You had something for me no other man who ever fell in love with me had. You had respect for me."

Her amber eyes were flicking about his face.

"You were awfully decent because I was so young. You never pawed me. You never tried to drag me up here after we'd had a few drinks. But I knew you were in love with me."

"Lynne!" Peter began.

"Let me finish. You know why I broke off my engagement to Jimmy Foster, don't you?"

"Lynne—"

"Well, you do now," Lynne said. "I was telling the field it was closed for everybody but you. You've been so decent that sometimes I've positively hated you—but I never stopped loving you, darling, and I never will. I don't know why you married this girl. But I do know it wasn't because you were in love with her. You got in some sort of a jam. And now you're sticking by your guns because you're in it and because you're so awfully decent. And I want to know."

"All right," Peter said, "I'll tell you. I'm terribly sorry you've felt this way. I didn't realize it. I thought we were playing around with each other because we enjoyed each other. I've never made love to you, or tried to drag you up here after a few drinks, not because I'm decent but because I didn't feel that way. And I'm sorry you're making an issue of something that isn't an issue."

Lynne's amber eyes had become vivid. Her mouth

was making small grimaces, and her hands were never still.

"We might as well have it understood," Peter said. He felt miserable, because there was nothing, really, to say. Anything made things worse.

"Oh, yes; oh, yes; oh, yes," she said lightly. "By all means."

He said wearily. "Lynne, I married this girl because she's the one girl I've ever known I've felt so deeply about."

Lynne was shaking her head. Then she changed its direction and began slowly nodding. "Darling, you aren't fooling me. I know you. Don't you remember me? I'm Lynne. I'm the girl you took to Bimini last winter. I'm the little fool who's so crazy about you that the whole town's talking about it. And now they're laughing about it. I know how decent you are. I know that that's behind your marrying this—this girl. What I'm trying to say is that I'm not going to stand for it. I'm going to get you out of it."

Peter had been crushing out his cigarette. He jerked his head up. He said incredulously: "You're—what?"

"I'm going to break it up," Lynne said breezily. "I'm going to make her divorce you."

Peter stared at her. "You must be nuts."

"I don't deny it. Half the Van Pells who ever lived ended their lives in insane asylums. But we're smart too. I'm going to that girl and I'm—"

"You're going to do nothing of the kind," Peter said.

"And I'm going to tell her about our trip to Bimini from Palm Beach last winter."

Peter shrugged. "Go ahead."

Lynne's mouth began to work. She flung herself at him. With her arms about his neck in what amounted to a strangle-hold, she panted: "You've got to do something about me. You've got to get rid of that girl! You did love me—you know you did! I can't stand it! You can't jilt me like this! People are laughing at me."

She kissed him four or five times on the mouth.

Peter disengaged himself and crossed the room. He said shakily: "Lynne, all you're doing is making me feel like an awful heel. I'm not a heel. For heaven's sake, cut it out."

She stood looking at him with her fists on her hips, her eyes partly closed, her lips clamped together.

"All right," she said. "So you mean it. All right, Peter. I'm going to go to her and I'm going to tell her just what happened in Bimini."

Peter said, "Well, what did happen? I thought we went there on a fishing trip. I thought we caught a lot of kingfish and groupers and barracudas. So what happened?"

"So we got tight one night and you seduced me."

Her face was entirely white. Her eyes were huge and amber and shining. She backed against a chair and did not take her eyes from his.

Peter said, in a voice harsh from shock: "Why, Lynne, you know damned well that's a lie."

"I don't care if it is a lie. I'll make her believe it!" Lynne said tensely. "I'll produce photostatic copies of the hotel register to prove it."

"To prove what? Our rooms were at opposite ends of the hotel. To prove what?" he demanded.

"That we were there three nights! That we flew over there alone! That you took me there deliberately! That you had only one idea!"

"Lynne, for heaven's sake, you must be out of your mind. People fly to Bimini for fishing every day of the winter."

"Yes—sometimes for fishing. But when a man with your reputation and a girl of my inexperience fly off alone to Bimini—"

"Lynne—"

"—for three days and three nights, what do you suppose people say?"

"Nothing—naturally, because—"

"You don't know what people said. You don't know how the tongues clacked!"

"I don't believe it."

"Your lovely bride will believe it!"

"Lynne, the only reason we could go was that Gertrude Sanders was at Bimini to chaperone you."

"Gertrude Sanders is dead."

Lynne dashed out her cigarette. Peter reflected: She's apparently direct and honest, but she slyly plans a course of action, then acts on it in a straight-from-the-shoulder way, so that she gives an honest impression. It's a talent.

"And she'll believe it," Lynne said rapidly, sinking into a chair. "And she'll divorce you."

"Don't excite yourself," said Peter, seizing her wrist.

Sandra, in the doorway, said lightly: "Well, heaven

knows I'm gullible, and I believe everything anyone tells me. But why will I divorce him? Hello, Lynne. You look ghastly."

Lynne, panting, stared at her. "So do you. You look awful. And you'll look worse when I tell you the truth about this husband of yours."

"Don't you mean when, as, and if you tell the truth?" Sandra said sweetly, ignoring Peter's startled gaze.

Lynne said huskily: "I mean what happened in Bimini last February."

Sandra, keeping her eyes on Lynne, gravely lighted a cigarette. "Well, what happened in Bimini last February?"

"He seduced me."

"Who seduced you?"

"Peter."

Sandra shrugged and lifted her hands, palms up, with fingers spread out. "Does that matter?" she said amiably.

"Does that matter!" Lynne cried. "You mean, it doesn't matter to you? You mean, you won't divorce him?"

"Certainly not. I don't care what happened between you two. Peter and I are concerned with nothing but the future. Peter's past is a closed book—and we burned the book. Peter, wipe the lipstick off your mouth."

Lynne took a deep breath. She glared at Sandra, and she glared at Peter.

"All right," she said, with the air of a fighter rallying and closing in for the kill. "I'll tell Peter something that you won't laugh off. You're not in love with him!"

"Really?" Sandra drawled.

"Well," Lynne said, controlling her voice a little, but talking so rapidly that her words reminded Peter of a snare drum, "whom did you have cocktails with the instant you hit town? Whose arms did you rush into? My brother's! Does Peter know about that? Does he know that you're so crazy mad about Brook that you can't think straight?"

"You mentioned it," Peter said gravely, "in your telegram."

Lynne stared at him. "Don't you believe she's in love with Brook?"

"Of course I believe it. It's true."

Lynne's air was one of helplessness. "You—you know she's in love with Brook and—and it's all right?"

"It's perfectly all right," Peter said. "You see, Lynne, we're extremely modern."

"And now, Lynne," Sandra said graciously, "now that everything's cleared up so nicely, perhaps you'd better run along."

Lynne stared at them a moment longer with an air of bewilderment. Then she snatched up her purse and walked rapidly out of the room. Watching the empty doorway, Peter heard the front door slam.

He turned to Sandra. She was biting her lower lip. She looked slightly apprehensive, slightly belligerent. "How long have you known about Brook?"

"Only since yesterday morning."

Sandra's color was returning. She said, with sudden indignation: "I think you revel in being mysterious."

Peter's green eyes slid over her face. "You said that in Las Vegas. I told you I sometimes find it practical.

And I'm relieved it's Brook Van Pell. I wasn't at first. But the more I thought about it, the more relieved I became. If Brook were as warm and human as he is good looking, I'd have plenty to worry about. As it is, when you fall out of love with him, as you will one of these days, it will be complete and final. You'll have no regrets. He sent you here to spy on me, didn't he?"

Sandra didn't answer. Her eyes remained calm and derisive.

"He's one of the few men I ever knew," Peter went on, "so cold-blooded that he'd risk sending the girl he's in love with to live with a man so she could spy on him."

Sandra said softly: "Don't you think you've said about enough on that subject?"

He was sorry he had mentioned it at all. Having gone as far as he had, he had given her an advantage. But Lynne had upset him so that he hardly cared what he said.

Henry came down the hall and announced dinner. They went into the dining-room. When Peter had seated Sandra at the table, she looked quickly up at him and smiled as if there had been no unpleasantness.

"Storm, I never saw you really embarrassed before. You're so darned sure of yourself, and you hate to be thrown off your poise. I thought nothing could fluster you. I thought that magnificent poise was unshakable."

Peter grinned wryly. "I'll let you in on a secret. The truth is, I have very little social assurance."

She looked at him with glowing eyes. "Really?" she drawled. "I'd say you're as socially assured as a merry-go-round with a steam calliope attachment. Maybe your tenacity fools people. Lynne is as tenacious as you are. You're really an awful lot alike, you know. You're both awful liars. Neither of you has any more conscience than a gila monster. You're both greedy. You're both ruthless. I think you'd make a lovely team."

Peter looked uncomfortable. Sandra's eyes were round and innocent.

"By the way, Storm, I didn't intend to eavesdrop, but I was just coming out of the kitchen and Lynne did raise her voice so. If it's any comfort, I heard a lot of that conversation. I especially heard her say, 'I don't care if it is a lie, I'll make her believe it.' You do get into the most awful messes, don't you?"

The corners of Sandra's mouth were twitching. Her eyes were shimmering. She suddenly began to laugh. With her face rosily aglow, her dark-blue eyes half-mooned and crinkling, she laughed and laughed. Peter watched her curiously, enjoying her lovely golden laugh, and finally began to grin. Her laughter relieved the tension. It always did.

"You haven't seen the last of her," she said presently.

"I'm afraid not."

"She'll be utterly wretched until she does something about it."

"I know," Peter said.

Henry brought in the steak for Peter to carve. Sandra said: "I broiled that myself. You haven't told me how you got out of Kingman. I heard they arrested you on a murder charge."

"They did. I was afraid they'd hold us both as witnesses. I finally made the sheriff gamble with me. We agreed that if I could produce an alibi, he'd free me. The deputy who arrested me mentioned that a doctor had found Ketzler's body immediately after we left for Needles. The doctor fixed the time of the murder, and Judge Jeffers supplied the alibi. We were being married while Ketzler was being murdered."

Sandra looked at him with wonderment. "Storm, you're a horrible person, but you're magnificent. I'm beginning to realize that to you, life is nothing but a poker game—with half the cards in the deck wild."

He gazed at her thoughtfully. He was carving the steak. "This steak is a beautiful job of broiling."

"I'm really a wonderful cook," Sandra admitted. "As a matter of fact, I do everything well."

"It doesn't seem to me you fall in love very intelligently."

She sent him a resentful glance. "I thought we'd agreed to skip that. Did you tell the sheriff we went to Needles?"

"No. I said we'd pulled off the road near Topock and came back to Kingman to beat the sandstorm."

Henry, finished with his serving, left the room.

Sandra gazed dreamily at the side of Peter's head, then at his amused green eyes, then at the shine of light on his smooth brown face. Her eyes became sapphire gleams. Peter could still smell the perfume in her hair. It went with her hair and her eyes and her mouth.

With her curling brown hair, with its reddish lights, her dreaming blue eyes, her rather large soft mouth, her clever sun-browned face, it still didn't make the slightest difference to him whether she was beautiful or not.

Looking at her eyes and her mouth and her smooth young throat, he had an almost uncontrollable desire to take her in his arms again. He imagined what it would be like to hold her in his arms, as he had in the living-room, and to have her suddenly become responsive.

Her eyes were moving dreamily over his face, as a girl's eyes move over the face of a man she loves, as if she were indulging herself with each familiar, beloved feature, almost as if she, too, were considering what it would be like if he took her in his arms again.

"I was wondering," she said, "what will be done about us when the police find that we did go to Needles."

"We will be questioned," Peter said. "And we will lie our way out of it."

Henry came into the room with a long, fat envelope in his hand. He said: "This just came, Mr. Storm."

It was an air mail special delivery letter—the one Peter had been waiting for since his arıval in New York. He excused himself and went into his study and opened it.

The report from Jim Severance, in Washington, on Scott Higgins, alias Professor John Medkin, alias Eric Donaldson, alias Donald Hough, supported his suspicions, and elaborated upon the report that Peter's legman, Ben Macklin, had made on the conversation he and Eddie Dolan had overheard between Brook Van Pell and Sandra in the Pelican.

According to this report, Scott Higgins' father had been an English remittance man, and his mother had been an Italian. He had worked on an Ethiopian oil deal before the Italians invaded Ethiopia. He had worked for Italian interests in Mexico. Other missions were listed—in Persia, in Greece, in Venezuela and in Rumania.

Always for Italy. And always more or less in collaboration with a certain Count Angelo Beretti, a man of apparently great versatility who was high in official councils in his own country.

A clipping from a New York paper was pasted to the last page of Jim Severance's report, with the marginal notation in pencil, "You might check this."

The clipping stated that Count Angelo Beretti was en route to New York on the Italian liner, "City of Naples," which would dock on Thursday evening.

This was Thursday evening. Peter rang for Henry and asked for the morning papers. When Henry brought them, Peter consulted the ship news columns and learned that the "City of Naples" would dock tonight at about nine o'clock.

17

WHEN Sandra opened her door in response to Henry's knock, he said, bowing: "Pardon me, but there's a call for you from Mr. Kenelm Colamore, the columnist. I've been hanging up on reporters all evening, on Mr. Storm's orders, but Mr. Colamore says it's personal and important."

Sandra hesitated, then said: "Oh, I'll talk to him."

"You can take it on this extension, Mrs. Storm. I'll throw the cam switch in the kitchen, so that this phone and the one in Mr. Storm's room and the one in his study—they're all on the same extension—will ring, if you wish. Or, if you don't wish to take any calls at all, I'll leave the cam off."

"Leave it on," Sandra said.

She picked up the telephone and listened. She waited until she heard Henry restore the kitchen telephone to its holder. Then she said: "Hi, Ken."

He said in his deep, sonorous voice: "My darling girl, I hope you'll pardon this untimely intrusion, but you are being entirely too elusive."

Kenelm Colamore was a gentle, dark rascal who, in Sandra's opinion, treated the English language with greater respect in his column than any newspaper writer she knew, and who dealt with his victims with greater viciousness than any columnist alive.

"What am I to say?"

"All I want," he answered, "is the low-down on this mystery marriage of yours."

Sandra laughed. "Is that all? Well, what's the low-down on any marriage? Don't people still just fall in love and get married?"

His responding laughter was so cynical that her throat tightened. "Sometimes," he said. "But if a certain lovely newspaper girl falls in love with a certain Park Avenue playboy and impulsively marries him, what is a certain column-conducting sharpshooter to say about the reactions of a certain corporation lawyer?"

"You might try asking him."

"I have. He, too, is elusive."

Sandra giggled. "All right, tell me all about this new law which says that a girl can't fall out of love with one man and marry another."

"Does that cover it, Sandra?"

"Ambiguously. But not for publication."

"Your choice of words," Colamore said in his sardonic drawl, "intrigues me. Let's try another angle. When a brand new Park Avenue matron arrives in New York on her honeymoon without her honey and dashes from her plane to the arms of her ex-lambie-pie."

"Look, Ken," Sandra stopped him, and her voice was jittery. "You can do me a great favor in return for one. Hold it a few days and I'll positively give you something screamingly exclusive."

"How many days?" he said suspiciously.

"I'll let you know. Is it a deal?"

"Tentatively. I've been hearing strange and fascinat-

ing rumors from the great and romantic State of
Arizona."

"And you'll hear others." Sandra said quickly. "Let
them pile up for a few days, and I will—it's a promise
—strike the conflagration. Meanwhile, you can do me
another great favor. You know I'm a straight shooter
and you know I'm a girl who likes the truth."

"If you must advertise yourself to your loving friends
—so what?"

"It's this. You know more truth about people in this
town than anyone I ever heard of. You know where
all the bodies are buried, and where all the skeletons are
hanging, and you have an elephant's memory. So I
want to know the truth about Peter Storm."

"Are you referring, by any chance, to the monster
you married?"

"I am."

"Who," Kenelm Colamore said cautiously, "should
know more about a man than the woman he marries?"

"Kenelm Colamore," she answered promptly.

He said ponderously: "You really want it straight?"

"Straight."

He growled: "You're tantalizing me, Sandra. It ain't
fair. I thought everybody knew that Peter Storm is
rich, that he went to the best schools, that he belongs
to the best clubs, knows the best—and the worst—
people, and was voted practically by acclaim the most
eligible young bachelor in New York—until you
grabbed him. You're annoying Sandra."

"So are you, Ken. I want the scandals. The inside
dope."

"This," said the columnist, "is probably the screwiest question I have ever been asked. Aren't you satisfied to let well enough alone?"

"I want to know all about the past only because of its possible bearing on the future. I want no messy surprises. A wise bride sees all, and says little."

"I still think it's a screwy question," Kenelm Colamore said, "although I grant that you're clever. Okay, my dove. Here it is. The brute you married is probably the most maligned man in New York. I have examined the inner seams of all his scandals with a powerful magnifying glass."

"First," Sandra said, "the Carol Dunbar scandal."

"All right. When Carol was tried for the murder of Max Pendleton, Pete had known the girl for some time casually around the night spots. He was very sorry for her because he thought she wasn't getting a square deal. So he hired the best lawyer available—Oscar Krugleman—to defend her. She was not his mistress. He doesn't play it that way. I've known other people he's helped. You wanted it straight, and there it is."

"Now the Grace Thorpe scandal," Sandra said.

"Okay. Peter went to Reno last week to testify for Grace Thorpe because he's known her since they were brats. The inside story is that her husband intended to bring a counter-suit with some perjured witnesses. If Ronnie Thorpe had got away with it, Grace's name would have been smeared over all the front pages. Pete plugged that maneuver, and Grace won a nice, clean-cut divorce. That's why Ronnie Thorpe insulted Pete on the courthouse steps in Reno, and that's why Pete blackened his eyes, broke his nose and knocked out four of his teeth. Are you disappointed or delighted?"

"Neither. Interested."

"The trouble with Pete, the reason he gets into these jams, is that he just doesn't give a damn. He's the kind of person that scandal-mongers like me are apt to say rotten things about because he's a big attractive guy, and he's rich, and we're envious. I could tell you a dozen rich, meaty, scandalous stories about him that I tracked down. Every one has proved to be a square egg. Why go on? There are no skeletons. In simple words, you have married a very fine guy and you are a very lucky girl. And if you have the brains of a half-wit, you'll throw that torch you're carrying into the river."

18

IT was beginning to rain when Peter reached the pier into which the "City of Naples," somewhat ahead of schedule, was just being warped. Floodlights blazed through fine slanting stripes of rain upon the black hull and the white faces packed along the rails.

Peter went into the shed and to the lattice which separated welcomers from the travelers who must go through customs.

He watched the gangway and presently saw Count Angelo Beretti. Count Beretti was a short, heavily-built man with gray hair and a gray military mustache. Although Peter had never met him or seen him before, he recognized him instantly from newspaper photographs.

The short, stout Italian in the brown suit was instantly surrounded by men whom Peter recognized as reporters. Count Beretti had evidently not been met by the ship news men at Quarantine, or his answers to their questions had not been satisfactory to city editors.

The Italian Count was brandishing his short arms as if he were angry or impatient. He presently broke away from the men. He walked to the lattice work, and was permitted to go out. He carried nothing but a malacca stick.

He scuttled through the rain to a taxicab and got into it. Peter, who had followed him along the sidewalk, did not hear the instructions he gave the driver. He returned to his own cab and said, "Follow that cab. Don't lose it. There's twenty dollars in it for you."

His driver said: "Okay, buddy. Peel it off and have it ready."

The cab which Beretti had entered was perhaps two hundred feet away when Peter's cab swung out to follow it. Another cab passed his and fell in behind the one ahead. Then another cab in which a pale, thin young man who wore tortoise-rimmed glasses was riding, came charging past Peter's cab and suddenly swung into it.

Peter's driver spun his wheel. The cab seemed to skid. The front wheels struck the curb and went up on the sidewalk. The other cab, only inches away, was stopped, still rocking on its springs.

As Peter got out, the thin young man in tortoise-rimmed glasses got out also. He seemed bewildered. He apologized to Peter. The two cab drivers were exchanging the sort of remarks which New York cab drivers exchange on such occasions.

Rain began to fall more heavily. Peter glanced anxiously about him for another cab, then he looked up and saw the cab containing Count Beretti, and the second cab which had pushed in ahead of his, round a corner and turn east.

It was all, he thought, pretty obvious. Certainly, it was not accidental. He suspected that the thin, apologetic young man blinking at him behind his tortoise-rimmed glasses was one of Brook Van Pell's men, and had arranged this incident with great care, and that the cab following Count Angelo Beretti contained another of Van Pell's men, or Van Pell himself.

At all events, whoever had hatched the scheme, had succeeded, and Peter had lost Count Beretti. He had, however, instructed Ben Macklin to tell Eddie Dolan that he was to trail Van Pell and to report anything of consequence immediately. Peter's remaining hope was that Van Pell might lead Eddie to Scott Higgins' hideout.

Peter entered his apartment the back way, to avoid reporters. He went into the kitchen and threw the cam switch on the telephone, so that, if Eddie Dolan called him, Sandra could not listen in on the call. Her door was closed, but she was evidently awake, for there was a light at the crack under her door.

He closed the kitchen door and waited. He had waited perhaps ten minutes when the phone rang. Eddie Dolan's deep voice said: "Mr. Storm, it's Eddie. I'm phoning from a drugstore on Madison near 58th. Van Pell's in a remodeled brownstone apartment house on the south side of 58th, and an ambulance has just driven up there. I don't know what's going on. A woman was screaming."

Peter said: "Wait a minute, Eddie. Has Van Pell come out?"

"No."

"What's the address?"

Eddie told him. Peter said: "Wait across the street. If Van Pell comes out, tail him."

"Okay, Mr. Storm."

Peter threw the cam switch so that, if Sandra wished, she could use the extension in her room. He went out the back way again, whistled to a passing taxi, got in and gave the driver the address.

A gray ambulance was backed into the curb when Peter got there. Two men in white were carrying a man out of the apartment doorway on a stretcher. A hasty bandage was wrapped about his head. It was blood-stained. The man's face was waxen. His mouth was open and his lips were white.

The man was Count Angelo Beretti.

Peter said to the interne: "Where did this happen?"

"On the third floor landing."

"Do you know what happened to him?"

"Somebody clouted him on the head."

Peter waited until they were clear of the doorway, then slipped in and ran up the stairs. At the third floor landing, he stopped. There were two doors facing each other. He tried one. It was locked. He tried the other and peered in from the hall upon a softly-lighted, well-furnished living-room.

Several tables and chairs had been overturned in what must have been a violent struggle. Blue, yellow and white sheets of note paper were scattered about the floor. And in the middle of the large, dull-red and blue, Afghan rug, lay the tall, handsome blond man whom Peter had been trying to find.

Scott Higgins, alias Professor John Medkin, alias Eric

Donaldson, lay sprawled on his back, with two bullet holes less than an inch apart in the right temple above his eye.

All his pockets had been rifled. Table and desk drawers had been yanked out and their contents scattered on the floor in what must have been a frantic search.

The dead man, the ransacked drawers, told an adequate and depressing story. It was, to Peter, quite obvious that Brook Van Pell had come here, had encountered Beretti on the landing and had knocked him unconscious, had delivered a blow on his skull that might result in death, for the face of the man Peter had seen on the stretcher had been that of a man seriously if not fatally hurt; and had entered this apartment, secured the platinum watch containing the loganite formula and killed this dangerous adventurer.

For the first time since he had gone to the Three Tree Ranch to test his theory that Dr. Logan's laboratory might have been dynamited, and to ascertain if the loganite formula was still in existence, Peter admitted defeat. Until now there had been some hope. If he could have come while Van Pell was still here, he might have had it out with him; he might still have got the formula. There was no hope left.

He had not entered the room. With the door opened, he was standing on the threshold when he heard heavy footfalls on the stairs. He turned and looked down. Two men in police uniform were coming up the stairs. One of them was a tall, heavily-built, red-faced man who wore a sergeant's chevrons. His face was familiar to Peter, although Peter did not know his name.

The sergeant smiled and said heartily: "Well! Hello, there, Mr. Storm!"

This might readily, Peter realized, lead to serious complications. He said: "Hello sergeant. There seems to be a dead man in here."

The sergeant said quickly: "A friend of yours?"

"No. I was passing this place a few minutes ago. And an ambulance stood at the curb. They were carrying a man out on a stretcher. I thought I recognized him as Count Angelo Beretti. The interne didn't know anything about it. I was curious, so I came up here and looked around. This door was partly opened, so—"

"How long have you been up here, Mr. Storm?"

"I should say less than a minute. Perhaps only a half minute."

The policeman said: "Well, all we got was an ambulance follow-up."

The sergeant said: "Do you know who this man is, Mr. Storm?"

Peter hesitated. He didn't believe that the police would link this man with the man who had vanished so mysteriously from the Three Tree Ranch night before last. "No," he said.

The sergeant said, "Well, I hope you haven't touched anything."

"Only the doorknob. I've just been standing here."

"You didn't go into the room at all?"

"No."

"Whoever did that," the policeman said, "must have been a pretty fair shot."

"I've got to run along," Peter said.

The sergeant had gone into the room. He went to the desk and picked up the telephone. He said, "Okay, Mr. Storm. It looks like this guy and Count Beretti didn't like each other much."

Peter went downstairs. He crossed the street and found Eddie Dolan in a doorway under an umbrella. He was smoking a pipe.

Peter said: "The man I've been trying to catch up with was just killed up there. Shot twice in the head. Did you hear shots?"

"No, sir. All I heard was a woman screaming. She screamed about three times."

"How long after Van Pell had gone up there?"

"I should say about five minutes. Either Van Pell came out while I was phoning you near the corner, or he ducked out a back way. I only saw him go in. Did you run into those cops up there?"

Eddie's dark eyes were alarmed. "How did you get away so fast?"

"I know the sergeant. I told him I was passing by, recognized the man they were putting into the ambulance, and went up to investigate."

Eddie said with concern: "Isn't this apt to catch up with you. Mr. Storm?"

"It may."

"But I was here. I saw—"

"You saw Van Pell go up. And you saw me go up. Did you see anything else?"

"No, sir. What'll I do now?"

"Go home and go to bed," Peter said wearily. "You might call up Ben Macklin. Tell him to stay in bed. Tell him it's all over."

Peter decided to walk home. The rain had diminished to a drizzle. He felt disgusted. He had failed, not through any fault of his own, but because Brook Van Pell had proved himself to be the cleverer man, because he was much better qualified for this sort of thing than Peter was. It had been Peter's most important job for Allied Metals.

"I failed actually because I'm not smart enough for this kind of work. And I've probably made some mistakes."

His mind went back and forth over what he had done and what he had tried to do. He returned each time to Sandra. If he had had nothing to do with her, if he had not taken her out to Dr. Logan's ranch with him, this might not have happened, for she had, in small but important ways, betrayed him.

If she had not deliberately delayed him by being impudent to the motorcop who stopped them in Sulphide, Peter might have overtaken Scott Higgins in the desert. Or, if he had not permitted her to make that telephone call in the Kingman Hotel, Scott Higgins might have been on the train when it reached La Junta, Colorado.

He thought bitterly: "I suppose it doesn't matter. Maybe if she hadn't been so fresh to that cop, if we'd gotten away and gone right on, I might have had to shoot it out with Higgins, and I might be dead."

His thoughts continued to rotate about Sandra.

Naturally, she was in love with Brook Van Pell. There was a man who got what he went after.

The drizzle on Peter's face was welcome. His face was so hot that the fine drops of moisture, it seemed to him, should sizzle.

"There's only one thing to do at a time like this, and that's to get roaring, so I'll get roaring."

He wondered what he would say to Sandra. Would he mention that the man she was in love with had killed Scott Higgins? He decided that the answer to that one was definitely no. He couldn't prove it. And she wouldn't believe him.

There was only one thing left to do—notify the F. B. I., tell them step by step what had happened; let them sift it out, let them do what they could in securing the formula from Van Pell.

Peter was still considering the advisability of this, and weighing its possible repercussions, when he reached his apartment. To avoid reporters, Peter went up in the service elevator. Henry let him into the apartment.

The Negro said: "Mr. Van Pell just phoned, Mr. Storm. He said it was very important. He'll phone again, he said, in a few minutes."

"Did he talk to Mrs. Storm?"

"Yes, sir."

"What did he say to her?"

"I don't know, sir."

Peter looked steadily at Henry's veined dark eyes. He said: "Henry, this is no time for ethics. It's a matter of life and death to me to know what he said to her."

Henry said unhappily: "Mr. Storm, I'm sorry; but I
didn't listen."

Peter poured himself a drink of Scotch and drank it
neat. "Has Mrs. Storm been out of her room?"

"Yes, sir. She came out awhile after you went out,
and she sort of looked around. She asked me where you
were and I told her I didn't know. After she talked to
Mr. Van Pell, she asked me when you had gone out,
and I said I wasn't sure of the time. She seemed very
upset. She's been in her room with the door closed
since."

Peter said: "When Mr. Van Pell calls, I'll take it in
my study."

He went into his study and closed the door. When
the phone rang, he picked up the instrument and said
hello.

The deep, resonant voice of Brook Van Pell said:
"Peter? This is Brook Van Pell. If you aren't busy, I'd
like to see you on a rather important matter for a few
minutes."

Peter tried to make his voice sound casual when he
said, "Where?"

"Supposing we say the Stirrup Cup. Can you meet
me there in fifteen minutes?"

"Yes," Peter answered. "I'll be there in fifteen
minutes."

Hanging up, he thought: "There should be a logical
reason for this. He wants something. What is it?"

He was still frowning over it when the telephone
rang again. He said, "Yes," guardedly.

The voice that answered was Lynne's. She said gaily:

"My darling little pumpkin face, how would you like to swap a pretty platinum watch with the initials H. L. engraved on the back of it for a divorce from that wench?"

Thinking of Brook Van Pell's mysterious request, Peter said amiably: "I'm fascinated, Lynne."

"All right. Come on up and we'll talk about it. You see, darling, I'm not nearly so dumb as I seem."

She laughed, and he was sure she was at least tight. "Well, I'm not dumb. Also I came well equipped with eyes and ears. What I mean, darling, is that I know all about Hilary Logan and loganite and everything else."

Peter felt as though he had been holding his breath for hours, Lynne laughed again and said: "Am I boring you?"

"You're doing all right," Peter said. "Keep it up."

"What do you suppose I've been doing this past week?" she cried. "I've been listening in on my brother's telephone conversations, and on his other conversations. Did you know how he tracked down Scott Higgins today?"

"No," Peter said. He was finding it difficult, keeping up with her. He was finding it hard to think.

"It was awfully clever. He knew he was coming in a private plane. So did you, darling. But Brook was smarter than you were. He had every automobile approach into Manhattan Island watched by scads of men, and he tracked him to his apartment that way. Do you know where Brook made his mistake?"

"Where?" Peter said weakly.

"He was too foxy. And he gave Higgins too much

rope. When Higgins went for that horseback ride, Brook should have waited in that apartment until he got back. But he didn't. He waited until a few minutes before Count Beretti was supposed to come there, then went. By that time, someone else had the pretty platinum watch."

"Who?" Peter asked.

"Who do you suppose, darling? I went there before Brook did. I got it."

"How? I don't quite understand."

"Simply by pointing a revolver at him. I said I'd shoot if he didn't give it to me, and I meant it, and he knew I meant it."

Peter said, "You're a remarkable girl," and he thought: "She's so sly. She's such an outrageous little liar. It's another of her gags."

Lynne said, "If you want the watch, darling, come and get it. But I mean what I said about the terms. You don't get the watch unless you promise word of honor to divorce her."

Peter said, "I've a terribly important appointment that won't keep. I can be there in an hour or so. Hold tight. Hold everything."

She laughed and said, "I'll be waiting, darling."

Someone knocked at the study door. Peter replaced the telephone in its stand and said, "Come in."

Henry came in. He said: "Mr. Storm, there's a gentleman here named Mr. Benton. He's from the New York sheriff's office and he says if you refuse to see him he'll come back with a warrant."

19

SANDRA had heard both of Peter's telephone conversations. Each time when the phone had rung, she had quickly picked up the telephone in her room and had listened. She was puzzled by Brook's request that Peter meet him in the Stirrup Cup, but not quite so puzzled as Peter had been.

Brook's conversation with her on the telephone a few minutes previously had been mystifying and upsetting but it had prepared her.

He had sounded agitated. He had said, "Is Storm there?" and when she had said that he wasn't, that he'd gone out, Brook had said angrily, "When? I must know."

She had not known. And he had said, "Everything's ruined. Higgins is dead. Someone shot him. He was dead when I got there."

Before she could question him, he had hung up. He had sounded terribly upset. She had tried in vain to reach him before Peter had come in.

Listening to Peter's conversation with Lynne, Sandra had had the same thoughts that he had had. She knew that Lynne was sly and that she would tell the most outrageous lies to gain a point. But Sandra's deductions had not been the same as Peter's.

Peter was a man, and knowing how sly Lynne was, he

believed that she was lying, Sandra, knowing that Lynne would go to any lengths to get Peter, believed that Lynne was telling the truth and did have Hilary Logan's platinum watch. What Brook had said to her on the phone before Peter had come in was sufficient confirmation.

Who had killed Scott Higgins? Not Brook, that was certain. Not Peter, or he would have the watch, and he would not have agreed to meet Brook, and he would have talked differently to Lynne.

Lynne? Sandra thought about it a moment. Lynne, when she had left here, had been on the verge of a tantrum. She had been furious enough to kill anyone. She was crazy enough about Peter to do almost anything.

Sandra decided to go to the Van Pell house, to see Lynne, and to try to get the watch away from her before Peter arrived there. She could not reach Brook. She would have to do it alone. He was, she knew, disappointed in her, although she had done her best.

As Sandra started on her way she visualized how delighted Brook would be if she could surprise him by saying, "Our worries are over, darling. Isn't it wonderful? Here's the watch."

Leaving her room, she heard Peter and another man talking in the living-room. She found Henry in the kitchen and asked him who the man was. When he told her it was a Mr. Benton from the New York sheriff's office, Sandra was delighted. Every minute he was delayed meant a minute more for her.

The Van Pell house was between Madison and Fifth. Arriving there, Sandra raced up the steps with beating heart.

She knew that Lynne Van Pell envied her and hated her, and she knew that Lynne could be merciless and extremely dangerous. Sandra had no plan for securing the fabulously valuable watch from her. She had only the fixed intention of getting it somehow and of surprising Brook with her resourcefulness.

She pressed the button, the door opened and she said: "Miss Van Pell is expecting me, Colton. I'll go right up, shall I?"

Without waiting for his answer, she walked briskly down the large and gloomy marble hall.

Sandra was looking forward to her marriage to Brook and to her occupancy of this house because, among other reasons, of what she firmly intended to do about remodeling it and cheering it up.

Entering the automatic elevator she went to the fourth floor and knocked at the door of Lynne's room.

Lynne's husky voice cried, "Come!" And Sandra turned the knob and walked in. Lynne's room had none of the gloom and dreariness of the rest of the house. Its air was one of delicacy, crispness and good taste.

Lynne was lying on one of two beds, facing the foot of the bed and the opening door. She wore a chiffon dressing gown over satin pajamas.

She was obviously dressed for receiving Peter Storm, and her eyes became perfectly round on seeing Sandra, and her face scarlet. She swung her feet to the floor and sat up, all in one swift jerk of motion.

Her amber eyes were alert and very hostile.

She said harshly: "What do you want? Where is Peter?"

Sandra tossed her raincoat across a chair. "I haven't the faintest idea, Lynne, I haven't seen him in hours. But he's why I'm here. I wanted to have a talk with you about Peter. Things can't go on this way. After all, we're a pair of civilized women."

"I'm not so sure of that," Lynne said. "I've been in love with Peter for over a year. You aren't in love with him. You're in love with my brother. I don't call that so damned civilized."

"But you don't understand."

Lynne was sitting stiffly on the edge of the bed, with her arms folded, each hand clasping an elbow as she bent slightly forward. She was still embarrassed and still furious at having been caught so beautifully prepared to receive Peter Storm.

"What don't I understand?"

"I'm married to Peter," Sandra said quietly. "I want it to work."

The amber eyes burned at her. "You're a · liar, Sandra."

"All right," Sandra said cheerfully, "let's put it another way. I'm not in love with him. Our marriage happened as the result of certain circumstances I won't bother to explain now. You can take my word that we were both forced into it. It's a marriage that can't and won't work. It must for a little while, until I can gracefully get out of it. I can't now, because I don't want a scandal. Is that enough?"

Lynne was plainly suspicious but intensely interested. "No."

"I can't elaborate it now," Sandra said. "All I can say is I know how you feel about Peter. And I'll tell you in the strictest confidence—have I your confidence?"

"Yes."

"Because I want to relieve your mind—that, although we're married legally, we are not married in any other sense."

Lynne stared at her and smiled slyly. "You're still lying, Sandra."

"Lynne, you're quite mistaken. I'm in love with only one man, and I'll never be in love with another man. That's Brook. I mean that, and you know I do."

Lynne stared at her for fully fifteen seconds, probing her eyes, then seemed to relax.

"I am not in love wth Peter," Sandra went on. "And I won't be. I dislike him, and he knows it. You've said yourself how decent he is. He's been terribly decent. He'll get over his feeling about me. Whether he does or not, you can trust me, even living on this basis with him. That's what I wanted you to know. And it won't be for long. You will have him, but you must be a little patient, or, so help me, Lynne, you'll spoil everything."

The girl on the bed was nodding, even smiling a little. She said: "I think you really mean that. Would you like a drink?"

"I'd love it."

"All I have is Scotch and water. You see, I was expecting Peter, and he doesn't drink anything else."

"I'll have Scotch and water. Not too much water."

"All right."

Lynne got up and went into an adjoining room. Sandra heard her making the drinks, and she wondered what she was to do next. Hidden somewhere in one of the rooms of this suite was the watch.

Lynne returned with the two highballs, one in each hand. She placed them on a table and said, "I'll get some cigarettes."

She crossed the room. Sandra reached out for her drink. Then she noticed on the base of the glass that Lynne had set down before her—obviously for her—a sprinkling of white powder. It might be nothing but powdered sugar, but why should Lynne put powdered sugar in Scotch and water?"

Before Lynne had crossed the room to another table on which was a golden cigarette box, Sandra had switched the drinks. As Lynne turned, Sandra picked up the highball which Lynne had intended for herself and thirstily drank some of it.

Lynne put the golden box down and picked up the drink she had intended for Sandra. She was watching Sandra curiously. She said: "Sit down, Sandra. I'd like to have this pretty definite. I don't trust you, but I distrust you a lot less than a lot of girls I know."

Sandra sat down and finished her drink. Lynne was drinking hers slowly, a sip at a time, as if she relished it.

"How definite," Sandra said pleasantly, "do you want it to be?"

"That's entirely up to you. How long will it take?"

"As soon as the hubbub over all this trouble has died

away," Sandra answered, "I'll move out of Peter's apartment. Let's say, a week, or ten days at the outside."

"And I'm to trust you," Lynne said, taking another sip, "that you'll stay away from him, and that you won't even let him kiss you?"

"You certainly can."

Lynne finished her highball quickly and said: "Will you have another?"

"Not just yet." It seemed to Sandra that Lynne's eyelids looked longer, and that her speech was already a little thick, yet she didn't believe it was possible, if there was a sleeping powder of some sort in the drink, that it would take effect so rapidly.

She glanced at her watch. She had already been here a half hour. Peter might arrive at any moment. She believed that his talk with Brook would be very brief. He would discover that Brook did not have the watch, and he would get away promptly.

"Very well," Lynne said. She rubbed the heel of her palm, trailing the fingers across her forehead. She seemed to make an effort to sit up straighter. She looked quickly at her glass, then at the one Sandra had emptied.

She said, swallowing, "Do you mind going now, Sandra?"

She got up. Her movements were uncertain. She swayed a little. She swallowed again. She caught her lower lip in her teeth and her eyes grew large. She blinked. She said, in a strange imitation of her usual rapid-fire way of talking: "You swapped those glasses."

Sandra looked at her with amazement. "Lynne, what are you talking about?"

Lynne took several deep breaths rapidly. She panted: "You contemptible, double-crossing—" She stopped and swallowed again. She made grimaces as if her mouth tasted bitter. "Get out of here!" she panted, frantically.

She threw herself at Sandra. Sandra caught her wrists and held her away. Lynne broke free and ran, lurching, toward the door, trying to get out of the room. Sandra ran ahead of her, placed her back to the door and cried out, "Get back!"

Lynne turned about, almost fell down, and ran back. She ran to the telephone on one of the bedside tables. As she picked it up, Sandra, on the other side of the bed, reached over and seized the cord. She pulled at it, but it did not come out or break. Sandra pulled the phone from her and dropped it back in the holder.

Lynne had fallen across the bed face down. She rolled over and pushed herself up on her elbows. She said laboringly: "You're not so smart. My brother isn't in love with you. He thinks you're nothing but a fool. He's in love with Carol Dunbar. She's his mistress. He's—"

Her voice had become slower and thicker until it stopped. Her eyes were glazed and long-lidded. She was breathing rapidly in short gasps, with her mouth open. Her eyes seemed to go perfectly blank of all intelligence just before they closed. She collapsed on the bed, with her head hanging down over the edge, her dark hair tumbling to the floor.

Sandra stared at her with fascination. She lifted Lynne by the shoulders and pulled her around so that her head was on the pillow. She arranged her feet. Then

Sandra ran to the door and locked it, trembling with the necessity of finding the platinum watch before Peter arrived, following his interview with the man from the sheriff's office and Brook Van Pell.

20

MR. BENTON, of the New York sheriff's office, was standing before the cabinet looking at Peter's collection of miniature horses when Peter went into the living-room.

Peter's caller was a large, calm-looking man in a blue serge suit. He wore gold-rimmed glasses.

He said pleasantly: "I hate to bother you, Mr. Storm, but we've just received a request from Kingman, Arizona, asking us to check up with you on some things that happened out there on your recent trip."

Mr. Benton took out a sheet of flimsy paper through which Peter could see notations.

The man from the sheriff's office studied the paper for a moment, then said. "It seems there was a certain blue sedan that was missing or unaccounted for when you started East," Mr. Benton looked up.

"Yes," Peter said.

"Sheriff Johnson of Kingman says it was found abandoned at the Needles, California, Santa Fe railroad station, and that it is registered in the name of Dr. Hilary Logan."

"Amazing," Peter murmured.

Mr. Benton looked at Peter over the tops of his glasses. "One of the things Sheriff Johnson wants to know is this: why did you say you did not recognize

228

this man who shot you in the head, when it is now definitely known that you went on to Needles and talked to the ticket agent and accurately described a man who must have been the man who shot you?"

"Because," Peter answered, "I did not recognize the man who shot me. I saw only a dim figure. I did not see him clearly."

"But why," Mr. Benton gently persisted, "did you tell the sheriff you had not gone to Needles but had parked beside the road just east of Topock, and had turned back to Kingman when a sandstorm came up?"

"Let's have the rest of them," Peter said.

"Very well, Mr. Storm. The man you described to the ticket agent at Needles is a man named Professor John Medkin. This man vanished from Logan's ranch on the night Ketzler was killed. Why did you deny, when Sheriff Johnston questioned you, that you had seen this Professor Medkin after you had left the ranch?

"It says here that you denied all knowledge of him. Yet you described him perfectly to the Needles ticket agent. You described him as a tall, big, blond man with a mustache, and a slight English accent, and you said he was wearing a pale-gray shirt and white trousers and white canvas oxfords. Is that correct?"

"Yes," Peter said. He was trying to think of a way around this, yet there was, he realized, no way around it. And that wasn't the worst of it.

"That description," Mr. Benton went on with gentle relentlessness, "tallies perfectly with the description Sheriff Johnston secured of Professor Medkin at Logan's ranch. Why, then, when Sheriff Johnston questioned you, did you deny all knowledge of Professor Medkin, and why did you say you and Mrs. Storm did not go to Needles?"

"Mr. Benton," Peter said, "nothing is to be gained by lying. I'll tell you just what happened. This man Professor Medkin killed, this Simon Ketzler, was a cold-blooded murderer who deliberately blew up that laboratory and murdered Dr. Logan. Professor Medkin was an old friend of Dr. Logan's. He followed Simon Ketzler and killed him, justifiably, I think, for his cold-blooded killing of Dr. Logan."

Mr. Benton was gazing at Peter thoughtfully. "Why didn't you tell this to Sheriff Johnston?"

"Because I was entirely in sympathy with what Professor Medkin did. Simon Ketzler deserved to be shot down. Furthermore," Peter said, "I knew that, even if Professor Medkin had been apprehended, he would never be brought to trial. No Arizona jury would convict a man who had tracked down and killed a cold-blooded murderer."

Mr. Benton was shaking his head. "I don't believe Sheriff Johnston will be satisfied with that explanation. I think he'll say you had no right to take the law into your own hands. Actually, you were aiding and abetting a murderer, by letting him escape, by failing to notify the police immediately, and especially by denying you knew where he was when Sheriff Johnston questioned you. Where is this man now?"

"I don't know."

Mr. Benton folded up the flimsy paper and returned it to his pocket. "I'll make a report immediately to

Sheriff Johnston, but," he said gravely, "I'm sure he will only confirm what I've said. You may face some very serious charges, Mr. Storm."

Peter saw him to the door. The situation was, he realized, even more serious than Mr. Benton had portrayed it. Modern police arms were marvelously coordinated. And Scott Higgins had been a man of very distinctive appearance. Peter's presence at the Fifty-eighth Street apartment immediately after Scott Higgins' murder would certainly be linked, in alert police minds, with his recent activities in Nevada and Arizona.

It was not at all unlikely that he would be arrested on the charge that he had murdered Scott Higgins.

The simplest solution, he realized, was to carry out the idea he had had on his walk home—to notify the F.B.I., to tell them every scrap of the truth. He had hesitated before because of the inevitable repercussions. It might be impossible to prove that Brook Van Pell had killed Scott Higgins. And perhaps he hadn't.

Circumstantial evidence indicated it, but circumstantial evidence was often an arrow pointing down the wrong road. Who had been in the cab that had followed Count Beretti's cab from the pier? That whole carefully-organized and successful attempt at preventing Peter from following the Italian might not have been Brook Van Pell's.

The situation, Peter realized, was now completely out of his control. His wisest move would be to communicate at once either with the New York Police or the F.B.I. Yet he hesitated.

One thing he must do was to warn Sandra that he

suspected Van Pell of having killed Scott Higgins. She would not believe him, but it would prepare her. Peter believed that Van Pell was not in love with her, but had all along deliberately used her because she was clever and because she was infatuated with him. If it were true that Van Pell had killed Higgins, then her position was suddenly dangerous. She already knew too much.

Peter went to her room. The door was open and the room was dark. Henry said that Mrs. Storm had gone out.

As he left the apartment to keep his appointment with Brook Van Pell at the Stirrup Cup, Peter decided not to notify the F.B.I. until he had heard why that cool and clever individual wanted to see him.

Every attempt had been made by the proprietors of the Stirrup Cup to reproduce the atmosphere of an old English hunting lodge. The rafters and walls had a smoked look. There was a large blackened fireplace. There were trophies and hunting prints about the walls, and old announcements of hunts and steeplechases.

There was a hat-check girl and there were telephone booths in the lobby. Peter gave up his hat and rain-coat, then pushed open the fumed oak door into the main room.

Brook Van Pell was sitting at the far end of the bar, watching the door. Peter's throat was dry and his nerves were tensed. He did not know Brook Van Pell very well. He had seen him once or twice at the house when he had called for Lynne to take her to some party or the theater, and he had encountered him casually at some club or other. Van Pell was some six or seven years older than Peter, and they moved in different circles.

As Peter walked down the long, dusky room, he had an impression of cool, clear gray eyes in a dark, lean, youthful face. Suddenly smiling, Brook Van Pell looked younger than thirty-six. He looked suave, clever, very capable. He was perhaps two inches taller than Peter, and with his wide shoulders, his trimness and his lean brown face, he had the look of a man in excellent physical condition; a man who, in a fight, would be fast and sure and dangerous. His hard smile was dangerous, and it did not go with his soft gray eyes or the whimsical twirk of his eyebrows.

The two men shook hands briefly, smiling while they did it, and Van Pell said: "Shall we sit at a table?"

"All right," Peter said indifferently.

A waiter followed them over. Van Pell said, as they seated themselves: "I know you're a very busy man. Shall we get straight to the point?"

"Yes," Peter said pleasantly. He was thinking, at that moment, less about Van Pell's reason for wanting to meet him here than of Sandra's infatuation with this man. It wasn't hard to understand. Brook Van Pell, with his height, his good looks, his dangerous and yet whimsical air was a man whom, Peter suspected, very few women would not be attracted to. He had the charm of civilized virility.

"What will you drink?"

"Scotch," Peter said.

"Soda or water?"

"Water."

"Waiter, bring two Scotch and waters."

It was probably typical of him, Peter thought, to flatter the man he was with by ordering the same drink, whether he preferred it or not.

When the waiter had gone, Van Pell said: "All right, let's get straight to the point. We'll admit, I think, without quibbling, that we're a pair of fairly clever men. The only trouble is, we're on opposite sides of the fence. My feeling is that the time has come to call a truce."

He hesitated. Peter grinned. "Go ahead."

"The certain thing we're both after," Van Pell went on in his deep voice, "is really worth so much money that there is no reason that I can see why we shouldn't combine forces."

He paused again, and Peter said, "I see."

"Certainly," Van Pell said, "it's foolish for two men as smart as we are to be at cross-purposes. Don't you think so?"

"I do definitely," Peter said.

The gray, cool eyes were searching his. He wanted to say the rest of what was on his mind, and Peter didn't care whether he said it or not.

"If we should pool all we know—" Van Pell began tentatively. It amused Peter. In his hotel bedroom, in Las Vegas, Sandra had said substantially the same thing.

The waiter brought their drinks. Peter promptly drank his, because his nervous system needed it, and his mouth and throat were dry. Also, he was so relieved that he felt he should celebrate to that extent. For it was obvious, whether or not this man had killed Scott Higgins, that he did not have the watch containing the loganite formula.

Peter realized that Lynne must have been telling the truth; that she had gone to Scott Higgins' apartment and had held him up, just as she said, and got the watch, before her brother arrived.

Peter put his empty glass down. "All right," he said briskly. "Let's put all our cards on the table. If you'll wait here a moment, there's something in my raincoat pocket that I want to show you."

Van Pell smiled and said, "That's fine. I hoped there might be."

Peter left the table. He went into the lobby. He secured his hat and raincoat, tipped the hat-check girl and went out.

There was an empty taxicab in the parking stand. Peter got into it and gave the driver the address of the Van Pell house.

21

HAVING exhausted all of the obvious and the less obvious hiding places for a watch in Lynne's bedroom, Sandra had gone into the adjoining dressing-room. On a table there were a bottle of Scotch, a vacuum gallon jug of ice cubes and an icebox carafe of water. And on this table, beside the water carafe, were the two cobalt-blue parts of a capsule. There was still a little white powder clinging to the wall of one of the capsule halves.

It must, Sandra reflected, be swift and deadly stuff—something that Lynne had doubtless acquired from one of the more dangerous of the young men she was reputed to go around with. Lynne had been, Sandra guessed, afraid of her, and had decided to dope her drink, so that she would be unconscious when Peter arrived and could decide what was to be done about her.

Sandra searched the dressing-room thoroughly. Then she searched the closets and the bathroom. She had, she was sure, exhausted every possible hiding place.

She returned to the dressing-table and methodically went through the drawers again. Then she removed the paper linings. Back of the lining of the first drawer she had searched she found a Grand Central baggage check.

Sandra considered it for a moment, then thought: "Of course! Lynne's clever. And she's devious."

She returned to the bedroom. Lynne was still asleep. Her face was pale and she was breathing deeply and regularly. Sandra picked up her purse, folded the baggage check and placed it in her change purse, unlocked the door and went out. She tiptoed to the stairs and started down them. Peter Storm, she was sure, would arrive at any moment. He would take the elevator, and she definitely did not want to encounter him. He would certainly be suspicious. He might even insist on searching her.

Reaching the ground floor, she started toward the door. Colton suddenly and silently appeared just ahead of her. She hesitated, but he hadn't seen her. He went on to the front door. Sandra slipped into the small drawing-room, which was in darkness. She heard the front door open, then Peter Storm's deep, rather harsh voice.

She did not hear what he said, but she distinctly heard what the butler said. He said: "Yes, sir. Will you go right up, Mr. Storm? Mrs. Storm is up there with her."

Peter said sharply: "When did she come?" He sounded agitated.

"It must have been fully an hour ago, Mr. Storm."

The two men passed the doorway of the small drawing-room on their way to the elevator. Peter was walking rapidly, almost running.

Sandra smiled in the darkness and waited until she heard the elevator door close, then she walked out into the gloomy hall.

Colton turned about from the closed elevator door. He said, with surprise: "Mrs. Storm, I didn't know you were here. Your husband just went up."

"It's quite all right," Sandra said brightly. "I've an errand to run for Miss Van Pell."

She walked to Madison, signalled a cruising taxi and was driven to the Grand Central Station. There, at the baggage room at the north end of the rotunda, she accepted a small, worn, brown leather suitcase in exchange for the baggage check.

She carried it up the stairs and out to a taxicab. She said to the driver: "Drive very slowly down Fifth Avenue to Washington Square. And I'll want this domelight."

She searched the suitcase as the cab went slowly south on Fifth Avenue. The watch was not in it. The suitcase contained nothing but a pair of worn green slippers, wads of newspaper and an empty gin bottle.

The cab was crossing Thirty-third Street before Sandra, growing somewhat desperate, had exhausted the possibilities of all the wads of newspaper. It was crossing Eighteenth Street when Sandra had an inspiration. She was thinking of the thoroughness with which Scott Higgins had ripped apart Simon Ketzler's two pieces of luggage.

She began to rip out the lining of the suitcase. She came presently to a place that had been recently pasted down. Under the lining at that place was a slip of paper.

It was a pawnbroker's receipt for a pawned article. The address of the pawnshop was printed across the top.

Sandra gave the driver the address. She knew nothing about pawnshops, but she assumed that this one might be open all night because, if this redemption slip concerned Hilary Logan's watch, Lynne must have taken it there shortly before, or even shortly after, she had telephoned Peter Storm.

And it was, as she had assumed, an all-night pawn-shop. Sandra went in and presented the pawn ticket. The amount was five dollars. Sandra gave a bored young man the redemption slip and a ten-dollar bill.

She thought excitedly: "This is terrific. If it's the watch—think of my casually buying it, a watch worth millions of dollars, for five dollars and a few cents!"

The young man gave her change and a man's platinum watch. Sandra turned it over. The initials H. L. were engraved in shaded block letters on the back.

She put the watch in her purse. She was so excited she could hardly breathe. Her heart was beating in a frantic sort of rhythm and now and then skipping a beat. She suddenly felt faint and giddy and feverish.

She wondered if anyone had followed her. For she had suddenly realized that everyone who had possessed this watch, with the single exception of Lynne, had been murdered.

She was trembling as she got into the cab and gave the driver the address of Peter's apartment. He wouldn't be there, he couldn't possibly be there, for at least an hour.

She gave the amazed driver a ten-dollar bill and told him the rest was his. She went up to Peter's apartment and went into her room and locked both doors. Then she opened the back of the watch with the end of a nail file.

The inner surface of the inner lid was covered with the finest engraving—lines and lines of tiny letters too

small to be read without a powerful glass. And there
were microscopic diagrams, too.

She thought: "This is the most dramatic thing that
will ever happen to me in my whole life. Here, in my
hand, I hold the destiny of nations. Actually, I do! And
if loganite is as good as all these wild, murderous men
seem to think it is, I might even be holding the destiny
of the world in my hand."

Gazing at it soberly, she shivered. A picture came
into her mind: moonlight playing pranks with the
Joshua tree that grew almost to the main entrance of
Three Tree Ranch, an old man skulking to a maroon
coupe and quietly driving off.

Simon Ketzler had discovered where Dr. Logan kept
his secret, and had unhesitatingly murdered him by
blowing up the laboratory.

She thought of that wild drive through the night
with Peter Storm, of their finding Ketzler dead, and of
her shocked surprise when she had heard the loud report
of the pistol that had almost killed Peter Storm.

And now Scott Higgins, after that clever attempt at
entering New York unseen, was dead.

Who had killed him? Lynne?

She returned the watch to her purse, looked up the
telephone number of the Stirrup Cup, and dialed it.
She intended to say to Brook, if he were still there:
"Darling, I have the most interesting piece of jewelry
to show you."

But the man who answered said that Mr. Van Pell
had left some time before. Trying to visualize where he
might have gone, she tried other places. She tried all

the places she could think of, but Brook Van Pell was at none of them.

A jittery feeling was coming over her. She had gone to all this trouble to get this watch for Brook, because she loved him. She did not want to have it in her possession any longer than was necessary. And she could think of no safe place to hide it.

The feeling that she was hunted, that everywhere she turned there would be crafty, greedy eyes and the ruthlessness of men, suddenly chilled her.

[22.]

PETER knocked at the door of Lynne's room and when she did not answer, opened the door a crack and called, "Lynne!" Then he pushed open the door and started into the room.

When he saw her on the bed, apparently asleep, he was alarmed. He knew, because Colton had told him so, that Sandra was here, or had been here. She could have left only in the past few minutes.

He called: "Lynne! Lynne!" But she did not open her eyes.

Peter went to the bed and said sternly, "Lynne! Wake up!" His first guess was that she had been drinking; had passed out.

She was relaxed, in a heavy, snoring sleep. He lifted her eyelids. The pupils were tightly contracted—brilliant black points. He went into her bathroom, found a bottle of aromatic spirits of ammonia, spilled about a teaspoonful into a half glass of water, returned to Lynne and set the drink down.

He propped her up on the pillows and slapped her face. This did not arouse her. With his thumbs he pressed hard against the two small depressions in the bone above the eyes. When this didn't arouse her, he slapped her face methodically until her eyelids fluttered.

Her eyes opened and closed. Her eyes opened and remained opened. She stared at him, but she was so stupefied by whatever drug Sandra had given her that she did not know who he was.

He made her drink the aromatic spirits of ammonia, then pulled her to her feet and said: "Go in there and take a cold shower. Stay under it until you're awake."

She said dully, "All right." And staggered into her bathroom. He heard the sound of the shower. It ran such a long time that he grew uneasy, then it stopped. Presently Lynne came out, folding the pale green dressing gown about her coral-satin pajamas. Her face was flushed and her eyes were clearer, but her mouth sagged. She looked sullen and sleepy.

Lynne sat down on the bed and looked up at him. She tried to smile, but the result was a wry grimace, as if her mouth had a bitter taste.

"What happened, Lynne?"

The girl said dully: "Sandra came up here and I was suspicious of her. I was scared of her. I had some knockout powders and I put one in a drink for her. But she switched the drinks and I got it."

"Where's that watch?"

"She has it by this time. I was afraid to keep it. I pawned it, then I put the pawn ticket in the lining of a suitcase and checked it at Grand Central, then I hid the baggage check behind the lining of a drawer in my dressing table. I just looked. It's gone." Her eyes filled with tears. "I'm sorry."

Peter said: "You needn't be. I'm sorry I was so long getting here. What's the name of that pawnshop?"

Lynne told him, and he picked up the telephone. He called the pawnshop and made inquiries. Presently he put the telephone back and said, "That's that. A young lady has redeemed the watch. Where's Brook? She'll go straight to him."

"I'll call Colton," Lynne said.

But Colton, appearing promptly, did not know where Mr. Van Pell was. He was not at home.

Peter called his own apartment. "Henry," he said, "is Mrs. Storm there?"

Henry said: "No, Mr. Storm. She hasn't come in yet."

Peter put down the telephone and Lynne sighed. "You didn't think I was telling the truth. You're a fool. Sandra knew. She's too smart for you, darling. I was going to give you that watch in return for your promise that you'd kick her out tonight."

Lynne got up from the bed. She pressed the fingers of each hand against the temple of each of her eyes. She said: "I feel terribly dopey." She went to the table for a cigarette. She lighted it, placed her back to the table and smiled wanly.

"I'm still going to make you do it. She says she doesn't love you, but I don't trust her and I don't trust the two of you together. You're a fool to let her stay there. She'll keep right on double-crossing you. She keeps saying she's afraid of a scandal. Well, what of it? It's only an excuse to keep on using you. If she hadn't got that watch, I could have forced you to give her up tonight. I can still do it. I can send you to a death cell, Peter."

Peter had dropped down to the arm of a chair. He was looking at her and speculating.

Lynne walked toward him, stopped a half dozen feet away. She puffed at her cigarette and considered him through narrowed eyes.

"Do you know who killed Scott Higgins?"

He nodded. "Your brother."

"You don't know it. You only suspect it. Can you prove it?"

"No."

Lynne folded her arms. "Darling, you're in an awfully tight spot. You were at Scott Higgins' apartment. I saw you when I came out of the areaway onto Fifty-eighth Street. You went up when they were taking Count Beretti out. I saw those policemen go up and I saw you come out again. You ran into them, didn't you?"

"Yes."

"Were you in Scott Higgins' room?"

"I was standing in the doorway."

"When they connect this with your doings out West, what will they do to you?"

Peter shrugged.

"Darling," Lynne said, "shall I tell you just what happened?"

"Were you there when Higgins was killed?"

"Yes. I went there with a revolver in my purse. When I knocked at the door, I had the revolver in my hand. Higgins was expecting no one but Count Beretti. I surprised him, just as Brook intended to. I told him if he didn't give me the watch I'd shoot him, and I meant

it, and he knew I meant it. He'd just given me the
watch when Brook knocked at the door. I slipped into
the back room. Did you notice that curtain in the
doorway?"

"Yes."

"I was back of that. I saw everything. Brook's hand
in his pocket was ominously clutching a gun. It was too
plain to be missed. He said, 'Where is that watch?' and
Higgins said, 'You ought to know, Van.' And Brook
said, 'You're not going to double-cross me again.' And
Higgins said, 'I wouldn't dream of trying, Van. She's
back there. Help yourself.'

"Brook started for the back room, and as he did,
Higgins reached into his pocket. And Brook shot him.
Twice. And while he was searching the apartment, I
slipped out the back window and down the fire escape.

"I think Brook must have started out the front door
and run into Count Beretti and slugged him with his
gun. I don't know. I didn't see Brook again. I haven't
seen him since."

"He doesn't realize, of course," Peter interrupted,
"that you were there."

"Of course not! He thought Higgins was just being
crafty. Brook started for the back room, then he
thought Higgins was tricking him into turning his back,
and when he looked and saw Higgins' hand going into
his pocket, presumably for a gun, he shot him. At least,
that's how it seemed to me. And, by the way, darling,
Brook wore a pair of gray gloves. And I doubt if anyone saw him go in, and certainly no one saw him go
out."

"One of my men saw him go in."

"Eddie Dolan?"

"Yes."

Lynne smiled and smashed out her cigarette in a tray. "Eddie's a jailbird, Peter. Would his word be any good in court?"

"It might."

"Don't be silly. They'll hang the murder on you, Peter. You can't wriggle out of it. And I'm the only one who can save you. I'll do it—on one condition."

Peter was nodding. "I know."

"That you get rid of Sandra tonight and divorce her as soon as possible. Darling, I mean it. I love you. If I can't have you, no one else shall."

Peter said, in a dry voice, "Would you let them electrocute me?"

Lynne studied his face. "They wouldn't electrocute you. They'd send you up for manslaughter, at the worst. After all, Higgins was a murderer, wanted for killing a man in Arizona. But on account of the way you've handled it, they'd be awfully rough on you. You'd certainly go to prison."

She shrugged. "Well, darling? I said I love you, and I meant it. But I'm selfish and I'm quite cruel. And I have something else to think about. If I can't have you, I'm not going to be an altruist and save you from prison, and go through what I'd have to go through as a consequence. My brother being tried for that murder, and convicted, would be a family scandal I'd never live down."

Peter was sure that she meant just what she was saying. He had not known until tonight that Lynne was in love with him, but he had known that she was selfish, unscrupulous and cruel.

She walked toward him until she was only a few inches away. Her eyes were wet with tears again. She put her hands on his shoulders. Her mouth trembled.

"Darling, look. That's one side of me. For over a year, I've wanted you. I've been hoping that you'd do something, or say something that would mean you felt as I do. Peter, there isn't anything I wouldn't do for you. When I realized tonight that I'd lost you, I was desperate. You've seen how desperate. There isn't anything I won't do. Then there's the other side. We've had loads of fun together. We get along beautifully, we're both clever. Life would be so much fun for us!"

Lynne dropped her hands. "If it weren't for that girl, you'd have come around to it eventually. You're crazy mad about her, aren't you?"

"Yes."

Lynne cried: "What has she got that I haven't got? She isn't any better looking than I am. Her figure isn't any better than mine, and she's the type that gets plump. She isn't any smarter that I am. And she doesn't love you at all. She doesn't even like you! She's crazy about Brook. What are you wasting your time for?"

Peter, from the depths of his discomfort, answered, "Does anyone ever know?"

Lynne looked at his eyes and her shoulders sagged. "No," she said softly. "We just go round making fools of ourselves."

She turned about, walked to the table and took another cigarette from the gold box. She tapped the end of it on the lid of the box, then tossed the cigarette on the table. She turned and walked toward Peter. Her eyes were wet again and her mouth was making grimaces.

She said brokenly: "Darling, I can't do it." She went close to him. She slipped her arms about his shoulders, then up around his neck. "Put your arms around me."

Peter put his arms about her. She snuggled against him. She put her cheek against his coat and she sighed. She looked up at him.

"Darling, you don't love me and you never will. No matter how it works out, you'll always be in love with her. Won't you?"

Peter said miserably: "I suppose so, honey."

"Maybe you can work it out with her. I don't know. I do know that Brook isn't really in love with her, although he thinks he is, and he wants to be. The only woman he's ever been really crazy about is Carol Dunbar. She's common and she's cheap, but he's crazy about her—and Carol's crazy about you."

"Don't be silly," Peter said.

"All right, darling; I won't be silly. Brook has been using Sandra just as unscrupulously as she's been using you. He's flattered because she has this yen for him. He always is, you know. He's horribly vain, and when a girl as smart as Sandra falls for that lovely, suave line of his, he's delighted. He plays he's in love with her, and he'll take all he can get, but he's awfully cruel to girls like Sandra when he gets tired of them."

Lynne spun out of Peter's arm and started again for

the table where the cigarettes were. She stopped and whirled about.

She said: "Do you realize that Sandra may be in grave danger? She'll deliver that watch to him, and she's a terribly honest person. She'll assume that Brook killed Scott Higgins, and she'll accuse him of it. And once she has accused him, her life is going to be in the greatest danger."

Peter said: "Why should she accuse him? She doesn't know anything about it."

"Because she's clever. She knows you didn't kill him. She knows I didn't kill him. She knows Count Beretti didn't kill him. Who's left?"

"Any number of possibilities."

"I think you're wrong, Peter. Besides, she knows too much. I tell you she's in great danger."

Peter went to the telephone and called his apartment. Henry said that Mrs. Storm had come home a few minutes ago, much excited, had done a great deal of phoning, and changed to other clothes.

"She told me," Henry said, "that she might not be back until morning, and she went out."

23

SANDRA had made ten or twelve telephone calls, trying to find Brook Van Pell, and she had finally found
him at his house. His voice sounded disagreeable until
she said, "Darling, are you sure no one's listening on
this wire? It's terribly important."

He said: "I'll call you back on a private line. Are you
at Storm's apartment?"

"Yes." She hung up and waited. He called her in a
few minutes. Sandra said: "Did you know that your
sister has been listening in on practically all of your
phone calls? She's known everything that's been going
on." She whispered: "Can you hear me?"

"Yes."

"I've got it!" She could not keep the excitement out
of her voice. Her throat choked with it. Her heart
drummed with it. Her whole body sang with it.

"The watch?" he said after a moment in which she
could visualize his expression of incredulity, then the
excitement enlivening his eyes and his face.

"Yes, darling." She added hastily: "Can't we go
somewhere and talk? I'll tell you all about it, and
there's another thing I want to discuss that's very important to me. I've heard about a girl named Carol
Dunbar."

He said impatiently, "What did you hear?"

"That you were having an affair with her and hadn't broken it off."

"That's ridiculous," he said indignantly. "I hear all sorts of things about all sorts of people. Are you going to take someone else's word against mine, or accept circumstantial evidence at its face value?"

"No, darling, I only—"

"Look, Sandra," he interrupted. "This is no time to discuss anything on the phone. I've got a suggestion. Let's drive out to my Connecticut place and have breakfast. We'll have a grand pow-wow about everything. I'll have the roadster gassed up and I'll take along bacon and eggs and butter and things. Grab a taxi and meet me in fifteen minutes on the corner of Sixty-first and Fifth. Will you?"

"Yes, darling. I'm scared to death of this thing. And Storm may be coming home any moment."

"He's still in Lynne's room," Van Pell said. "But hurry."

Sandra changed to a light suit and with the watch in her purse, left the apartment. On the way to Sixty-first Street and Fifth, she bought a late extra. The front page headline made her heart jump:

COUNT BERETTI IN MYSTERY BRAWL—MAY DIE.

She had no time to read the details, although, in a two-column drop, she gleaned that a man named Scott Higgins had been found shot to death in his apartment off the stair landing on which the well-known Italian had been found unconscious.

She was just beginning to read the account of it when

her taxi stopped at Sixty-first Street and Fifth. When the cab stopped and she looked up, she saw Brook's roadster coming along Sixty-first.

Sandra paid her driver and got into the roadster beside Brook. His face was flushed. At first she thought he had been drinking, then she realized it was nothing but excitement.

He said, with the air of a man trying to control impatience and excitement: "Have you got it?"

"Yes, darling." She cuddled against him. "You told me over the phone when I was in Kingman that I'm a smart girl. I've just gone ahead and proved it."

"Let me see it."

The curtness of his tone surprised her a little, but she could understand his excitement. She opened her purse. She held it under the cowl light. The watch was lying on the other things in her purse. The shaded block letters were visible.

"Good," he said heavily. "Did you look inside?"

"Yes. The inner side of the inner lid is covered with microscopic writing and tiny diagrams. There's no question about it."

Van Pell laughed shortly. "Yes," he said quietly, "you're a smart girl. How did you do it?"

She told him, first, about overhearing Lynne's telephone conversation with Peter, then of her visit with Lynne, of the doctored highball, and of her frantic search of Lynne's suite.

Van Pell made no comment until she had finished, then he said, "It's amazing, simply amazing. I thought Storm had it."

"You said Higgins was dead when you got there," Sandra mentioned.

"Yes. Someone got there just ahead of me."

"Beretti?"

"I didn't see him. I opened the door of Higgins' apartment and he was lying there, dead. I supposed it was Storm."

Sandra argued: "I don't believe it could have been. If he had the watch, why should he have met you at the Stirrup Cup?"

"Did you listen in on that call, too?"

"Yes."

"I thought he had it," Van Pell said. "I was willing to make any kind of terms with him. When he found I definitely didn't have it, he went hot-footing it out of there. My theory is that Storm killed him first, then looked for the watch afterward. When he didn't find it, he made a pretty frantic search. The place was in confusion."

"But you didn't go in?"

"No. What I saw from the door told the story. I didn't want to be seen hanging around there, so I ducked."

Sandra said thoughtfully: "I don't believe Storm killed him. I think it happened before he got there."

Van Pell said: "Well, we may never know. It's a murder that will certainly puzzle the police, with all their scientific gadgets. And it doesn't concern us. We've got the watch, and that's all that matters."

"And I'm a smart girl," Sandra said contentedly. With her head against his shoulder, she sighed happily.

"By the way, darling, who told you this rot about the Dunbar girl and me?"

"Lynne."

He chuckled. Sandra laughed softly. "Just before she passed out from that doped highball that was intended for me."

"I hope you didn't take it seriously."

"I didn't. All I wanted was your assurance."

He chuckled again. "Sandra, I adore you."

"I was hoping you'd eventually get around to that," she said, as they sped toward Van Pell's place in Connecticut.

24

BROOK VAN PELL'S Connecticut house was in a thinly-settled area on the outskirts of Westport. It was not at all pretentious. It was a small Colonial farmhouse of the saltbox pattern more than one hundred and fifty years old, and it nestled in a large grove of elms and maples.

He had bought it some months ago as a retreat, because he liked its solitude. It had been only slightly modernized, and he intended to leave it just as it was, because he liked its simplicity. He had bought up about a hundred acres around it, to protect its isolation. In the dooryard were old, unkempt rose bushes and a ragged lawn, and in back was a dilapidated barn. He intended to change none of it.

Sandra had never before visited his farm, as he called it. She had been curious to see the place, and she was delighted when the roadster stopped before a picket fence not in the best of repair, and he said, "Well, darling, this is it."

She thought it was charming. She had not expected anything like it; had been prepared on the contrary, for a larger place, one more in keeping with the austerity and stateliness of the Sixty-first Street house.

"When I'm in the midst of a tough case, I bring all the papers out here and work on it," he said. "I do my own cooking and housekeeping. I have a secret vice—I love to cook. But, I'm warning you, my pet—the place is a mess."

He unlocked the door and they went into a long, low living-room, simply but well furnished with maple and old mahogany. There were hooked rugs on the floor.

Van Pell went about, turning on lamps. He said, "Now, let me examine that watch."

Sandra took it out of her purse and gave it to him. He held it under a lamp, opened the back with a blade of his penknife, and opened the inner lid. He found a magnifying glass and studied the finely engraved lettering and diagrams. He finally chuckled and said, "You're a smart girl. Are you hungry?"

Sandra discovered, now that the strain was over, that she was ravenous. "Starved," she said.

"I'll make you an omelette," Van Pell said. "Make yourself comfortable, my dear. One of America's great unsung chefs is about to produce an omelette that you'll never forget. Coffee?"

"I'd love it."

He picked up the basket he had carried in from the car and took it into the kitchen. Sandra sat down near a table lamp and opened the extra which she had brought in, rolled up in her hand.

She read the rest of the story rapidly. Count Angelo Beretti had been found unconscious on the third-floor landing of a remodeled brownstone front apartment house on Fifty-eighth Street, and been taken to the hospital suffering from a possibly fractured skull. His condition was very serious.

A Mrs. Sarah Malin, who resided on the floor above, had come upon the recumbent Italian on her way downstairs, and had summoned an ambulance. He had evidently been struck with some blunt object at the base of the skull, and he had not yet recovered consciousness. The Italian Consul could shed no light on the mystery. He had not, he said, been officially informed that Count Beretti was coming to this country.

It was presumed that he had had a fight with a man who lived in an apartment off the third floor landing where Count Beretti had been found. The door of the apartment, Mrs. Malin was certain, had been closed when she came downstairs.

Police were mystified by the fact that the man in the apartment was lying dead in the middle of his livingroom with two bullet holes in his forehead. A search of his papers had indicated that his name was either Professor John Medkin, or Scott Higgins.

The mystery was heightened by the absence of a revolver, or automatic pistol, with which Count Beretti had supposedly shot Scott Higgins. The police were inclined to the theory that it was impossible for Count Beretti, in his condition, to have fired the two shots which had killed Higgins, and they suspected that there had been a third man, who has escaped, after shooting Higgins and knocking Count Beretti unconscious.

Nothing was known about Scott Higgins' background. Because of Count Beretti's importance, and the mystery surrounding his visit to this country, it was likely that the State Department would take up the case.

Sandra turned to an inside page where the account was continued.

She read that Scott Higgins had been dressed in riding clothes when found. Then came this sentence: "Police are interested in the discovery of a small silver luck charm, a dachshund, with one ruby eye and one sapphire eye, which was found in a fold of the dead man's shirt, as it may have been dropped there by his assailant."

Sandra read that sentence again. She read it a third time. Her heart had almost stopped beating the first time she read it. Then it had given a painful thump and begun to beat wildly.

She jumped up and ran into the kitchen with the paper in her hand. Van Pell had just taken the frying pan containing the omelette off the stove, and had turned off the gas under the coffee pot.

He smiled at her, then stopped smiling when he saw how white her face was, how enormous her eyes were.

"What's the matter, darling?"

She said, trying to control her voice: "When you went up to Scott Higgins' apartment, he was dead, wasn't he?"

"Yes, Sandra. Why?"

"You didn't go in, you said. The door was unlocked. You just looked in, you said. He was lying in the middle of the room, dead."

"Exactly, Sandra. Why? What's wrong?"

"You positively didn't go into that room?"

"No."

"You just looked in, realized that someone had been

there before you, had killed him and either found or not found the watch?"

"Yes, Sandra." He was watching her alertly. "Why? What's this all about?"

"Brook," she said in a breaking voice, "you're lying. You killed him."

He stared at her. "Darling, are you crazy?"

"Read this," she said. And she held out the newspaper, indicating the sentence with her thumbnail. "I gave you that silver dachshund as a pocket charm. I bought it in Paris a year ago. One of its sapphire eyes was missing, and I thought it would be funny to have a ruby put in instead. There can't be the slightest question that that's the silver dachshund I gave you. And you always carried it in your right hand hip pocket, where you'd naturally carry a pistol."

She stopped. She was out of breath. Her heart was beating so frantically that it ached.

He said gravely, "Go on, Sandra."

She panted: "You must have pulled it out of your pocket somehow when you pulled out your pistol and shot him. It—it could have caught in a fold of your coat, and dropped on him when you were searching him for that watch."

Van Pell was smiling thinly. "Darling," he said quietly, "that's perfectly amazing reasoning."

"It's true!" she cried. "How else could it have got there? You said you didn't go into that room. You said you just looked in. You were lying. You killed him!"

He looked at her steadily, still with that faint smile.

He said gently: "Darling, let's go into the other room and talk this over."

She cried: "Then you did kill him!"

He said in a tired voice: "Sandra, I want to tell you all about it."

He took her by the arm and led her into the living-room. He sat her down on a couch and seated himself beside her. She stared into his suddenly tired face with frightened, busy eyes. He seemed to come to a decision. The muscles about his mouth tightened.

He said: "It's a very strange situation. No one else in the world knows, or can ever know, that I killed him. That silver piece can't possibly be traced to me."

"How did it happen?"

He sighed heavily. "It was an accident, Sandra. I went up there to get that watch. He didn't expect me. When he opened the door, and saw me, he ran back across the room for his gun. When he picked it up, I shot him. And now it's in your hands, darling. I know how you feel. It was an accident, it wasn't pre-meditated. The whole situation is perfectly horrible. What shall I do? It ruins my life. It ruins everything."

"You've got to tell the police!" Sandra said. "If you don't, we're all going to be involved. Especially Storm. He was up there. He's in trouble already over the lies he had to tell to get out of Kingman. The New York sheriff's office sent a man up to question him this evening. They know he was after Higgins. They know it was Higgins who shot at him in the desert. It says here that his name may be Higgins or Medkin. You've got to tell the police."

Van Pell was shaking his head. "No, Sandra. There's very little likelihood that Storm will be blamed for this."

"Did you knock out Beretti in the hall?"

Van Pell hesitated and said, "Yes."

"He must have seen you."

"No. He was in the hall when I went upstairs. He was facing Higgins' door. He didn't turn. He didn't see me. I hit him, then knocked on the door."

"But he may die, too! This paper says he may have a fractured skull. Storm will be charged with that, too."

"Stop worrying about Storm!" Van Pell cried. The sudden violence of his tone startled her. "Why do you consider him?"

He was white with anger. His mouth was thin and his eyebrows were drawn flat above his eyes. She stared at his unfamiliar face, saw it relax. He took a deep breath. He touched her hand. She snatched her hand away.

He said in a tone that was meant to be soothing, "Darling, listen to me. What I told you this afternoon still applies. I told you I would lay down my life to get this watch, this formula, for America's sake. You know how I meant it. What is a life or two compared to the thousands, the millions that loganite will save if this country should ever go on a war footing?"

Sandra did not like the expression in his eyes. This afternoon she had believed him when he had talked so largely of patriotism. She didn't believe him now. She might have, in time, found sufficient rationalization for him in the killing of Scott Higgins. That might have been accidental, or, as he claimed, a killing committed in self defense. But his striking down of Count Beretti could not be rationalized. Certainly not on patriotic grounds, for she was now convinced that his motives were anything but patriotic.

She said passionately: "Brook, I don't believe a word of that. You've killed one man and possibly a second. And Storm will be blamed for both. There is nothing you can do but explain it to the police. You can't let an innocent person be blamed. I won't stand for it!"

Again fury flared brightly in his eyes, but when he spoke his tone was patient. "Darling, listen to me. If I were to go to the police, this watch, this formula would have to be explained. You would be involved. So would my sister."

"I don't care," Sandra said recklessly. "You've got to tell them."

"And," he said quietly, "there would be other complications. International complications."

Sandra said swiftly: "How could there be? You intend to manufacture loganite for this country, don't you? You said so." She stared at him wonderingly. "Or do you, Brook? Were you lying about that, too?"

"No, darling." He tried to take her hand again, and again she withdrew it from his reach. She was seeing, for the first time, with clear eyes, a man who was something much worse than a hypocrite. Not quite the first time. She had sensed something like it this afternoon in the Pelican when she had seen him, for the first time, dispassionately, as a cool, driving personality who ruthlessly got what he wanted.

"Look," he said. "You're missing a very important point. If our positions were reversed, if for any reason you had killed a person, or two or three persons, my only thought would be to save you from detection. We are faced with a situation that countless people must have faced before us. People are murdered every day.

"The murderer may have a close friend who knows about it, or to whom he can go and trust. I refuse to see it as a moral issue. It was an accident. If you had come to me under similar circumstances, I wouldn't become righteous and begin urging you to go to the police. I'd move heaven and earth to keep you out of it. And you know it, Sandra!"

"I'm not being righteous," Sandra said calmly. "I say you must tell the police the truth so that innocent people won't be blamed."

"If innocent people are blamed," he said quickly, "I'll promise on my honor to tell the truth."

Sandra was shaking her head. "No, Brook. It's gone too far. We're going back to New York now, and we're going straight to headquarters."

She was watching his eyes when she finished. She had never seen them so clear, so gray, so cold. She realized, first, that this man did not love her, and never had loved her. She realized, then, that she was the only person who knew and could prove that he had killed Scott Higgins. And with this went the realization that he intended to kill her.

Lynne said: "I'm horribly sorry to wake you up, Colton, but it may be a matter of life and death."

"Just a moment, Miss Van Pell," the butler said. "I'll slip on a robe."

Colton came out into the hall from his room a minute later, blinking his eyes sleepily against the light, hugging the blue dressing gown about his skinny figure.

"Haven't you any idea where my brother might be?"

"No, Miss Van Pell. But after you inquired about him he was here for a short time in the library. Then he rang for me and told me to have his roadster gassed up and the tires checked, and to have a basket packed. He wanted things for breakfast, he said—eggs, bacon, bread, coffee, butter and so on."

Lynne said hysterically: "Peter, that means only one place—his farm up in Connecticut. It's just outside Westport. Colton, how long ago did he leave?"

"About a half hour ago, Miss Van Pell. I went to bed immediately afterward."

Lynne said: "Call the garage and have them send my coupe around at once. Have them gas it and check the oil and tires. Tell them to hurry. I'll put on some clothes, Peter. I'll be down in a jiff. Wait for me downstairs."

Peter's face was white and strained, but he grinned at her and patted her hand. "Good girl," he said.

When Sandra realized that she alone knew that Brook had killed Scott Higgins, and possibly killed Count Beretti, and that he intended to kill her, she jumped up from the couch. Her intention was to reach the front door before he could catch her, to get outdoors and to run as fast as she could to the nearest house to wake up the occupants and to demand protection.

She did not reach the front door. He must have been prepared for such action. He must have arisen from the couch a split-second after she did. She was half-way to the door when his hand fell on her shoulder, and his fingers dug into her flesh so deeply that she cried out with the pain.

He said, "Sandra, what is this all about? We were discussing a very difficult and delicate situation, and we hadn't talked it out. Where were you going?"

She dropped her shoulder, to free herself of that painful grip, and slipped behind a table. Facing him over a low table lamp, with the light shining into his face, she was suddenly so frightened that she almost screamed.

Her first wild and possibly hysterical conviction that . he intended to kill her, might have been imagination. But what she saw in his clear gray eyes across the table lamp was not imagination. His eyes were the eyes of a killer. She could not have explained why she was so sure of it. She had, to her knowledge, never before seen the eyes of a man intent on killing another person. It was a deadly intentness, a fixed and inescapable determination.

His face was gray, his lips were pale, but she hardly saw them. His intention was wholly centered in his eyes. The pupils were contracted to dazzling black points which caught light from the lamp and gleamed.

It ran through her thoughts in a hopeless wail: "This man is going to kill me. And there's nothing I can do."

Her only hope was, so she thought then, to escape somehow from this house.

She thought: "He's insane. He's always been a little insane, but I never realized it."

She realized it now. He said, in a soothing voice: "Sandra, what's got into you, darling?"

Sandra cried: "You're not going to do it!"

He said gently, "I'm going to kill you. You don't leave me any alternative. I gave you your chance. I'm in love with you. I've never loved anyone as I love you, Sandra. I understand fully how your conscience is working. Darling, come here."

She cried in terror: "Keep away from me!"

He began to edge toward the table. As he moved, she moved correspondingly. His eyes never left her face.

She looked frantically about for something with which to defend herself. There was nothing on this side of the room. On the other side, by the fireplace, were the fire irons—tongs and a heavy, black iron poker. But before she could reach them, he would have her. The table lamp was flimsy. It would not do. There was nothing within reach.

His voice went on, suddenly a heavy dead voice that sent pricklings into her scalp. "I love you, Sandra. I've been in love with you from the first time I met you. I wanted to marry you. You know that."

He was still moving toward the end of the table. Sandra continued to move, an inch at a time, prepared to run if he should make a lunge for her. There was a heavy vase on a table halfway to the door. If she could reach the vase, if she could hit him with it hard enough—

She saw the gathering determination in his eyes just

before he made the lunge. She leaped away, toward the other table, just when he was about to catch her.

Sandra ran to the table on which the vase stood. She snatched it up as he ran toward her. She waited an instant, then lifted it up and brought it down with all her force on his head.

The vase shattered into a thousand pieces. He did not even stagger. He paused for a moment. The look in his eyes had not changed. A trickle of blood ran down the left side of his square forehead, and down beside the eye and along the cheek. He did not seem to notice it.

"Sandra, I want to talk this out with you."

She slipped behind the table. He faced her across it.

He said, in the voice of a man thoughtfully arguing a complex case: "Darling, I told you that nothing can stand between me and my getting what I want. I wanted this watch, but you're still standing between me and what I want. I don't want to kill you, but I have to. But before I kill you, just once, darling, I want to hold you in my arms. I love you. I want to hold you close to me. I want you to love me as much as I love you."

She had been horrified by her realization that he intended to kill her. She had been horrified by his cold-blooded announcement that he intended to kill her. Now she realized, with growing terror, that this man, this murderer, was actually making love to her while he was planning to kill her.

There was another fear in her mind—that she would be unable to defend herself against him. Her heart, which had, at the beginning of this, begun to beat with a frantic rhythm, was now missing beats and fluttering.

She felt a coldness rising in her body, and a growing faintness. She was afraid she would, at any moment, fall unconscious.

Facing him across the table, prepared to run, or dodge, if he came toward her again, she watched the trickle of blood reach his chin and she thought of Peter Storm. Pictures of him were vivid in her mind.

She saw him as he had looked with the bandage she had made from strips of a dead man's shirt about his head at a rakish angle. She heard him saying, as clearly as if he were here in this room: "You're a liar, Mrs. Storm . . ." In Kingman, he was saying to the reporters, "What we really want you to say is that we're very, very happy now that we're finally married . . ." Upstairs, in her hotel room, he was saying, "People who are really frightened prop chairs under doorknobs."

And then he was looking at her with steady green eyes, saying, "Go to the devil."

Brook Van Pell was staring at her steadily, never moving his eyes. He said quietly, "Come with me, Sandra."

And there was nothing more on the table to throw at him. If she could maneuver him around the table, to where she was now, then race across the room to the fireplace!

She moved a few inches along the table. But he only stared and waited for her to move.

Her heart gave another flutter. Her mouth and throat were dry. She thought: "Just a moment ago he was making an omelette for me. Why did I say such things? I should have realized."

"Brook," she said, "on my word of honor, I won't talk."

"You're lying now," he said quietly.

"I'm not lying!" she cried desperately.

He shook his head slowly. "I wish you weren't. I don't want to do this. There is no other way, Sandra."

She was seeing Peter Storm in a dozen situations, saying dozens of different things. She saw him carving a steak, saying: "It doesn't seem to me you fall in love very intelligently."

She thought wildly: "I don't! I don't! Or do I? I don't know. I thought I was in love with this man, but all along I've been falling in love with Storm. I must have been, to feel like this now."

Staring across the table into Van Pell's clear, gray, relentless eyes, she realized that this change of heart had actually begun this afternoon, when she had seen Brook so clearly, so dispassionately; that, actually, she had begun to fall in love with Peter Storm before that. In Kingman? It was hard to say. But it made little difference. It was too late now. Everything was too late, now.

Peter Storm was saying: "I've never had so many emotions stirred up at once by any one girl—admiration and respect and a desire to be terribly helpful."

And she remembered that she had said, "If you feel it so deeply, then why don't you do something about it?"

And Peter had kissed her.

"Storm!" she was thinking. Now, in her hysteria, in her terror of this man with the deadly gray eyes across the table from her, it seemed foolish to be calling for her husband by his last name.

"If I had only realized— If I had only dreamed that this was nothing but a dreadful fascination. I knew it this afternoon, but I wouldn't acknowledge it. I knew it, everything went to pieces, when he insisted that I was to live at Peter's apartment, to spy on him. No man who really loved a girl would tolerate such a situation. Peter was right. He's always been right. *If I had lived,*" she thought, "I might have got around to calling him Peter. Or just 'darling' . . ."

The words almost forced themselves past her clamped lips. "Oh, darling! . . ."

With terror flowing over her in icy waves, she watched the steady, merciless gray eyes across the table. He was in no hurry. A few more minutes of this—

It was nothing but her thinking of Peter that vitalized her, and gave her the courage to act boldly. She gave the table a sudden, violent push. She ran around the end of it and across the room to the fireplace. She snatched up the heavy fire-tongs.

Before she could lift them, he had knocked them from her hand. He reached for her hair, but she jumped out of his reach. She seized a table lamp and threw it at him. It hit his shoulder. He came toward her. She snatched up a wooden bookend and threw it at him. It struck his face. He came toward her in the same slow, deliberate, relentless way.

She cried helplessly: "Keep away from me!"

"Sandra—darling," he said.

She backed away. She bumped into a table. Her fingers found a metal cigarette box. It was heavy. His head was forward, and his eyes held steadily to hers. She threw the box. It struck his shoulder. His eyes did not flicker. He came toward her in the same slow, determined, relentless way.

[25.]

SANDRA did not hear the coupe stop. Afterward, she dimly recalled having heard a sound like the slamming of a car door. But her first sharp impression was the crash of breaking glass, as a window burst.

She was in a corner of the room. She had tried to back into the kitchen, intending to run to the back door. But she had misjudged the distance and backed into the corner, where he got his hands on her shoulders again. He was pulling her into his arms when the sound of breaking glass came.

Then she was free, and spinning away from him, whirling past a chair, a table, a love-seat. She saw Peter Storm come through the window, and she thought it was her own imagination again, she had been seeing him so vividly.

But there was no mistaking the reality of the impact of the bodies of the two men. They exchanged no words. With one accord, they settled down to the grim business of destroying each other.

She saw Peter strike Brook Van Pell in the face, and she saw that it affected him as slightly as had all the things she had thrown at him. She saw him strike Peter in the chest, and the force of the blow sent Peter staggering back eight or ten feet, against a table, which overturned as Peter pushed against it and threw himself with swinging fists at Van Pell again. And then Sandra was aware that Peter was not alone.

Lynne had crawled through the broken window, white-faced and grim. She was reaching into her open pocketbook.

She took out a pistol and lifted it and aimed it at one of the two men. Her hand holding the pistol was shaking. Then the determination seemed to run out of her.

Her hand, still shaking, so that the pistol muzzle danced from side to side, came slowly down. She squeezed her eyes shut and compressed her lips in a tortured grimace.

The two men were still fighting. They were locked together now. Sandra had a glimpse of Brook Van Pell's face, his eyes, over Peter's wide shoulders. His lower lip was sagging and his eyes were a gray blaze of murder.

He pushed Peter away, and as he did so, he quickly bent down for the heavy black fire-tongs. Sandra saw his foot shoot out, then the quick movement of his left hand. He tripped Peter, and Peter, trying to regain his balance, fell to the floor with such force that he was momentarily stunned.

He half lay against a table, helpless, and on his face was the empty look Sandra had seen on the faces of fighters who are knocked down.

Then Brook Van Pell started toward him in the same slow, determined, remorseless way that had frightened her so when he had pursued her. The heavy fire-tongs were gripped tightly in his right hand, and he slowly raised them as he advanced to strike the half-stunned man on the floor.

Sandra screamed: "Brook! Brook!" If he heard her, he paid not the slightest heed.

Sandra snatched the pistol from Lynne's limp hand. She raised it until Brook Van Pell's dark handsome head was centered along the sight. She pulled the trigger once as Lynne put her hands over her eyes.

Brook Van Pell suddenly fell to the floor and rolled over. And Lynne was saying, in her husky voice: "You had to do that, Sandra. I tried to. I couldn't."

Sandra saw the pistol on the floor near her right foot. She had not known she had dropped it. She said dully: "He was going to kill Peter."

She had not seen Peter get up off the floor. He was standing close beside her, with his arm about her shoulders. "Sandy, are you all right?"

She looked at him a moment, still finding it hard to believe that he had not been struck by the tongs, and said: "Thanks, Storm. I'm all right."

Then she fell into a chair. But she didn't faint.

Peter kneeled beside the long, still man on the floor.

Lynne said calmly: "Dead?"

"Yes."

"There wasn't any other way."

Sandra said: "It's in his left-hand coat pocket. That one. For Allied Metals Corporation—with my compliments."

Then she covered her face with her hands, for it suddenly felt full of icy-hot needles.

Peter had the watch in his hand. He was looking at it and shaking his head. Sandra wished he would come over and take her in his arms and say, "There's been enough of this nonsense," but he didn't.

He was looking at her sadly. She had never seen such sadness in his eyes. She knew what was in his mind. He thought she was shattered because she had had to kill the man she loved.

She said steadily: "Peter, I'm not sorry I killed him. I'll never be. He was trying to kill me. He was about to kill you."

Still with that look in his eyes, he said: "I understand."

But he didn't. He still had the same thought.

Then Lynne said wearily, "It's not a very nice thing to have to kill your own brother."

"Don't be silly," Peter said impatiently. "Why should you take the blame? It isn't necessary. You weren't even here. This man was threatening to kill my wife."

"And you," Sandra said. "And I shot him."

"No," Peter said. "I shot him. Get out of here, Lynne. Get in your car and drive back to New York. And drive moderately. And keep your mouth shut."

The icy-hot needles had stopped. Sandra took her hands away from her cheeks. "You see, Lynne," she said, "it's all so simple and clean-cut. Leave it to Storm. Always leave everything to Storm. And why not?"

She got up. She felt limp. Her knees were wobbly but she knew she wasn't going to faint. That was all over. The nightmarish things remained, but Peter's presence, his firm way of handling things was restorative.

He said gently, "Sandy, I'm awfully afraid this is that scandal."

"Maybe," she said, "it's time to have a scandal and get it over with."

"This scandal," Lynne said, "will take an awful lot of getting over."

"You don't understand Storm," Sandra said. "He has an unlimited capacity for absorbing publicity. Honestly, Storm, the jams you get into. And this is just about the way you get into all of them, isn't it? Lynne, you'd better bow before his superior judgment and get out of here."

Peter said, with a hint of anger: "Stop being funny, Sandy. I'll telephone the police. Lynne, you can't leave, after all. If you did, there would be no way of explaining how I got here."

Lynne nodded. "I saw it all. I'll make a good witness. You can say you shot him, and I'll swear to that."

To Sandra their voices were suddenly like voices in a large auditorium. A dozen different reactions were setting in. She wanted to go outdoors and run down the road. She wanted to scream. She wanted to get off by herself and cry. But mostly, she wanted Peter to take her in his arms and comfort her.

But Peter was remote, and curt. And she realized why. He believed she was shattered because the man she loved had betrayed her. He was reconciled to the countless number of things she had said, all adding up to the one—how she detested him.

If she told him how she felt about him, he wouldn't like it. He would think she was flying from the arms of one man to the arms of another, and his idealism would resent it.

Peter was telephoning the State Police. Lynne was smoking a cigarette, coolly looking about the room at the things Sandra had thrown, at the broken vase, the cigarette box, the lamp, the book-end.

And Sandra was realizing that, to convince this man that she loved him and that Brook was nothing to her but a dreadful experience that she wanted to forget, might be exceedingly difficult.

Peter hung up the phone and walked over to her. She looked at him hopelessly. It seemed to her there was nothing she could say that would be even remotely right.

He said gravely: "You'd better have a drink. You'll have to pull yourself together. We've got to agree on a story and stick to it, because they'll question us separately."

Lynne said sharply: "What will we say?"

"The truth, except that I shot him. We suspected he was bringing Sandra out here to kill her, because she knew too much.

"We arrived in time. He was about to kill her, so I shot him. All the details are the same."

"It's my gun," Lynne said. "And they're awfully clever."

Peter said: "Yes, you gave it to me just before we got out of the car. He came at me and I shot him."

"I can't stand it in here," Sandra said suddenly.

She opened the front door and walked out quickly. The night breeze was cool on her hot cheeks. She walked to the end of the dooryard, to a stone fence.

Then she heard Peter following. He came up beside

her. She turned. She could hardly see his face in the
glow from the windows. She felt weak and expectant
and miserable.

She said: "What's going to happen?"

"Publicity," he said dryly. "Plenty of publicity. The
police may hold us a couple of days, but it will be
routine. Lynne saw him kill Scott Higgins. She'll testify
to it. We'll have to tell the truth about our hunt for
loganite—with one exception. You were working with
me, not Van Pell. We'll have to go to Kingman and
clear up that business. There's no escaping that. I won't
mind. It will be nice escaping the reporters."

"There will always be reporters," Sandra said.

He said nothing. She wished she could see his face.
She hoped he wasn't looking at the pale blur where her
face was with amusement. It was his defense against
everything—against any kind of hurt.

He said: "Sandy, I've been trying to find some way
of saying how sorry I am about this. What happened
out here was an awful thing for you to go through,
but even that wasn't as bad as seeing the man you're in
love with—"

He hesitated. She said: "Dead—by my own hand?"

"That's what I was trying to say."

Her heart began to beat rapidly. "But I wasn't in
love with him. I don't think I ever was in love with
him, except just at first. Whatever it was, it wasn't love.
I realized it this afternoon, but I wouldn't admit it. I
saw him this afternoon as he really was, and what happened tonight only confirmed it."

She thought that Peter had suddenly moved closer to her, but it was her imagination again.

She went on painfully, "I suppose you'll never forgive me for the hateful things I've said to you. I can't explain them. You've been so decent and so kind."

"Don't try," Peter said.

"Now you detest me."

He said nothing for a moment. Then: "Sandy, what are you trying to say?"

She was trying, she realized, to say things that were impossible to say. She was trying to tell him she must have been in love with him practically since the moment they had met.

She said: "Peter, look. He told me he was going to kill me. He said he had to, because I knew too much. I knew he'd killed Scott Higgins, and he thought I was the only one who knew. I knew he intended to kill me before he said it. I didn't think there was any hope for me. And all that went through my mind was how decent you'd been to me, and how much I loved you."

He suddenly had her by the elbows. He said harshly: "Sandy, take it easy."

"I knew he'd kill me, and I knew there wasn't any way to escape, and all I could think of was you. Darling, it's going to take me days to make you realize that what I'm saying is true. I simply had to make a start."

He was trying to see her face. He was bending his head, but there wasn't enough light.

Sandra said, in the same level voice: "I'm going to spend the rest of my life making it up to you—if you'll let me. I know what you're thinking now, that I'm still all confused and mixed up. I'm not, darling. I have been confused and mixed up, but I'm not any more."

His face was only inches away. He was still holding her elbows, still trying to see her face. His hands were trembling.

He said huskily: "Sandy, if you really mean what you're saying—"

She wailed: "I do, darling! All I want is to clear up everything between us. Do you think I can? Do you want me to?"

"Keep right on," he said.

"I'm glad we're going back to Kingman," she said. "I have a very sentimental idea about our catching up with our honeymoon where it should have started."

The End

www.ingramcontent.com/pod-product-compliance
Lightning Source LLC
Chambersburg PA
CBHW020735250626

47155CB00003B/769